THE
SISTER
PACT

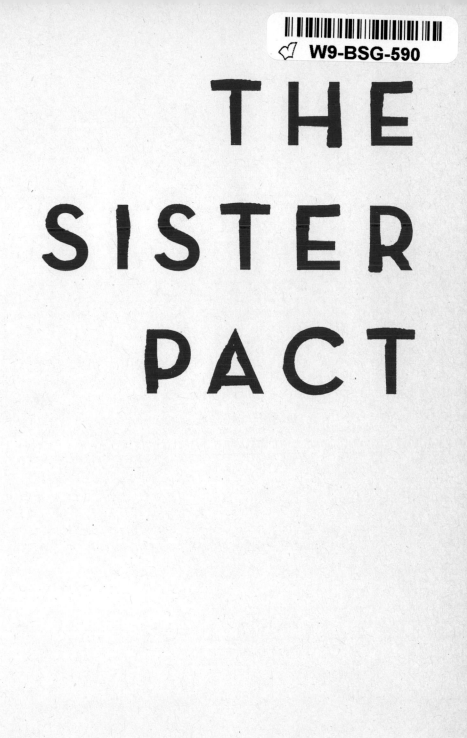

THE SISTER PACT

STACIE RAMEY

sourcebooks
fire

Published by Sourcebooks Fire, an imprint of Sourcebooks, Inc.
P.O. Box 4410, Naperville, Illinois 60567–4410
(630) 961–3900
Fax: (630) 961–2168
www.sourcebooks.com

Library of Congress Cataloging-in-Publication data is on file with the publisher.

Printed and bound in the United States of America.
VP 10 9 8 7 6 5 4 3

*This book is dedicated to Mom and Dad
because they are everything, still.*

CHAPTER 1

The last thing we did as a family was bury my sister. That makes this meeting even harder to face.

I don't have to be a psychic to know what everyone thinks when they look at me. Why did she do it? Why didn't I? And the thing is, after all that happened, I'm not sure I know the answer to either.

Mom walks behind me, her hand gently curled around my bicep. Dad motions to show us where to sit, even though the guidance office is new ground for him.

I force myself to look into the faces of my judges and feel immediate relief. The principal, Mrs. Pendrick, smiles, warm and sweet, and the wrinkly skin around her eyes and lips lifts as she does. Mr. Hicks, my guidance counselor, the one the girls think is sort of cute, stands next to her. Where Mrs. Pendrick is all soft creases, he's wide shoulders, built for dealing with bad kids or bad parents, but he winks at me like he wants me to know he's on my side.

Mrs. Pendrick places a hand on mine. "It's nice to see you, Allie. We're so glad you're back."

Her hand is like an island of safe in a sea of danger. I smile at her so she thinks I'm okay. I smile so it looks like I'm not breaking. Like everything that happened was a mistake and I'm ready for a do-over.

Mr. Kispert, my art teacher, comes barreling into the room, carrying his iced coffee and my portfolio. "Sorry I'm late," he says. He nods at me and I try to nod back, but my body's kind of frozen. I had no idea he'd be here too.

"We were just getting started." Mrs. Pendrick opens a file, my name written on the tab. "I pulled Allie's records. She's on track for graduation next year, of course."

I tell myself to pay attention. I try to focus on Mrs. Pendrick, whose Southern accent makes her sound as misplaced as "the wrong Alice" in the new version of *Alice in Wonderland*, but it's hard.

"We may want to take a look at the courses she's chosen for this year." Mrs. Pendrick adjusts her reading glasses and flips through the pages.

My eyes hurt, the start of a migraine. I blink.

"We want to make certain we're not asking too much of her." Mr. Hicks shifts forward, his hands loosely steepled on the fake mahogany table in front of him.

The surface of the table is so shiny, I see my face in it, distorted and strange. I blink again. Caught somewhere between the blink and the reflection, I see her, Leah, in her black leotard and pink tights, like she's waiting in the wings for her cue.

Even though I realize it's just a trick of the light, I can't help staring at not-real-Leah, waiting to see if she's going to dance. I'm staring so hard, I must have stopped paying attention to what's going on around me because Dad's voice is stern. "Sit up, Allie. These people are here for you."

I square myself in my seat, horrified by the look of pity that crosses Mr. Hicks's face.

Mrs. Pendrick reaches across the table and takes my hand again, her touch soft as butter. "Are you okay, dear?"

"I'm fine. I just have a headache."

Dad shoots me a look like he wants me to behave, to make up for Leah. As if I could.

"Mr. Blackmore, we have to be patient with Allie," Mrs. Pendrick insists.

I should probably warn Mrs. Pendrick that Dad doesn't believe in being patient. It's all about domination and war games with him. He's the general. I'm the soldier he commands, and he will not lose this hill. No matter what. When I look at him, I see dried blood caked on his hands. Mom's. Leah's. Mine.

I shake that image out of my head and try to find my Happy. I think about everyone's colors. Mrs. Pendrick would be creamy yellow, icing pink, powder blue. And Mr. Hicks would be something easy too, like golf-course-turf green. I try to think about how I would paint them if I still painted. And just like that, Happy has left the building. Like Leah did.

"It's her junior year." Dad leans forward, his not-giving-an-inch stance making my stomach knot. I already know his colors: muddy brown, gray black, the color of pissed. "We need to get her back on track."

"We understand that." Mr. Hicks folds his hands again like a tent. "But this is going to be a very hard year for Allie."

It *is* going to be a hard year. And no meeting is going to change that. So instead of listening to them, I close my eyes and call to my mind the sound of Leah's ballet shoes shuffling against the floor. Eight weeks after, I can still hear them, but who knows for how long? Right now, I'm so grateful for the soft slide, slide, slide that is so real and strong that it fills me with unreasonable hope. Maybe she hasn't left me. Maybe it didn't happen. Maybe she'll forgive me.

"Maybe we could keep just two of the AP classes?" Mom suggests.

I open my eyes and pray I'm not crazy. It's hard to know if you are. Nobody really thinks they are. But I can almost hear Leah laughing with me—so like her to laugh when I'm in the hot seat and she's not.

Mr. Kispert takes out my portfolio and lays it on the table next to a brochure from the Rhode Island School of Design. The requirements are highlighted in crime-scene-tape yellow. "Allie should keep her AP Studio Art class. I'll supervise her. She'll do fine, and she needs it to work on her application."

Reading upside down, I can make out all the things I need to do to make that happen. Last year it all seemed easy. Now each step feels like a mountain I'm not equipped to climb. Mr. Kispert looks at me and winks. I smile back, even though I feel like a complete fake. I can't do art anymore, and I don't know how to tell him.

Mom puts her hand out to take the brochure, and it shakes. *Please don't let Dad notice. Please.* Dad grunts and takes it instead. "I'm not giving up on my daughter. Even if you guys are."

"Nobody's giving up on her," Mr. Hicks says. "We just want her to be okay."

"She wants to go to RISD. How do you expect her to get into a top art school if you don't give her the right classes?" His voice strains, and for a second I think he's going to cry, which I've never seen him do—except when we buried Leah.

"David, please." Mom says.

He slams the table hard. "Goddammit, Karen, this is what you do, what you always do. You give into the girls." He clears his throat. "Her. You give into her."

Mom's eyes well at Dad's obvious stumble. They've been calling Leah and I *them* or *the girls* for so long. It must be hard to adjust, but seeing Dad struggle with the math makes me feel horrible. We did this. We cut his regiment in half. Maybe his heart too. I want to reach out to him. I want to tell him I'm sorry. That I didn't think she meant it. That I definitely didn't—until I did. But that's a cop-out. Truth is, I don't remember most of that night.

Dad's voice sounds like he's surrendering. "What do you want me to do, Karen? Let her fail? That's not exactly going to fix her, is it?"

Everybody gets quiet. I can feel the silence like a noose around my neck. Dad's pain radiates off him. Mom's shame makes her sink into the chair. Mr. Hicks and Mrs. Pendrick sit, waiting for the right thing to say to heal this family. But there isn't anything to be said after all this. After what Leah did and what I almost did.

I close my eyes and wish Leah were here. I wish so hard, I can almost feel her holding my hand. Sometimes she did that when Mom and Dad fought. Sometimes she held my hand and I'd play with her silver flower ring, the one she always wore. They buried her with that ring. Mom said she wanted to give it to me, but I wanted Leah to have it. I lay my head on the table, the cool feeling enough to calm me for a minute.

"Jesus, Allie, can you try to focus?" I lift my head to see Dad close his eyes, and I know I've pushed him too hard. He shakes his head like a bull. He does that when he's done. He stares at the ceiling. "Is this how it's going to be now? Are you going to give up?"

And just like that he makes me want to disappear, makes me wish I could be wherever Leah is now, away from him and his shit. Away from everyone's expectations. Away from his stupid war with Mom.

And more than ever, I wish Leah were here. If she were here, really here, she'd stop Dad from being a jerk. She'd make Mom sit up straight and actually have an opinion. She'd take over this meeting and make them stop talking about my life as if I'm not even in it. Leah could totally do that. She was epic.

Until she killed herself.

Mrs. Pendrick clears her throat. "I understand your concerns, Mr. Blackmore. Junior year *is* a very important year. But Allie needs to heal."

We Blackmores? We don't heal. We patch up and make do. We Blackmores move on. It's in some contract that Dad made us sign when we were born. Leah's in breach. Now I'm the one in the spotlight. Thanks, Sis.

"Allie's seeing someone." Dad clears his throat. "A psychiatrist."

Mom nods quickly to show they're on the same page, which has been a ridiculously rare occurrence since Mom's Xanax addiction made the scene. Or since Dad's girlfriend, Danielle, did. The one that has texted him three times since he picked Mom and me up today. I guess she was mad he didn't let her come. To *my* meeting. My head starts pounding. I reach into my backpack and pull out an Excedrin pack and a Gatorade.

"What are you doing?" Mom's face gets red.

"I have a headache," I explain.

"You're supposed to tell me, and I give it to you." She shuffles around in her purse.

"It's just Excedrin." Does she honestly want to become my personal med vending machine? Like a human PEZ dispenser? I rip open the packet and put the pills on my tongue. Everyone gets quiet and looks at me like I just bit the head off a bat.

This is so outrageous. I can't deal with it alone. Leah should be facing this horrible aftermath with me. Every suicide pact needs a fallback for prisoners of war. Apparently.

Dad's hand goes on Mom's. It's a small gesture but so foreign in their full-scale battle that I can't pull my eyes from the spectacle. Mom puts her purse back on the arm of her chair. I'm not sure if I've imagined it, but I think I hear the sound of the pills rattling in their bottles, and that worries me greatly. Now that Leah's gone AWOL, I don't think I'd follow her, but if I'm so solid, why the hell am I wondering how many pills Mom has on her?

"I want to hear how Allie feels," Mr. Hicks says, breaking my reverie.

I swallow hard. How do I feel? I feel like I'm breaking inside. I can't see colors anymore. It's like when Leah left, she took the best of me. I feel like if one of us should have lived, it should have been her. She'd be way better in the role of surviving sister than I am. She'd have better hair too.

"Allie?" Dad prompts. "Mr. Hicks asked you a question. How do you feel?"

Sometimes I feel like I'm no more here than Leah is. Sometimes I forget. I think it didn't happen. I wait for my cell to ring. I think she's going to burst into the room, full of life and pissed at me for having borrowed one of her things. But then I remember. And it's like that night all over again. And I get mad—at her for going, and them for not even knowing that I'm not just mad she went, but also that she didn't take me with her. Like she promised. Like we promised each other.

"Allie?" Dad's voice gets tighter.

But I can't tell them any of that. They don't want to hear about that. Everyone's so sick of death, they want me to lighten the mood. It's up to me. I'm on stage now. Dad's beating the drum. Mom's cowering. My teachers and the guidance counselors are waiting like revival attendees ready to be preached to, ready to clap. I can't disappoint them. So I try to be like Leah. I sit up tall. I "dance." "It's fine." I look at Mom so she'll know I mean it. Mostly. "AP art classes. Everything else honors."

"You sure you can do that, sweetie?" I hear the relief in Mom's voice. She wants to believe it's all over. I guess I can't really blame her.

Mrs. Pendrick's face screws up. "I think this is a mistake."

"I agree," Mr. Hicks says. "But let's do this. How about we move forward with that schedule and keep an eye on you, Allie? That sound okay? We're here whenever you need."

"Perfect." Dad stands.

Mom follows his lead.

I stand too, not wanting to break rank, especially when there's been a break in the fighting. It's not that I think it's so perfect, but I'm playing the part of the foot soldier, as usual. We soldiers march and follow orders. We soldiers act like it's all good. Hup, two, three, four. Even when we're breaking.

CHAPTER 2

I meet Emery outside her house. She's in tiny running shorts and a sports bra, letting her island-girl skin take center stage. Muscles look better in tan than white. They just do. But Emery's long legs and tight booty would be fierce in any color. She gathers up her long, curly hair in a ponytail, then makes a messy bun and asks. "So, how was it?"

"Fine." I get one last look at my cell, see no new texts, and stash it in my pocket. "Why are we doing this again?"

Emery frowns. She knows whose text I'm waiting for. The same one I always wait for. The unspoken issue between Emery and me that I need to get over—Max. I'm glad she doesn't confront that monster but instead simply says, "I've gotta get in shape. You know Mr. Carbon doesn't cast fat actresses."

It's not like Emery's even close to fat. She's not in the ZIP code of fat. She knows this. So do I, but I also know that she's right about the drama teacher at our school. Leah used to say that he picked out the girls who gave up their ambitions over the summer for ice cream and pizza.

"Okay, but why am *I* doing this?" I ask.

"Because you're my best friend and you're supporting me."

"More like being left behind." Once we get going, Emery will lap me for sure.

"I'll stay with you this time. I swear."

True to her word, Emery starts slow. At first I feel like I can do it. I can run the six miles she's got mapped out for us. "You just want to run by Taylor's house. Admit it," I pant between breaths.

"So what? I look hot when I run."

She's right. She does. Her hair stays in place. Her face stays the same perfect olive color. Her muscles propel her forward. She travels across the landscape more than she runs. Watching her do anything physical is like watching Leah dance.

We round the corner. "So tell me," she says, her breath even.

"Mr. Kispert was there."

Emery glances at the house we're running past and the thin woods behind it. On the other side of those trees is my yard. My backyard with my studio. The one Dad had built for me. At the time I was ecstatic. It felt important, as if he saw me— really saw me—and he knew I was special. But now, I get it. It wasn't a gift. It was an obligation. A promise I made to be the talented daughter who would make him proud.

We pick up the pace, and I am grateful to be moving away from all that, at least for now. My good mood sours as soon as we pass Max's house. His car is parked out front, meaning he's home. And he didn't text. He didn't check in to see how I was, even though he knew how hard today would be.

Emery reads my mood like a psychic at the county fair. "You know how he is."

"Whatever." This time I increase the pace, as if tiring myself out will prove I'm over him.

"Maybe you need to broaden your field."

I concentrate on my legs, which are starting to feel like lead. I tell myself to keep going. I tell my legs to push off like Emery's do. I tell myself that if Leah were here, she'd race me to the end of the street, beat me, then taunt me the rest of the way.

She's still so with me, I can almost hear her saying, *You're slow, Baby Sister. Sloppy Seconds.*

So I start racing. I sprint to the end of the street. Emery's long legs outpace me without even a struggle. I bend over and hold my side, try to catch my breath. Breathe. Breathe. Breathe.

A group of guys jog our way, keeping in a tight formation, teammates in training. They're too far away to see which team. My heart skips a little. I try not to hope Max is with them. As they get closer, I see they aren't the swimmers but baseball players.

They mostly ignore me as they pass, which is totally cool. Except one of them doesn't. Nick Larsons stops, comes closer. Nick Larsons—part baseball player, part artist. I'm not sure the exact proportions of each. He has a tight first-baseman build and warm hazel eyes. He paints more realistic than I like but still decent.

Emery gives me an approving look and then takes off running alongside the baseball team, faster than she and I were running but still not even a challenge for her.

Nick looks at me like he's so glad to see me. He actually looks happy that I'm here, which, in a way, surprises me. "Hey, Allie. What's up?"

I don't answer, just start running again. "I'm slow. You can go ahead."

He runs next to me, easy jock strides, all muscle and strength. Everything I wish I were. He turns and faces backward, jogging the whole time. "You taking studio?" he asks.

"Yeah. You?"

He smiles. "Yeah. Can't believe they let me in. Kispert's cool. But I'm in way over my head."

I pick up my speed, and Nick turns so he's running forward again and adjusts to my new pace. "You won't have any trouble with it though," he says.

"You have no idea."

He laughs. I don't.

When we get to the end of the street, I stop again. I motion behind me. "I'm gonna go home. This is way too much exercise for me."

He puts the brakes on too. "Okay. See you tomorrow. I'll look for you."

"Sure thing." I make myself face him, make myself ignore Max, who has just stepped out of his house. It's like I have some kind of Max radar that I couldn't turn off even if I wanted to.

"Is that okay?" Nick trips a little over the words, making me smile.

I act like I don't see Max standing in the driveway, watching me. I act like I want to flirt with Nick, like it means something to me. "Yeah. More than okay."

Nick's turn to smile. Sweet. I wish I could make my heart skip knowing I made him smile. But I can't. It's his turn to motion behind him. "I'm gonna go catch up…"

"Yeah. Sure."

He jogs away, turning to look at me one more time. I wave, and I tell myself not to turn around. Not to look at Max. Watch Nick, who has that silly smile pasted on his face. He turns on the jets, turbo-ing himself forward.

"So you're into baseball players now?" Max's voice comes from behind me. "That's a completely valid choice. You know, if you don't mind your men a little small."

I still don't turn to face him. "Thanks for your approval. Not that you actually get a say."

He drapes his arms over me, leaning his body against mine. I try not to feel how ripped he is, but I can't. It's not like his body's the only thing I love about Max, but I'd have to be dead not to notice. He whispers in my ear. "How was it?"

Tears spring to my eyes. I want to push him away and run home, pretend that jogging is my new passion. It's not like what he says to me is so profound—it's just that his concern gets inside me. Deep. It blankets me, hugging my ribs hard, massaging my heart. Max does this without even trying. He turns me, so I have to face him. He sees my tears. But it's not like he needed to. Max knows. He holds me against him, and I bury my face in his neck.

14

"Shh. It's okay. It's going to be okay."

I cry more, not caring. He holds me closer. It's like there's no space between us. I want to turn my face up to his. I want to kiss him. I feel that need in every cell of my body—my Max need. Bottomless and aching and just plain stupid because I know it's not going to happen. Not after that one time last spring. That thought is the slap in the face and the punch in the gut I need to stop the tears. I pull away from him so he won't know—as if he doesn't already.

He wipes one of my tears away with his thumb. His eyes are so intense, I have to look away. "How 'bout I walk you home?" he asks.

I nod. That I can do.

CHAPTER 3

I walk into my house, look at my school schedule on the counter where Mom left it for me. She's always doing that, thinking that if I can just prepare for things, I'll be okay. As if you could prepare for anything. What a joke. Leah and I planned. And see where that got us? Or at least her.

I hold the schedule in my hand and stare at the teachers and subjects I'll be taking. Junior year is my *make it or break it* year. Looking at my classes, I have no idea how I'll get into any college, let alone RISD. No one I know takes regular classes, and honors are for people headed for state colleges. Not for elite art schools.

My head throbs. The silence in the house is so loud I can't think. Anger. Shame. Guilt. Denial. Put that in a blender and mix it up. Drink it down with a calm-down pill. Keep going. Just. Keep. Going.

Lights out through the house means Mom's probably lying down. Her deal-with-it cocktail already in her. Part of me wishes that she would give it up, that after everything that happened, she would have stopped. Or Dad would have come back and stopped her. Part of me remembers how it used to be when Mom and Dad still pretended to be happy. Or maybe they actually were. It's stupid to think about the things I wish, because Mom's not going to stop taking pills and Dad's not going to change. Leah always said I was stupid about people. She was right. Clearly.

The reverberation of Leah's voice leaks into my brain, like a drumbeat synchronizing with my migraine. *You were always so starstruck, Baby Sister.*

I trudge upstairs to my room. I need something to calm me down too. I need to find a little Relief.

I reach into the back of my closet. In one of my old Michael Kors bags, I've hidden the bottle of NyQuil I had Mom get me two weeks ago when I told her I had a cold. I roll it in my palm and play the game Leah and I used to: *I'll stop if.* This time it's a one-player game, but I don't let that get to me. If Max calls, I'll stop. If Leah were here, she'd call me a cheater because that's not even in the realm of possibilities. So I go again. If Emery calls, I'll stop. If Mom wakes up, I'll stop. If the phone rings in the next ten seconds, from anyone, a solicitor, a creditor, the school, I'll stop. I breathe out and count to ten. No calls. No texts. No reason to stop. I strip the plastic off and unscrew the top, breaking the seal as I do.

NyQuil is part of my emergency arsenal, strictly for code-red situations. Or when I need help sleeping. But right now, I need it to make the headache stop. I need to find some Escape. I need to heal, like Mrs. Pendrick said. I'm living my life in tiny squares, doing the best I can.

And I know how bad this is. Of course I do, after Leah, but

it's not Mom drugs. It's only the over-the-counter stuff. Just as I bring the lip of the bottle to my mouth, I get a flash from that last night I saw Leah alive, the party I can't remember. God, that sucks. I suck. My last night with her, and I blew it in so many ways.

I tip the bottle and drink a big swig. The sickening medicine taste almost chokes me, but I keep it in. I drink some more and walk to the window. From here I can see my studio. It's waiting for me, but I'm not ready. So I turn up the music and drink some more.

I lie back on my bed and think about Leah. The questions I can't get out of my mind: Why did she do it without following our plan? Why didn't she tell me? Why? Why? Why? The tears threaten, but I push them away. Crying doesn't help. Nothing does except the medicine that's just starting to kick in and make the grip on my head loosen.

I look around my room, blue-haze walls and beach-white trim. Leah picked out the colors. My hands go to my head, trying to make the pain stop. But I hear her voice, a memory filling my head with its soft tones and pretty scents. I hear my sister like it's in real time, even though it was years ago.

"You need something to make your work pop," Leah said as I painted squares of color samples from the paint store over the babyish purple I had in middle school. "I like this one." She pointed to the blue patch.

I remember being annoyed at first. Shouldn't I get to pick the color for *my* room? But she was right. It was perfect. Like she was. She could always talk me into anything. My sister made me a little starstruck. She never minded, as long as it was her star I was following.

Liquid inspiration from the NyQuil strikes. I should paint something for Leah, let her know I get it now. Maybe I didn't when she was alive. Maybe I didn't listen when she tried to tell me things.

I open the door and look out into the hallway—lights off, TV on downstairs. Mom's checkout gives me the clear shot I need. In the garage, I find the white paint from the trim and the brushes. Everything seems really clear right now. And brilliant. I feel sort of brilliant. Like every part of my brain is working.

Back in my room, I shake the can of paint and open it with a screwdriver and hammer, trying hard not to spill it on my hardwood floors. Too late.

My curtains are in the way, so I rip them off the rod. I have to stand on my window seat to reach as high as I need. I start to paint, not knowing what I'm doing until the image forms on the wall, like magic. By the time I've painted the point of convergence on my window where the pink diamond goes, I recognize it. I painted it like it was burned into my brain. Leah's ring.

I sit back and admire my work. I hope, wherever she is, she sees this and knows I'm sorry. A pain shoots through my head and I squint at the blinding light of the setting sun. Spiky rays angle in through my painting, making it seem like it's alive.

I close my eyes against the brightness. When I open them again, I'm confused. Because I see Leah standing there. Really standing there. I'm not imagining it. She's there, surrounded by light, kind of outlined in it. Like one of my rendering sketches.

I go to reach for her, ask her if she's really here, but her image disappears, and I know it's just my guilt and need that's bringing her to me. Even if she can't stay.

I close up the paint can and take it and the medicine bottle downstairs. The paint and tools go back into the garage, and the brush gets washed in the sink. I run my hand over its stainless steel surface, careful that all the evidence goes down the drain. Finally I wrap the medicine bottle in newspaper and push it to the bottom of the trash can, making certain that it's completely covered. One thing Leah taught me was how to hide your party.

When I'm done, I walk back up to my bathroom and brush my teeth, trying not to look in the mirror, as if my crazy will show. I crawl into bed and try not to think about tomorrow. First day of school. I put my hands together in the prayer position and put them under my cheek. I try not to think about what I just did or worry about what it means. Sleep will help. I know I'm not coping. I'm living my life in tiny squares. Checkerboard moves. Each play means something. Each turn matters. The most important thing is to keep moving. To not get jumped. Sometimes a little NyQuil helps that. They don't call it medicine for nothing.

CHAPTER 4

I'm almost ready for school when I hear the front door open and Emery booming up the steps. Guess she's already had her daily dose of double espresso, two sugars. Emery on caffeine is way too much to handle—especially after my binge last night. I go into my bathroom and grab some aspirin. This is going to be a long day.

"Hey, girl," Emery calls. "Where are…"

I find her staring at my wall, pointing—as if just staring isn't enough. As if pointing will change anything. "Wow," she says.

"Yeah."

"Is that… Is it…"

"It's her ring."

Emery's brow furrows. I know what she's thinking.

"I didn't mean anything by it," I say. "It's just a painting."

"It just looks kind of like a portal, you know?"

"It's just a painting. I was just screwing around."

"Allie, I don't know, it's kind of…" Emery's eyes wet, and I feel bad.

"I'm serious. I'm not going anywhere. I promise."

Emery stares at my stupid paint on the wall. "You have no idea what it was like finding out." She turns her stare on me.

"How awful it felt not to know you two had planned… I mean, I still don't know what that was all about."

"It was a stupid game. Leah and I… We just used to talk about it sometimes. When things were bad. But we didn't mean it." I stop talking, because obviously Leah *did* think about it. Obviously she was serious.

Emery kisses me on the cheek. "I miss her too. She was an excellent big sister."

Emery, an only child, suffered from wanting what I had. Leah. And Leah was happy to lord over the two of us. She used to say having Emery was like a buy one, get one free deal.

"Come on." I grab my lip gloss, Trident Layers gum, and a to-go pack of aspirin for later. "We're going to be late. And you know you hate that."

"I do." She nods her head. "I hate not being there when it all starts."

"And you think *I'm* messed up?" I take one last glance at my painting, thinking about what Emery said. *A portal. If only…* I turn off the light.

"Hey, your mom left you something," Emery calls from the kitchen. I hustle to catch up and see Mom pulled her usual, leaving a note and a twenty. I wonder where she thinks I eat at school that I need twenty dollars. Is it her version of buying my forgiveness for her not making it out of bed to tell me to have a good first day? She shouldn't worry. It's not like I was counting on her.

I ignore the note and take the money.

"Where is she anyway?" Emery asks.

"Sleeping." I push her out the door.

Emery starts the car, and I slide into the passenger seat. We both stare at my studio. I hope she doesn't say anything. But I know she will.

"Have you…"

"No. Not yet."

She turns to me. "You will."

I nod.

"Okay, let's do this." She adjusts her mirror. I look at her and see her eyes fill.

Leah's left a wake of pain. I wonder if she knew it would be like this. I wonder if she got how many people would be hurt.

As we turn into the traffic jam that is the road to our high school, she says, "Oh, I totally forgot. Text Max. He wants to meet us."

My face heats. How come she knew that and I didn't? I pull my phone out and see two texts from Max last night and a bunch from Emery that I ignored. I open up his thread.

U ok?

Then, Meet up in the parking lot tom?

I breathe out and text him.

On our way

Emery pulls into a parking spot, slamming on her brakes last minute so we don't run into the concrete parking divider. As if it snuck up on her. As if she didn't expect it. Despite the headache that I woke up with that is building thanks to

Emery's whiplash-inducing braking session, I'm glad that some things haven't changed. Namely Emery.

She looks in the mirror and paints on her starlet-red lips. It's a ritual that starts with pencil lip liner, proceeds to lipstick, and finishes with a sheer gloss.

"It's Bang-Bang Red. You like?"

"What happened to Crush?" Her favorite color last year.

"I'm over it." She winks.

Max's face appears in my window, and I jump. I look at his dark, curly hair, deep blue eyes, and pink face, now tanned terra cotta after his summer gig as lifeguard at our community pool. Max's colors are all about warmth—red, orange, pink.

He opens my door and waits as I get out. He and Em exchange a quick glance that I catch just before she shoves her sunglasses in place.

"I'm fine," I say.

Max puts his arm around me and part of me wants to play wounded so he won't let me go. He pulls his schedule out of his pocket. "Show you mine if you show me yours?" He smiles at me lecherously.

I have already scanned his classes. None of ours match. I'm going to be a social pariah, in all the lower classes now.

Emery pulls her schedule out of her purse, the new Michael Kors one, tan with gold MKs all over it. Her going-back-to-school purse. Emery's happy. She holds her schedule up to Max's. I can see they already have two matches. Honors chem and AP psychology. I groan.

The two of them sharing something just makes me feel even more left out. I get that Max isn't one hundred percent mine. I just wish he were.

"Hey, Iron Man," one of Max's swimming friends calls from behind us.

He holds up a hand in a wave, then snakes his arms around both Em and I. Max is just using us as props. The guys behind us, the pack, laugh.

Emery pulls his arm off her. "Go be with your friends."

He leans into me. "I'll find you later. Be good." He kisses my cheek and then moves on.

"Where's your first?" Emery asks.

"Honors English with Miss Lafrance."

"I've got drama."

Emery stops walking and so do I. She grabs my schedule. "Cool, we have lunch together. Find me later, okay?"

"Sure."

Emery shoots me one last look as I veer toward the two-hundred building. I pass Jennifer Skelton and Vanessa Waters. My eyes drop to the floor before I have to register the look of disdain I'm sure Vanessa will shoot me. It's bad enough I have to be back in school without Leah, surrounded by her friends and frenemies. I hate that I have to face Vanessa. Everything shouldn't be hard.

My head stays down the rest of the way to class. I hear pieces of conversation, current and memories. Old and new mixing together as if in a blender. Like the one they had at the party.

The night she did it. Where was I when she was thinking about dying? Drinking with her friends. Bile rises in my throat.

"*It's a strawberry daiquiri. You'll like it,*" Jason saying as he handed me one. Leah looking at me like she approved. Jason was one of the football players. Sean's friend.

Max today saying "*Be good*" and then kissing me.

Emery saying "*It's called Bang-Bang Red. You like?*"

Vanessa at the party. "*Ask your sister why she's not on the team anymore. Ask her.*"

The words *ask her* reverberate in my head, making me dizzy. What I wouldn't give to ask her now. The dance team. The rumors. Even if half of them were true, does that add up to killing yourself?

The headache ramps up to full force by the time I make it to class, but more than that, my body feels like it's been hit by a truck. Smacked and slapped and stung with all the memories and the murmurs. I should have packed a little something. Maybe a Benadryl or two to get through today. Not NyQuil or Robitussin or anything major. Just a little numb. And I know how wrong that is, how stupid it is to rely on chemicals to get through the day, but it sucks being back without her. Leah used to own this school. Now she's gone, and they've moved in to fill in the space she used to occupy. If that's not depressing, I don't know what is.

"Hey, Allie," a voice breaks me out of my haze. Nick. "You have Lafrance too?" he asks, his head tilting toward the door.

"Yeah."

"Let's get in before all the back-of-the-room seats are taken. Or are you one of those front-of-the-room suck-ups?"

"Hardly." I laugh.

"Come on." He grabs my arm.

I let him lead me to the back of the room, and I wonder when I became like this—so easily led. Or was I always? I look at Nick and think maybe he'd be rusts and greens. But not just because of his copper-colored hair. It's more than that. It seems like maybe those are the colors of his laughs, quiet but honest. And his energy—crisp and clean like fresh-cut grass. Seeing his colors, or at least feeling them, is like a gift. If Nick Larsons, part-artist, part–first baseman is making me think about art, that's a good thing. For the first time today, I've found a little Happy. Legit.

Miss Lafrance walks to the front of the class. She holds up a copy of *The Alchemist*. I groan. We read it last year in AP Language and Composition. But maybe that helps me? Maybe I can coast through this class and give my brain a rest. Obviously it needs one.

CHAPTER 5

The day's finally over, and I can't wait to get home. Emery's staying after for drama club, and only freshmen and sophomores take the bus. So, iPod in my ears, I walk. I pass the little market that Em and I used to walk to when we were trying to be grown-up and independent. I stop in front of it. Maybe I'll go in, look at the cards, the funny little hamsters that play "Kung Fu Fighting" if you press the button on their paws. Leah used to do that—press all their buttons and we'd laugh and clap as they sang just out of sync, moving their little nunchucks the whole time. That memory warms me. I decide I'm going in. The bell on the door rings, and the old lady working the counter looks up at me, a small smile on her face as she does.

But now that I'm here, I feel sort of disoriented. Leah's not here, not even in my mind. Emery's got drama. Max has swimming. I'm here all alone.

I walk past the cards. Past the hamster toys. Past the summer clearance aisle, the doughnuts, the wine bottles, the cheeses, the apples and bananas, the desserts—to the cold medicine aisle, where I grab a bottle of NyQuil without even thinking. As my hand closes around it, as I march up to the counter, I tell myself, *Just because I am buying this, doesn't mean I have to take it. It's just a backup in case I need one. I'm just being prepared.*

"Is that all, honey?" the woman at the counter asks.

"Yes." I force myself to look at her. "Mom's pretty sick."

"That's nice you're getting this for her then."

I walk out of the store, bag in my backpack, feeling like a total idiot because I just lied to this stranger. And because I'm stockpiling meds now for no apparent reason. Everything is so confusing in my head, and I need some clarity. I need to remember what happened. Not just that night. Right before. Volcanoes don't just erupt out of nowhere. The fire and the heat and the pain build. The same is true for me.

I take out my phone and toggle to the notes section, where I've saved the texts Max sent me last spring.

I think we should try.

I want us to.

You know how I feel about you.

I pass the library and the post office. I cut through the golf course and climb down the hill, taking me to the back of my yard, pushing back the Max scab I've picked at now. I was so stupid to believe him. So stupid.

I walk through the thin trees at the back of our property and past my studio. I don't have the key with me because I stopped carrying it, but my hand goes into my pocket as if expecting to find it.

I stop and look in the window. It's dark, and I can't see much—just my paintings covered in sheets. My paintings.

And then it happens. I see her. Leah's in my studio, warming up as if she's getting ready for dance class. I bang on the window. She doesn't look up, just keeps going. First position, arm straight. Second position, leaning over. She's dressed in a black leotard with ballerina-pink tights and a black see-through skirt. I push my face against the window so I can listen to the sound her ballet shoes make as they slide across the concrete, but I can't make them out. My head starts throbbing. I steady myself against the wall.

I close my eyes for just a second, and when I open them again, she's gone. Like she was never there. Was it just in my cracked mind? I almost bang on the window, but I know she won't be there—I do. But knowing something and accepting it are two totally different animals. Like with Max last spring. I knew. But I still wanted him.

The sadness that descends on me makes it hard to climb up the stairs, through the mudroom, and into the kitchen, where Sophie is there waiting for me, her tail wagging like crazy.

I bend down and let her climb on me. Then I pick her up and let her kiss my face. "I missed you too, puppy."

Sophie was Leah's baby. Now I guess she's mine. We got her three years ago for Leah's birthday.

"But she's both of ours," Leah had told me as we drove home from the breeder. "Our dog, right?"

Sophie had climbed into my lap and kissed my face, her puppy breath filling my nose.

"You're such a freak!" Leah had said, but her eyes crinkled

and her voice was happy. "Come back to Mommy." She'd lifted Sophie off my lap and onto hers.

I'd thought it was nice of her to share with me. Of course, she also meant ours to walk, ours to bathe, ours to clean up after. That never mattered to me, even though I ended up doing most of the disgusting work. I still thought it was a nice gesture. Always starstruck, that's me. Leah didn't mind as long as it was her star I was following.

Mom slides into the kitchen. Her movements seem careful, calculated, which annoys me. "How was your day?"

I push past her, go to the refrigerator, and grab a bottle of cold water. Without thinking, I push the tips of my fingers into my temple.

"Headache again?"

I can almost hear her watching me. Her stare feels thick and heavy, like the slurring of her words. Did I really expect her to change? Stupid. Leah always said I was stupid about people.

"I'll get you a pill," she offers.

Mom goes to the cabinet and opens the one that has my rescue medication in it. Her hands shake as she pops out one of my pills, then drops it.

My head throbs as I stare at her clumsy attempt to medicate me. Mom finds the pill and cups it in her hands, reaching out toward me. I don't see the pill. I only see her shaking hands. She notices me staring. She tries to still her trembling fingers, but it's too late. I already saw. I know I should give Mom a break. I realize that. Leah was always so mad at Mom, but I always took her side. Now I don't even feel like doing that.

"I have to go out for a bit," Mom says. "You want something special for dinner?"

"No." I go upstairs, Sophie on my heels, glad to have space but not sure why it matters when Mom's gone most of the time in one way or another. Then I feel bad. So I call down to her, "Pizza would be good."

"Great," she says. "Pizza and maybe a salad."

"Fine." When I get to the top of the steps, I stand at Leah's door. I'm not supposed to go in there, but it's like I'm being summoned.

Sitting in her chair, I play the game I've played since I was little. I pretend I'm her. I open her top drawer and trail my fingers over her nail polish bottles, lined up in a neat row. Leah's colors: I'm a Pisa Work, Beach Party, and Silver Shatter. Not me, but perfect. And it hits me. There's no mess. Her desk drawer is perfectly organized, even more than usual. Like she cleaned it. Before. I get chills and wonder again why she didn't tell me. I knew about her little pill habit and about our arsenal, but I really never thought she'd use it. Not without me.

I turn on her computer. Her password: notsocommonwhite-bitch. Her screen saver is a montage of her favorite pictures. I scan them, like when you get your yearbook and you look to make sure that there are pictures of you in there. There aren't any of me on Leah's slide show. I know. I've looked a hundred times. Each time I wish it were different. But it's not. And with her gone, it never will be. The proof is right in front of me. I wasn't that important to her. I was more background than forefront. I sucked. Which must be why she left me behind.

"I'm sorry." Leah's voice comes to me. At first I think I'm imagining her, but I hear her. It's as if my head clears and just her voice is piped in.

I start to cry because I know this can't be real and I can't be sane. But I still want her with me.

"I'm here. You're not imagining it." She's still just voice and no body.

My head throbs, and I close my eyes. White lights flash and my migraine kicks up a notch. My stomach feels queasy. I go to our bathroom, the one we used to share, and open the medicine cabinet. Phenergan is the only thing that keeps me from puking. I put the pill in my mouth, cup my hand, and turn on the water. A memory of Leah standing in front of this mirror flashes in my mind.

We were getting ready to go out to the movies for one of the forced family outings Mom thought would help save the marriage.

"This is sooo lame," Leah moaned. "I was supposed to go out with Sean."

"I know," I said even though I was happy to be spending time with her, but I didn't want to sound like her dorky little sister. "It totally sucks."

Leah stood in front of her full-length mirror, her face tight, holding a prescription bottle.

"These pills are making me fat." She threw the bottle across the room and missed her trash can by an inch.

"Don't you need them?" I reached down to pick them up for her, the name Dr. Gates written on the label. Her psychiatrist. Mom wanted her to see a counselor, but Dad insisted on a psychiatrist because whatever Leah had was that bad. I had overheard him say "Crazy runs in families." He was talking about Mom's side. Of course.

Leah's face turned dark. She brushed back her hair with both hands. "Nah, I'm good. Hey, wanna grab my Chap?" she asked.

I reached into her drawer, pulled out her tube, and found the pills. Three of them in a plastic bag, all rolled up.

"What's this for?"

Leah blushed pink, then came across the room and grabbed it out of my hand. "Just a little pick-me-up. These are the best. I can go for days without eating on these little babies." She grabbed one and threw it into the back of her throat, chasing it down with a chug of sugar-free Rockstar. She winked at me.

I wanted to ask her where she got them, but I knew she wouldn't tell me. I wanted to tell her she was doing exactly what Mom does, but that would make her furious. Instead, I just sat on her bed, quietly agreeing with whatever stupid thing she chose to do.

"It's no big," she said. "I'm gonna need something to get through tonight with Mom and Dad anyway, and I told you, I'm getting fat. I won't get the lead in *Fame* if I'm a cow."

I snap out of the memory and flop on her bed. My eyes close, and I'm asleep almost immediately.

"Allie?"

Mom's voice startles me.

I hear her on the stairs. I don't want her to find me in Leah's room. She and Dad are a little weird on that subject. I push myself up, my head still fuzzy from the Phenergan. Leah's comforter is wrinkled. I have to fix that.

"Allie?"

Mom's made it to my room. Not good.

I lean over to turn off her computer and realize I don't have enough time. So I just switch off the monitor.

When Mom rounds the corner and appears in Leah's doorway, her face registers disappointment.

"I brought you your next pill."

"I don't need it."

Mom looks at me, standing over Leah's computer, the one they searched afterward for answers. Like Leah would leave some secret suicide file on her desktop. Like she wouldn't cover her tracks. It was part of the plan we'd made. Make everything look clean because Leah didn't want people to know why she did it. She wanted to stay perfect in everyone's eyes. She wanted to dance off stage as a tragic and mysterious heroine. Cue the curtain.

"I thought your father and I said we didn't want you spending so much time in here," Mom says.

"I was just looking for a book." Lie. Stupid one.

"Emery and Max are here to see you. Are you up to seeing them?"

"Sure."

"I'll tell them to meet you in your room." She retreats out of the doorway and walks unsteadily down the hall. I hear her steps, small, reticent. And I get as mad at her as Leah used to.

I walk out of Leah's room, turning the light off as I go, hoping that'll prove to Mom that I have no intention of coming back. Emery and Max bound up the stairs and rush through my door.

"You okay?" Emery asks. "You look like you just saw a ghost."

"I just didn't know you guys were coming together."

"Met up downstairs. How are you doing?" Max asks.

"Okay," I lie.

Max throws himself on my bed, making it bend under his weight—one hundred and eighty pounds, all muscle. He tells me all the time. Like I couldn't tell on my own. My mind goes over those texts.

I think we should try.

I want us to.

You know how I feel about you.

The meds have turned me floaty and loose, and I pretend it didn't end badly that time. I let them fill me with heat and hope, like they did when he sent them, instead of how stupid I felt after it all went down.

"Coach was hyper today, a total idiot. I'm beat." Max stretches his arms over his head, showing his guns like he likes to. I try not to smile, but he's so obvious.

Emery sits at my computer, eating some kind of PowerBar

36

and drinking the special tea that's supposed to cleanse her body but really just has a ton of caffeine, already surfing.

I sit on my window seat. My phone vibrates.

hi

"Who's that?" Max asks.

"Have no idea." It seems like such a good question that I type Who is this? and push Send.

The phone nearly jumps out of my hand.

Nick

"Whoever it is, they're lightning fast," Emery calls.

"It's Nick." I aim my words at Emery but hope they hit Max, hard.

"Nick Larsons?" Max asks.

"Yeah."

"Baseball player Nick? Again? What's with that guy?" he asks.

I stay quiet, enjoying Max's jealousy.

"He's okay, if you like baseball players. If that's your thing." Max thinks swimmers are the only real athletes.

I ignore Max and type back. Hi Nick.

U busy?

Max gets off the bed and comes over to me. He kneels down and moves the hair away from my eyes. "You okay, really? You look tired."

Sometimes I wonder what Max's thinking when he looks at me like that. Sometimes I think that he still wants to be more than friends—like last spring when we tried. We met at the park, both of us shy with each other at first. Then came shots of gin he'd stolen from his parents. Followed by Gatorade chasers. The swings. Then the merry-go-round. We'd laughed. We'd drunk. We'd kissed. His lips on mine, soft and sweet.

"Headache," I say.

"You wouldn't be holding out on me, would you?" Max's beautiful eyes take me in. I swear he wants to kiss me like that night. His fingers trace my face.

"I…"

Max's eyes shoot to the phone in my hand. "He asked you out in a text? Wow."

I look down.

I mean Friday night. You want to go out?

"Just be careful, okay? Guys suck. Just saying." Max gets up and crosses the room.

And just like that, he shuts me out like the week after our park hookup. After I froze up and couldn't give him what he wanted. I remember his hands on me in ways I never thought could feel so good. But then I hesitated and then he stopped. And the next day we were both sober and embarrassed. He could barely look at me as he said the things I'll never forget. The words I don't have to save in my phone, because they are written on my heart. *We're better as friends. I can't lose you. Maybe when we're older and less stupid.* Despite his excuses, I knew it was because I couldn't grow up.

Emery brings me back to the present. "She's almost like a nun these days. She couldn't *be* any more careful. Besides, he's cute. I kind of like redheads."

Max makes a face.

K I type back and hit Send.

I push Max out of the way and lie down on my bed. I put the pillow over my face and drown out the sound of Max and Emery's chatter. I close my eyes. God, I'm so tired.

Max lies down next to me, his body sending mine comfort, because our bodies do that. Without the worries about the future and what this means, with just straight-up contact, Max settles me. And even though I wish Max were with me, really with me, he's still my Max.

"Allie, Allie, Allie," Max whispers. "You need to sleep."

He's right, I do.

"Sweet dreams." Max throws his arm around me, and I let myself fall away from my room and the sad that lives here.

The colors come to me when I'm almost totally out—deep, rich blues and foamy greens, beach-washed whites, cedar grays. The colors from my better past surround me till I'm safe and happy and I can let go for a little while.

CHAPTER 6

I'm totally surprised when I find Mom in the kitchen waiting for me in her bathrobe, hair wild and messy, clutching her coffee cup in both hands. I used to tell her that when she drank coffee, she looked like she was praying. Today is definitely one of her hail-coffee-full-of-grace days.

"Morning," she manages as she brings the cup to her mouth.

"Morning." I push past her and open the fridge, hoping she remembered to go shopping. That's not always a given with Mom.

Surprisingly, there's a huge amount of food. I grab a Chobani black cherry yogurt for breakfast and a Gatorade for later. I move to the pantry to get the crunchy cereal I like to mix in and lean against the counter. Mom hands me a spoon and a brown bag.

"What's this?"

"Lunch. I packed you lunch."

I try not to choke.

"Organic peanut butter and jelly, carrot sticks, and a cut-up apple," she says. "I don't think you're eating right."

I seriously can't remember the last time she packed a lunch for me. "Thanks" is all I can manage. The yogurt now feels weird in my mouth.

A car beeps. Mom and I both look out the front window. Emery.

"Allie…" Mom says as I turn to go.

"Yeah?"

She hands me a business card with the name of a lab on it.

"What's this?"

She looks down at it, like my stare is way too hard to hold. "Come on, Allie. You know we agreed to this."

Blood tests. To see if I'm taking my anti-crazy meds. They can't be serious. "I didn't agree to anything." I'm not doing it. And it's not just because I'm not taking those stupid-ass meds. It's the principle.

I put the paper bag on the counter and with it the card from the lab. I don't need her guilt lunch with a side of accusation.

"We want to be sure—"

"We? Who's we?"

She doesn't answer, just stands there. Her eyes finally find mine. At least she looked me in the eye. Usually she's too impaired to do that.

"Allie, please. Your dad and I are trying to take care of you."

"How 'bout you guys try to trust me? How 'bout that?"

I feel like a total creep. Like a complete hypocrite. She's right. Hell, he's right too. I am not now nor do I ever intend to take that medicine. They forced me when I was in the hospital. It made me feel numb and stupid, as if I were looking at the world through some kind of gauze.

I look at the card and blink. My head tightens like I'm some kind of gear that's being wound. The appointment is right after school. Mom always waits to give me bad news when I won't have time to argue. She's a pro at this game—sneaky-Mom timing. Hate that shit. I should have known.

"Your father set this up. I wanted to tell you last night, but you fell asleep so early, I didn't have a chance."

"It's *today*? After school?"

"Yes. I'll pick you up if you want and take you."

"Gee, thanks."

"Allie—"

"I've gotta go." I walk toward the front door, yank it open, wave to Em, and turn back to Mom. "I'm not doing a stupid blood test and you can't make me."

"Allie, your father thinks…"

I hold up my hand. I know what Dad thinks. He's told me a hundred times: I'm too obsessed with Leah. I need to have a good year. He's afraid I'm throwing away my life. Like Leah did.

Dad says. Mom delivers. He's such a bully. She's such a victim. I'm so over them both.

———◦———

I used to love art class. Now I dread it. It's not just Mr. Kispert's expectations. Or Dad's. Or mine. It's also that Nick is in that class too. And even if I'm not into him like I am Max, I don't want him to see me struggle. The first week of any semester in art is about mixing colors and making choices. That means I'm officially screwed.

Piper Mason is already sitting at the back of the room, looking through art books when I walk in. Piper is a senior who could have gotten into any art school she wanted as a junior. She's this ridiculous phenom I will never be able to equal. Her focus is sculpture. She nods as I approach, and part of me feels honored she's letting me share the same space. I sit on the industrial-green patterned couch across from hers, this part of the room strictly for us AP students, which may just be Nick and Piper and me.

"I'm done with this one." Piper hands me the book she was looking through. "I'm thinking of doing portraits as my concentration, but I wonder if that's lame." She grabs another art book. "You know what you're doing?" She looks up at me from behind the bangs that have fallen over her face.

"No idea," I answer.

"God, I hate this." She leans forward. "You know what? If this art thing doesn't work out, maybe I'll just be an engineer or something. How hard could *that* be?"

I laugh, amazed she's treating me like her equal, which I am not, and also that she's unsure herself. "Or a heart surgeon," I suggest.

Her turn to laugh, though she's moved back into her previous position, with legs drawn in and her book balanced on her knees. "Truly."

The bell rings and Nick trots to the back of the room. "Hey." He slides his baseball bag off his shoulder and onto the floor. "We ready for the insanity? Although you two have probably solved the whole world peace thing by now."

"Yeah, but not our concentration topics," Piper says.

He smiles. "You guys as stuck as I am?"

"It's not due till next week," I offer.

"Just a stay of execution really." Nick drags two fingers across his throat, closes his eyes, and sticks his tongue out.

Piper stops her page flipping and faces him. "A little insensitive?"

His face turns bright red. His eyes go to me. "I'm sorry, Allie. I didn't mean—"

"No, it's okay. I know you didn't..." Silence surrounds me, chokes me. My throat swells with the knowledge of what they want from me. How, like everyone, they want me to tell them how it happened. What went down with Leah and me and the pact. "Can we just forget it?"

They go back to perusing the books, but I still feel the heat of their curiosity. I close my eyes and think about how it felt to find her. How it felt afterward. How it felt when I realized I was the one who'd bailed, even though she was the one who forgot to invite me.

I press my fingers into my eyelids and sigh.

Nick gets up and grabs the bathroom pass.

Piper lays the book flat in her lap and looks up at me. I pray she doesn't say anything mean. I don't know her that well, but she doesn't seem the type. Still, right now my world is filled with land mines. "Leah and I had English together last year. She was so cool."

I don't know what to say.

Piper goes back to flipping through the pages but keeps talking. "Use the pain for your art. Use it to make something real. I know that's what Leah did."

My head tilts. What is she talking about? How well did she know Leah? Her honesty shocks me. "I'm not sure I can anymore. I feel…"

"Blocked?" she asks.

"Yeah."

"That happens." Piper talks without looking up. "If your art's a little lost right now, you gotta find it. Find it any way you can. I mean, look at all the greats. Pain fueled them. Pain and maybe some *pain medicine*." She puts air quotes around the words, then continues. "Andy Warhol, Vincent van Gogh, hell, even Charles Schulz dabbled when the muse was playing hide-and-seek."

I sit there, mute and dumb in front of the coolest, most talented person I know. She yelled at Nick for being insensitive, but recommending I use the same meds that killed Leah might just take the cake for insensitivity. Doesn't it?

"The point is, find your art, Allie. Anyway you can."

Nick returns and Piper pulls back into herself, and I wonder if I imagined that entire conversation.

I close my eyes and think about the colors. That's how I used to find my art. The colors.

"I'm so pink." Leah's voice finds me from when I painted her this summer. I wanted to start on my concentration early, surprise Mr. Kispert. She offered to be my subject. Big surprise. Leah was all in when it was about her.

"It's *innocence* mixed with *reverie*. You look good like that," I said.

"Is that how you see me?" she asked.

I nodded. I saw her just that way. Perfect. Flawless. Mine.

"I remember when I looked like that," she said, wistfully.

I didn't know what she meant by that then and now I wish I had asked.

Piper's words loop around my brain. *Use the pain for your art. I know that's what Leah did.* When did Leah use her dancing to get over things? What things? The bell rings before I can get any answers.

———•———

Mom is waiting for me out in front of the school. Part of me is impressed she's sticking to her guns. The other part is panicked. I can't take that blood test.

Emery emerges from the front of the school, surrounded by kids I don't recognize. Probably freshies. Drama kids by the looks of it. Every color hair ever made and a few I've never seen before. I wait for her to make it to where I'm standing. Her eyes scan to Mom's car.

"What's up?"

"Stupid blood test."

"What for?"

"You know."

She raises her eyebrows. "I thought you were going to try to take them."

"I don't need them."

"She's just worried. Like we all are," Emery says.

"I don't need your worry. I didn't actually do anything. Remember? I was the one who lived?"

Emery lays her hand on my arm. "I'm sorry. This sucks."

"Guess there's no getting around it. Wish me luck."

She nods, and I leave her standing there as I walk toward Mom's car, a silver Mercedes SUV. In case she has to go off-roading. I open the door and have to hold onto the handle to hoist myself up and in.

Mom waits till I've buckled my seat belt before switching the car into drive, and for some reason that totally pisses me off. As if she didn't trust me to do my seat belt. As if I could possibly commit suicide by hard stop. Visions of me flying out the front windshield as Mom gets a little too feisty with the brakes fills my head and I almost laugh out loud.

"You still don't want to do the test?" She adjusts the rearview mirror and pulls out.

"No."

She uses the red light we're stopped at as an opportunity to look at me. Her eyes are full of tears I know I've put there. That Leah and I have. The light turns green. She nudges the car forward until we are moving in this slow, painful progression toward the thing I don't want to do and the thing she feels compelled to force me to.

47

"You know the test is pointless," I say.

"Because you're not taking the meds?"

I don't answer. She checks me with one of those sideways "Mom" looks.

"You need those meds. If Leah had…" She grips the wheel tighter. Her pale hands turn white under the pressure.

I stare at the road in front of us.

Mom brakes at another light. She rotates to face me. "Can you tell me why you don't want to take them?"

I try to talk, but the words are stuck inside me. I want to tell her I don't need them. That maybe Leah did, but I don't. I want to tell her I can't live like she does, pacing out her life from one dose to the next. I want to tell her I'm sorry I've made her life harder and sadder.

"I'm scared, Allie. Really scared…"

"I'm okay. I'm fine."

She reaches out to pat my hand. "Okay. No test today. But you'll have to do one in two weeks. Two weeks is the time it takes to build it up in your system." The light turns green.

Gratitude fills me. Then it's replaced by fear. "What about Dad?"

"I'll handle him. Don't worry."

"Thanks, Mom."

"Don't leave me, Allie. Stay."

My breath catches. I want to tell her I'm trying. I want to tell her I never planned to leave. She doesn't want to hear that. She wants me to promise. "I will," I say.

CHAPTER 7

The smell of Dr. Applegate's building gets inside me as soon as I open the door to the lobby. Clean. Antiseptic. The scent of hygiene makes me feel like I'm choking on mental health.

I sign in and nod at the receptionist, who is so small and meek, it's like she's trying not to take up too much space. I duck into the bathroom and lock the door. My hands shake as I pull out the bottle of NyQuil and think about not drinking any. Maybe I could white-knuckle it through this session? I look at the bottle, then in the mirror. Its beveled edge makes my face seem cracked and messed up, like a Picasso painting. I take that as a sign and unscrew the cap. I bring it to my lips. There's still time to stop. I don't have to do this.

There's a knock on the door. "Allie? Are you okay in there?"

"I'm fine," I bark. "I'll be right out."

"Okay, just checking."

My lips open this time. I take a drink, letting the gaggy cherry taste slide down my throat. Just three sips. No more. Just three. How bad could three gulps be? I close it, turn on the water, and splash some on my face. I open my mouth and wipe off my tongue with one of the paper towels from the basket. I grab a mint, flush the toilet, and push the door open.

I flop on one of the waiting room chairs and take my phone out. I feel like such a cheat and a liar, but honestly, I'm doing the best I can.

Mom picks up a *Good Housekeeping* magazine and pretends to read it. I pretend to not notice the irony. The cough medicine needs a good twenty minutes to kick in. Till then, I look at my phone. A new text blinks at me.

I slide my fingers across the screen.

Hey. Allie? This is Nick.

The next one, also from him. Was thinking about our concentration. We need twelve paintings? We could do the months of the year.

I curl my fingers over my lips. Send him a smiley face text back.

Or maybe the apostles?

This time I laugh out loud. Mom turns to look at me. "It's good to see you smile," she says.

The receptionist appears at the opened door, leans on it to let me know Dr. Applegate is ready to see me. We walk down the hallway to her office. The walls are lined with black-and-white pictures of oversized flowers, stock photo art that's insultingly generic. The door opens and Dr. Applegate comes forward, hand outstretched. "Come on in, Allie."

I duck into the room and take my place on the couch I hate. Burgundy. The worst color in the world. Dr. Applegate stands in front of me, all stiff colors: super-white skin, black-cherry lips, and chemically whitened teeth. Her hair is pulled back in a severe ponytail. She's dressed in a tight, gray pencil skirt and a crisp white shirt. Dr. Applegate is wearing her perfection like a talisman. I hate to tell her how ridiculous that is. If that worked, Leah would still be here.

She sits. "So, Allie, what would you like to talk about today?"

I look out the window and try to buy time. Her window faces a courtyard. There's never anyone out there and generally nothing to see, but it's a pretty green courtyard with a small maple tree that someone planted next to the window. Its leaves are vibrant, tree-frog green. God, I love greens. Greens and blues are the best colors in the world.

"Allie?" Dr. Applegate tries to make me pay attention. She sits in her sleek black chair, her posture perfect. Her pen taps a pad of lined paper. Her nails are Opi Red. She's so completely refined. So perfect. She's all about power and control. Like Dad. And Leah.

Until she killed herself.

"I'll start. First question, are you taking your meds?" Dr. Applegate shifts in her chair, her crossed leg pointed at me like an accusation.

I stare at the framed certificates on her wall, and the writing goes a little blurry, like my head. I don't answer. The thing is, she doesn't expect me to, because she's got her next bullet loaded and ready to fire.

"Okay, moving on. How was your first day at school?"

That one I'll answer. "Fine."

"Allie," Dr. Applegate starts again. "In order to get the full benefits of therapy, you have to participate. This is your time. For you."

I want to ask if her friend, Dr. Gates, gave Leah the "benefit" of therapy. Does she think he was successful with my sister? I want to ask her, but I don't, because Dr. Applegate isn't who I'm mad at, despite the burgundy couch. She didn't know about Leah's and my pact. I remind myself that she had no idea. And so far, she's stayed far enough away from the danger zone. She deserves something.

"It was weird," I say. "It felt like everyone was staring at me."

"That made you uncomfortable?"

I hate this crap. Of course it made me uncomfortable. She's using these questions to settle me down, to lull me. I know this trick. I can't let Dr. Applegate get to me. I can't let her break into the vault. I can't tell her that I'm seeing Leah and hearing her, not just in my memories but as if she's alive. With me. Now.

"We talked about how it was going to be hard to go back. You said you were ready."

"I am ready. It was just hard."

Dr. Applegate lasers her attention on me. "Let's talk about the medication. I'm going to ask you again, are you taking the meds?"

I consider lying. But right now, that's not the secret I need to keep. "No. I'm not."

"Can you tell me why?"

"Because I'm not depressed. No matter what you guys think. I'm the one who didn't do it. Remember?"

Dr. Applegate leans forward. We've danced around this point

for weeks. I know she thinks it's time for her to make progress on this. I brace myself for her next question. "Do you think Leah was depressed?"

"I guess so. I mean, obviously, she must have been. Right?"

"You and Leah were close, weren't you?"

I nod. She knows we were.

"She called you her 'bunker buddy.' Do you know what that means?"

Leah told Dr. Gates. I can't believe it.

"She said it was like a war with your mom and dad always fighting. How was it like a war?"

"They were always so mad at each other. They were ruthless. Horrible." The tears are building up. I almost don't even care. My mouth feels weird, as if my tongue is swollen. I take a drink of Gatorade and choke on it. "They acted like they wanted to kill each other."

Dr. Applegate's voice softens. "Like they hated each other?"

I nod. "They acted like they'd never even cared. Like everything that happened between them was a mistake. Even though it wasn't always like that."

Dr. Applegate shoulders relax and she clasps her hands in front of her like Mr. Hicks did in our meeting. Like she didn't hear my screwup referring to Leah and I as *we* still. "So you devised a battle plan, right?"

"Leah did."

"Just Leah?"

I nod. It's not quite true, but it's mostly on target.

Dr. Applegate gets up, goes to her desk, and brings back a chart with Leah's name on it. "Dr. Gates gave this to me to help you." She makes this big pretense like she's flipping through the pages, trying to find the right words, even though I know she's already read the chart, that she already knows what she's looking for, maybe has the passage highlighted. "She decided because she was the 'general,' you were the 'foot soldier'?"

My face heats. I feel the rage build. Why would Leah tell them these things and give them ammunition against me? Why did she always break team? I'm not going to answer Dr. Applegate's insulting questions. I shouldn't have to.

"Was Leah the general?"

I shake my head. Not always. She wasn't always in charge.

"Did Leah take her meds? The ones you don't want to take?"

I stand and turn away from her. "I don't know. You have the chart. What did Dr. Gates say?"

"I thought you and Leah were close."

"No, she didn't take the meds. She didn't want to."

"Was that a good decision? Not taking her meds?"

I bat at a tear that's gone rogue. "No. I guess not. But we don't know exactly why she did what she did. She might have had other reasons."

Dr. Applegate nods. "She might have. But what's a good enough reason to kill yourself?"

"I don't know."

"Do you have reasons to kill yourself?"

"No."

Dr. Applegate pauses as if she's considering my response. Then before I can tell myself this portion of the session is officially over and we're changing topics, Dr. Applegate says, "If Leah made all your decisions before, who decides now?"

Anger wells inside me. I feel it build, and I can't stop it. Leah said I was stupid about people. She was right. I was stupid to trust Dr. Applegate when this whole time she was ready to pounce on me, using our secret code against me. That was our language. Mine and Leah's—until Leah gave it up to the enemy. She may as well have painted a big bull's-eye on my chest.

"Allie? Who makes the decisions now?"

"I do."

"You do? You are deciding not to take your meds. Just you? Not Leah's voice in your head telling you not to?"

The room spins with her allegation, but I steel myself. "No. Of course not."

"Sometimes when people lose someone they love, they continue to see them, hear them, feel them long after that person's gone. It's completely normal."

I breathe in. Breathe out. Breathe in again. I need to stay calm. Not get rattled.

"I think it's important that you see the difference between you and Leah. Even if you were 'bunker buddies,' you were also different. She danced; you paint."

She died. I didn't.

"She was depressed; you say you're not."

"I'm not. I'm just sad. My sister killed herself. Aren't I allowed to be sad?"

"You certainly are, Allie. But what I want to know is why you agreed to the pact to begin with."

I press my hands into my head.

"Are you getting a headache?"

"Yes."

"You need to take something?"

"No. It's not bad."

"Your mother said you need to take your pills when you get headaches."

I push in harder. As much as I want the headache to stop, I might need it. I might be able to use it to get to Leah. Because I feel her there, behind the headache, like she's backstage waiting for her cue. "No. Don't need them."

"So why does your mom think you do?"

"Because that's what she does. Whenever anything hurts or is hard, she takes a pill or gives us one. You think that worked for my sister? Is that what you want for me? Because I'm not okay with that. I saw what my parents did and didn't do with Leah. They gave her pills. Like Mom takes. And now she's dead."

I collapse back into my chair, stunned by the words that came out of me, worried that the firestorm that runs through my veins when I think about Mom and Dad will consume me. And then there is Leah. My hands go to my face, which is hot with shame on top of the huge pile of mad. I should be stronger than this. Leah was.

Until she killed herself.

"I know that was hard, Allie. But it's important to talk about what happened and how you are feeling. That's why we have to find ways to help you cope."

I nod and I'm not even faking it. Coping would be good. I'm all in for coping. Now that I've been stripped raw and beaten bloody with my own admissions, a little coping might be in order. Suddenly, coping sounds fun.

"Let's try some relaxation exercises. They can help. Go ahead and lean back." Her voice shifts to a lower register.

I don't think it's going to work, but there's no arguing. After all, she did go to a recent workshop on the subject, the certificate of attendance already proudly displayed in a jet-black frame. Her wall is like her Girl Scout vest with her merit badges, all lined up. Dr. Applegate loves her some workshops. And credentials. She's a freak show of cred, my psychiatrist. Lucky me.

"Let your shoulders relax." Dr. Applegate's voice is low and steady.

Despite my reservations, I feel myself sink into the leather. It's cool and envelopes me. My body's already on board with her agenda. The cough medicine has made me obedient. They should list that on the label as a side effect.

"Let your body go loose. Feel yourself floating." Her voice soothes me, and my mind starts to unwind.

My mind takes me straight to snapshots of Leah that pass one by one. I see her posing for me in my studio. Leah laying on her stomach on her bed, holding her new iPhone, the one Dad gave us on his way out the door to live with his girlfriend. The girlfriend he lied to us about. The girlfriend he lied to Mom about. The girlfriend he left us for.

"Let your mind completely relax and find a happy time. Go there."

Leah looks up at me, her phone in her hand. She starts to talk, but the memory disintegrates till it becomes something else. Till I can't see her anymore, but I can hear her. "I can come back," her voice loops around me, making me happier than I've been since she did it. "Is that what you want?" she whispers.

She can come back? What does she mean? How?

"Will you do it? Will you bring me back?"

I want to ask her what she's talking about, but I'm so distracted by the scent of mangoes and another smell layered underneath it. Cherry ChapStick. The kind Leah used.

I feel myself nodding.

"That's it, Allie, stay with it," Dr. Applegate coos.

Leah laughs. I hear her voice so clear and strong that it makes a vision form in my head, like in a movie or a dream. My feet follow a path that seems so real, I can feel the ground under me as I walk barefoot through the woods. Leah is just ahead of me. My mind paints a scene that my heart is happy to follow. I see gray, brown, blue, and green hues. A bird chirps in the distance. A twig underfoot bends and snaps, but I don't care, because I know when I make it through the thicket, I'll find her. I call to her with my mind. *Wait for me.*

"You have to find me," Leah whispers.

This is some kind of game to her. My head starts to pound, and my heart matches the rhythm. I start to run, but no matter how fast I go, she's faster.

"Okay, Allie, let's wake up now." Dr. Applegate's voice leaks in.

I resist. I'm not ready to come back. I want to stay with Leah. I want to catch her, but Dr. Applegate's voice destroys my trance and I have no choice.

"Find me. Any way you can." It's Leah's voice saying pretty much the same thing Piper did earlier.

And then the spell is broken. Leah's gone, and in her wake there's just this huge hole inside me. And the questions. Always the questions. Why? Why did she leave me? Why didn't she take me with her?

"You all right?" Dr. Applegate asks.

I don't answer. I can't. I'm sitting here totally broken, completely defeated. I concentrate on breathing. Just breathing.

"You went very deep." She sits ramrod and writes in my file. "Sometimes it's hard to pull out of that."

I barely register what she's saying.

She leans forward, concern painted across her brow, deep lined and ugly. "Allie? Are you back?"

I sit up straighter and lick my lips. My mouth is so dry. I take a drink of Gatorade and try to clear my head. "Yes."

"Okay, Allie, time's almost up. You did really well today."

I sit there, numbed and mute, wondering what the eff just

happened and if any of it was real. Leah and her promises and her games. She's still playing them even though she's dead.

———————•———————

The minute we get home, I rush upstairs to my room. Sophie barks at my heels, and I pick her up. Together we lie on my bed. She kisses my face, which is in full migraine mode. I pet her so she'll lie down and close my eyes to try to stop the pain.

Sometimes distracting myself helps. I send my mind back to the memory I saw in Dr. Applegate's office. I'm careful not to read anything into it, but I let it play out as if it's happening, buying time till the headache pill Mom gave me in the car starts working.

We were in Leah's room that day. Mom had been crying in the bedroom; we could hear her all the way down the hall. Dad's steps were confident, strong, unquestioning. Leah was painting her nails I'm Not Really a Waitress red. I was sitting on her window seat. She let me stay in her room that day. She always did when it was bad.

Dad's footsteps stopped at the doorway. I didn't look up. I couldn't. "Here," he said, slipping in the room just enough to put an Apple bag on the bed for Leah and one on the floor for me. "Take care of your mom," he said. Then he was gone.

We listened to him walk down the stairs and out the door. I remember how heavy the air felt as I tried to wrap my head around the fact that this time, it was really it. This time he was gone for good. He chose her over us. Not just Mom. Us too. I started to cry.

"You have to accept it," Leah said as she began unwrapping her new phone. "It's not going to change. May as well benefit." She showed me the shiny new case Dad included with the phone. "Can't say as I blame him anyway."

I sat there, floored. Leah always did that, surprised me. I stood up and opened the window seat, grabbed our battle plan book. I flipped through it, looking at all the entries we'd made over the years. The skirmishes fought in our family war documented by me, the foot soldier. I looked up at Leah. "How's our arsenal doing?"

"Actually, I'm thinking of scrapping the mission," she said, still working on her phone.

Just like that. But I guessed that was the prerogative of the general.

"I'm serious." She nodded to the book in my hand. "We don't need that anymore. Things are going to get better now. With Dad gone, things will get better."

"How can you say that?"

She sat up and looked me in the eye. "Promise me you won't think about it. It was a stupid idea. We were stupid. Promise me." As a foot soldier, she didn't want my opinion, only my obedience. Then she pushed herself so her legs draped over the bed. "Hey, after we get these set up, I'm gonna go shopping. You can come with. Want a new dress for Brady's July Fourth party? It's gonna be killer."

I believed her. At the time I believed her. And looking back, I think I still do. Three weeks before she killed herself, she didn't want to. Things were going to get better.

I crawl out of bed, to my desk, open my backpack, and take out the bottle of NyQuil. I know it's not smart to mix these, I get that, but the pain is unbearable. I take a small sip and then a bigger one. I roll over, push my hand under my mattress, and pull out the notebook I hid after that conversation. I didn't want her to throw it out, even if she was canceling the combat. I wanted proof that we had been in the trenches together. Our war diary.

I lie back down and close my eyes. Like in Dr. Applegate's office, I try to find me some happiness. A sound comes to me, lingers on the edge of my consciousness. Whatever it is, it's coming from Leah's room. I walk out into the hall. My head is foggy and my eyes burn, but my ears zoom in. I know this sound. I've heard it a hundred times. A thousand. A million. In real life when Leah was alive. Then in my head after she died.

But these sounds are real. They are happening now. I can tell they are not happening in my head. I can hear them come from the other room, where my head is not.

I step into her room. The sunlight pours through the window, creating a sunburst that hurts to look at. I shield my eyes. She's standing in the light. I blink away the brightness, expecting her to disappear, but she doesn't. Leah is standing at her bar, wearing a black leotard and pink tights. She has on her ballet slippers, the pink ones, worn and cracked.

"It's amazing, isn't it?" She looks at her arms, more outline than substance. "I'm back."

She lifts her arms above her head and then sweeps them down in front of her again. She looks at her hand, the silver ring solid compared to her body. But still, even partially inked, she is flawless, just like when she was alive.

She turns to look at me, standing tall, as if she's ready to perform. Her arms glide over her head. Mom always said Leah had the perfect dancer's body. And she's right. Even dead, she is taller and straighter than me. Even dead, she wins.

I try to think about how much cough medicine I took. In Dr. Applegate's office. Then again in my room. I don't think it was much, but maybe it's like a cumulative effect. Maybe I'm killing my brain one dose at a time.

Leah laughs as she twirls in place. "You could never hold your drugs." Her arms are held in a circle as she spins, her ballet skirt floating away from her legs. Leah is half-in, half-out of this world. And I summoned her here. I get excited. I can ask her all the things I want to know. I can find out if I let her down or if it was the other way around.

She finishes her pirouette and stares me, arms crossed in front of her. "You're crazy, definitely. You're totally crazy if you think you can grill me like some stupid bitch on *Pretty Little Liars*."

She *fouettés* in front of me, turning and spinning till I'm sure she'll take off like a top. I can't stop watching her until I'm so dizzy, I feel as if I'm going to puke. Leah laughs, and I start to get a little mad. I'm sitting here dazed, confused, dizzy, drunk, sorry, and Leah's laughing and dancing. Just like when she was alive.

"You worry too much," Leah says. "It's not good for you."

I find myself nodding. Obviously this isn't normal. Even a little groggy from cold medicine, I can tell that. Even completely fucked up, this isn't normal. You don't just go around willing your dead sister back into this world. And then watch her dance.

"Leah?" I ask when she stops to sit on her window seat and adjust her tights. This time, she's more than outline, as if she's getting better at it. "Can other people see you?"

"No, of course not. Just you. And only when you want to." She smooths her black see-through skirt over her black leotard. Just like when she was in my studio. She reaches up to check her bun, but no hair has gone rogue. She looks at me, her eyes warm, brown. I always wished mine were brown too, but I got blue.

"I'm just worried. Maybe I've really lost it."

"You know it runs in the family." She laughs as if that's funny.

I start to think that maybe I can keep her like this for a little bit, and the thought makes me so happy, I don't care if I'm crazy. Because if I have to choose crazy with my sister or sane without her, I'm choosing crazy. Every time.

CHAPTER 8

I walk to lunch, grateful for forty minutes of no expectations. My head is swimmy from the NyQuil–headache-meds cocktail I took yesterday. My stomach is queasy, and there's a constant buzzing in my ears. The pressure behind my eyes is intense. I don't know how Mom does this.

I pass John Strickland, and he makes eye contact. I've got no idea why. John's a major dealer. I've never talked with him or had a class with him or even thought about him till now. I've heard things—that he got suspended last year for taking a crowbar to some guy's car and that he once beat up a guy who was making fun of an autistic kid so bad that he ended up in the hospital. John's like some kind of drug-dealing Batman that most people avoid unless they're in need of a little weed. I try not to stare as he passes me.

Emery grabs my arm from behind and twirls me around to face her. "Hey, girl. Guess what!"

I peel my gaze off of John and glue it to her face instead. "What?"

She pulls me into her so our faces are inches apart, and I can smell the strawberry Layers gum she's chewing. "The new drama teacher is even cuter than Carbon, and I'm trying out for the lead this year."

Emery loads her tray with a tuna sandwich on whole wheat, a Granny Smith apple, and a bag of Nacho Cheese Doritos, which she opens and starts eating as she pushes her tray across the metal counter leading to the cashier. The screeching sound of her tray makes my ears ring. "Aren't you eating?" she asks.

I point to my backpack. "Mom packed. Again."

"So weird."

When we get to our table, I see the rain. The drops collecting on the window remind me of the last time the three of us broke out of the house. Emery was sleeping over. Two weeks before Leah killed herself. It was raining that night too. Drizzling off and on. Leah had just gotten back from a date with Sean.

"Hey, Emery." Leah had smiled as she opened my bedroom door. "You got anything?"

"A little," Emery said. She always had a little. Said it helped her chill. Acting was tense work apparently. But I hadn't known Leah was into weed. I looked and saw Leah's hands shaking. But not like Mom's. Kind of like they were vibrating. Like she couldn't make them stop.

"Bring it?" Leah asked. "I could use a little mellow."

"Sure." Emery grabbed her purse, and I grabbed Sophie.

I remember feeling kind of annoyed that Leah ignored me for Em and wondering when Leah started smoking weed. I felt left out. Like a tagalong. When we got to the playground, Emery lowered herself onto the merry-go-round. Her long legs trailed on the ground as she started rolling a joint from the bag of weed. Leah sat across from her, their faces close. She lit it like they were sharing a secret.

"Come on, try it." Emery turned to me, hand outstretched.

I held up my hand. "I'm good." I hated when they pushed me into things.

"No use." Leah laughed. "She's a weed virgin too."

Heat spread through me like wildfire. I started to wonder when this became an intervention.

"Come on, Allie, you know we love you," Em said.

"We are the *only* ones who do." Leah leaned into Em. "Obviously."

Emery covered her mouth but couldn't hold in her giggles. Eventually she gave in, and the two of them bent over. I couldn't take it, the two of them hanging all over each other, laughing at me.

"You're messed up," I said, getting off the swing. I started to walk home, but Leah blocked my way.

"It's just sex, Allie. What the hell are you waiting for?" Leah was clearly mad at somebody, and I was the closest target. Not good. Like Dad, Leah was about war games. Like Mom, my role was to cower. "Why are you making it this big deal?"

I backed up. "I'm not. It just hasn't happened."

"Good. Because open your eyes, Allie. You want a shot at Max, you gotta grow up. He's not exactly dating the pure and innocent girls," Leah said. "He's a guy; he wants a little fun."

I aimed my stare at Emery. "You told her?"

Emery's mouth opened a little. "Ruh roh."

"It's not funny," I said.

"Nobody's laughing." Leah stood in front of me. "You've wanted Max forever. If not him, who?"

I opened my mouth, but I couldn't make the words come out. Angry tears streamed down my face.

Leah wiped them off. I tried to pull away, but she grabbed my arms. "You have to grow up. If you can't with Max, then pick someone else. Someone you don't care about. Then go back to him. Show him you can play with the big boys."

I wanted to smack her. Shouldn't Max care enough to wait for me? The day after our failed hookup, he was with Randi Flanders, so question answered. Max wasn't going to wait for anyone. Not even me. Especially not me.

"He's a guy," Leah explained as if I didn't know that. "He is just a guy. Not a god. Not a love. Just a guy."

I pushed past them and walked home by myself. Emery came in about a half an hour later. I didn't know if she came with Leah. And I didn't care.

"I'm sorry, Allie," Emery had whispered.

I pretended to be asleep.

"I think it's cool that you want it to be special. It's just not. Not the way you think."

I had wondered what she meant by that. But I hadn't asked.

I look at Emery now, talking with Violet Cunningham and Lindsey Clark, who put their trays down noisily in front of me. They are talking so fast that all I see is the flash, flash, flash of their super-white teeth, and all I hear is the dizzying loudness of their laughing. Lindsey crunches a chip. Emery crunches her apple. I start to sweat. Head to toe, I feel sick.

Emery leans into me. "You okay?"

"Fine."

It's difficult to hear what they're saying. Everything sounds fuzzy. Everything feels fuzzy. Everything is overwhelming. Including the smell of the food everyone's eating—Dorito smell, burrito smell, salad dressing, ketchup, fries. Gagging me. Making me feel like I want to die.

"Bathroom," I mumble. I go to get up. The room spins. I brace myself on the table.

"Allie?" Nick's voice comes from behind me. "You okay?"

"Nurse."

His arm goes around me, and he supports me as he walks me to the clinic.

Nurse Debbie comes out to greet me. "Oh, Allie, a headache?"

I groan.

"Let's just have you lie down for a little. I'll get you some ice. Bring her here."

Nick guides me to the cot and helps me lie down. I hear Nurse Debbie closing the blinds, which sounds like whips being cracked. Nick puts an ice pack on my forehead.

"You're scaring me, Allie," he whispers. "You look bad. Really bad."

And just like that, the guilt rushes in. God, I suck. I start to cry. Small tears. Because I don't deserve the big therapeutic kind. I did this. To myself. I need to stop.

"You better get back to class. Allie needs quiet."

He reaches down and kisses the top of my head. "Text me later. Okay?"

I nod. Then close I my eyes and think about the choices I'm making. Am I being smart? I fall asleep, Leah's voice washing over me like a wave on the beach.

"Just keep moving," she says. "Watch your checkerboard. Don't get jumped."

———————⋅———————

Mom is waiting in the front office to sign me out of school. We walk to the car in silence, thankfully. I close my eyes.

"Are you okay?" Mom asks. "I mean, is it because it's too hard? Are we pushing you too much?"

"It's all hard, Mom," I say.

"I know."

What I wouldn't give to go back in time, never make the pact. Or tell someone about it. What I wouldn't give to argue with Leah and say it was stupid.

Mom's car stops, jolting me conscious. We're parked in front of a CVS.

"Why are we stopping?"

"Just have to pick up your script; you're almost out. You wait here."

"That's okay. I'll go. I'm faster."

Mom hesitates, then opens her purse and grabs her wallet. She takes out her debit card and hands it to me. "Get yourself something if you like," she says.

I walk into the store and head toward the prescription counter, passing the makeup, then the nail polish, then the hair products. I walk past the rows of cold medicines. Small red pills. Bright-pink Benadryls. Yellow Coricidins. Followed by bottles of cough syrups. Syrups—as if you'd put it on pancakes or waffles. Words are important. They mean things. When the drug companies called cough medicine "syrup," they opened up a possibility that their product would sweeten something bitter. Like my life.

I run my fingers over the bottles like when Leah and I used to go for mani-pedis and I couldn't decide which color to pick. Only now there's no Leah.

Mom's words "*Get yourself something*" run through my head. I *am* out of Robitussin. It claims multisymptom, nighttime formula relief. These products are all offering them. Shouldn't I accept a little Help? When it's right here in front of me?

"Come on, Allie, we don't have all day. Pick one. Any one. Just pick," Leah's voice is sweet but slightly annoyed. The day of the party. She took me to get our nails done. Because I had agreed. It was time I grew up. And Leah was going to help me with that. I remember she was so good to me that day. And that felt so great. More intoxicating than Robitussin. More fun than gin shots chased with Gatorade. Leah choosing me was a drug. My favorite high.

I held up a red bottle of polish. "I'm Not Really a Waitress?"

She shook her head. "Too bad they don't have one called I'm Not Really a Virgin." She laughed so hard that she started to choke. I went along with the joke. She *was* helping me out after all, wasn't she?

Standing in the drugstore now, I do exactly what I did that day at the nail salon—and that night at the party. I close my eyes, reach out, and pick. My hand closes around the Delsym. I feel good about that choice because orange is one of my favorite colors. Orange is Max. And pumpkins. And Creamsicles. Orange is the color of warm. Orange will coat you and protect you and keep you safe. Like a life jacket, orange will lift you up.

I take it to the back of the store and put it on the counter.

"Hi, Allie," Mrs. Simpson, the cashier, says to me. Her hair is carrot and wheat and gold, and she has freckles on her face. She looks like a sunset. She reaches behind her, then places three prescription bags on the counter. Three. Mine plus two others.

She points to the cough medicine. "That also?"

"Yes. Oh and these…" I throw a pack of gum on the counter and turn around to pull a vitaminwater out of the cooler.

"You have a cough?" She inspects the bottle.

"Just at night."

"A little honey will take care of that too, you know."

I look at her and wonder if she knows about me. I mean, obviously she does. I wonder if she's going to refuse to ring me up. Tell me to put the Delsym back. Part of me hopes she will. But she rings it all up and points to the place to swipe the debit card. I type in the code. Transaction complete, she puts everything in a bag and hands it to me.

"Oh, sweetie?" she calls as I walk away.

I turn.

"Feel better."

"Thanks." And once again, I feel like a fake.

On my way out the door, I take the cough medicine out of the bag and transfer it into my backpack before I get to the car. I leave Mom's two prescriptions in the bag but crumple the receipt and shove it in my pocket. Mom's two scripts are the real reason she wanted to go in and pick these up. She didn't want me to know. As if I didn't.

Leah always said Mom had the best pharmacy on the block. It's where she "shopped" to get through a test or a breakup. It never bothered me back then if Leah sampled a little. It's not like she was hooked like Mom was, and why suffer when you could take a little Happy and move on? But maybe that wasn't the best plan. I mean, obviously, considering Leah's overdose and all.

———◦———

The receptionist tells me I can go back before I even sit down. That means no trip to the bathroom for me. No battle armor. I take my place on the burgundy love seat, even though it's hard to feel safe when I'm sitting on a big sea the color of death.

Dr. Applegate comes into the room. She's wearing dark-blue

pinstriped pants and another crisp white shirt. "How are you today, Allie?" Dr. Applegate asks as she settles into her chair.

"Okay, I guess."

"You look tired."

How bad must I look for her to say that? I think about making up an excuse, but I don't. Instead I slump lower in the chair and say, simply, "I am."

"I want to talk about something important, something we've avoided talking about for a long time now."

I close my eyes.

"Leah and you had a plan. You made a plan together."

I draw my knees up to my chin. I shake my head.

"You said you had one."

At least this time she doesn't flip through the pages. At least this time she doesn't pretend she's trying to remember. "You had a battle plan. You told the police that. You tried to take the pills she'd thrown up. You said you were supposed to go with her."

I lay my cheek in my hand. "No." I shake my head. "That's not true."

"Which part isn't true?"

I sniff, wipe my nose with a tissue. "I didn't want to go with her."

Dr. Applegate smiles at me. It's a small one but genuine. "I believe that, Allie."

We sit in silence for three and a half minutes. Then Dr. Applegate gives in. She can't stand silence; she thinks it's the enemy, so she slaughters it with this whisper. "We need to talk about the first time you discussed the pact."

I shake my head.

"I know this is hard, so don't answer me. Just think. Try to remember."

I don't have to think. I know. We were at the Cape. We'd gone up with Dad early. Two hours in the car with Dad in the best mood I'd seen him in forever. Leah sat up front, of course. She was wearing the new gold bracelet Dad had given her for being the youngest Robert Frost High School dance captain. It was this really *heavy hearts/kissing hearts* thing, and I knew it cost a fortune. I stretched out in back, headphones in, watching a movie on my tablet. I was thirteen. Leah was fifteen. Just turned.

We got to the house, and I let all the air in my lungs go out, just to make room for more Cape air. The breeze blew and the trees rustled. "Race ya." Leah bolted out of the car.

"Put the food away before you head to the beach," Dad called from his bedroom, where he'd wheeled his suitcase.

"What's got him so happy?" I asked Leah.

"Who cares? Just roll with it."

It was early in the season. The weekend before Memorial Day. The kids on the beach were wearing sweatshirts, but Leah stripped to her bathing suit.

"You're not serious. It's gotta be freezing."

"So what? It only hurts for a minute." She pointed to the water. "Besides, it's easier when you do it with someone."

Dr. Applegate's voice cuts through the mist. "Look around you. What colors do you see? Try to remember it all."

We were standing on the beach. The rocks were gray and blue—shimmery water, inky black in parts, and navy in others. Sea foam and sand and the sun overhead. Leah stood at the edge of the water. It slapped against her legs, and she held her hand out. Leah was a dancer. Her body was used to pain. The icy water would feel like knives to me, but to her, it was relief.

"Come on, I'll give you the blue dress. The one you like."

I stayed still in the sun on the sand. I let it bake on me and make me feel warm and loved. "You were going to give me that one anyway."

"Okay, then I'll give you the Kate Spade purse with all the colors to go with it."

I took my sweatshirt off. "How bad is it?"

"Not bad at all."

"Liar." I inched closer. Just the spray on my feet was too much. I shrieked and ran away.

She laughed so hard. I remember thinking she had the best laugh. She wrapped her arms around me and started dragging me to the water. "A deal's a deal." I shrieked the whole way in, screaming with each spanking of the waves against my skin.

"Don't you love it now?" she lowered herself so that the water was up her neck.

"Now that my body is numb, yeah."

"Numb is way better than feeling most times anyway."

The water splashed against us, and we bobbed up and down

with the waves. Then we rode some in toward the shore, like Dad had taught us when we were little. Finally, we straggled onto the beach, exhausted and freezing. I wrapped up in my towel, and she put her arm around me. "You wanna know a secret?" she asked.

"Yeah."

"I think I'm in love."

"Who this week?"

"No. Seriously."

"Who?"

"It's a secret, but it's real. Not like those stupid throwaway guys, you know?"

"How do *you* know?"

"Because I feel it. And because when I'm with him, I'm myself. I don't have to keep proving myself. Being me is good enough."

I looked at her. Leah feeling like she wasn't good enough? That thought blew my mind. I felt this immediate gratitude for whoever this guy was whom she loved. The one that Leah let fix her. "Wow. That sounds amazing."

"I'm thinking of giving up dancing."

I put my hand over my mouth. "Oh my God, Dad is going to freak!"

She laughed. "I know. But I'm so tired. And I just want to be. You know? I want to be left alone."

We walked back to the house.

"When are you going to tell them?"

"Maybe this weekend." She looked nervous but also kind of excited. I remember I thought she was so brave, and I wanted to be like her. "That's the point."

"What is?"

"I don't want to end up like they are, with the wrong person. I want to love and be loved and have that be the most important thing. Because this kind of love I'm talking about, it possesses you."

"That doesn't sound good."

"No, I'm not explaining it right. It's that nothing matters other than being with this person. Even the things you thought were important aren't. Every second you aren't with this person is like being slowly suffocated."

She put her hands around my neck and faked-choked me till we both almost fell over laughing.

I remember thinking my sister really trusted me to tell me this before she told my parents. Even if she didn't say who, I'd know soon anyway. Everyone would when they saw what she gave up to be with him. Whoever he was.

When we turned the corner, we saw two extra cars in the driveway. Two was wrong. Even one extra car was. Mom wasn't supposed to be here till tomorrow.

Dr. Applegate interrupts again. "You there, Allie? You see how it started?"

I nod.

"And you know why you started the plan? What made you?"

I open my eyes and looked at Dr. Applegate head-on. "Love."

Her eyes look at me like she totally gets me. She nods. "Okay, Allie, time's up."

Thankfully Mom doesn't feel the need to fill the ride back from Dr. Applegate's office with conversation. It isn't till we pull into the driveway that she asks, "You want Chinese food for dinner? I could run and get you lo mein." Mom unlocks the front door. "Just let me grab the coupon book."

I'm just about to answer when I see him standing there— Dad. In the hallway. When did he get here? And more importantly, why?

"David?" Mom asks. "Did you tell me you'd be coming over?"

"I saw what you did in your room." His face is tight and worn, as if commanding this platoon is killing him. "Come here, Allie. We need to talk."

My whole body wants to turn and run out the front door. Sophie stands next to me, not wanting to commit until I do. My little soldier.

"Let's find out what this is about." Mom walks into the living room, allowing him to take a seat in his spot. It burns me that he still gets to have one after he left us. Just like it burns me that he still has a key to the house.

"We need to talk about the paintings."

First pain. Then heat. Then hate. How could he? The paintings are mine. They have no right.

"I think your paintings are keeping you out of your studio…"

"They're not."

"Let me finish. We could store them somewhere."

"No!"

"Just until you're ready to see them again." He holds his hands in front of him, two twin stop signs like he's negotiating with a crazy person. Like he's trying to talk me off the ledge. "Then we'll bring them back."

Playing Dad is like playing poker against the house. I can't win. He holds all the cards except the ones he deals to me—the losing ones. Then he smiles as he collects his chips. And I sit here, alone, wishing like mad for a little backup. Not the Mom *folding her hand so she can get this over with and get back to her pills* backup either. I need my sister.

And then it hits me. Maybe I do hold some of the cards.

"If you take my paintings, I'll stop doing art altogether. You can't make me. If you touch them, I swear, my painting days will be done."

Dad turns greenish gray—camo colors. He didn't have a sound battle plan. I turn and walk up the stairs. They can talk about this all they want. I'm out.

He can't make me paint. I've finally got him. But in reality it's not much of a threat. It's not as if I'm creating much anyway. Just like that, the wind goes out of my sails. I open my backpack and take out my new artillery. My Delsym. Piper said I had to find my art. Leah too. I open the top and take a big gulp. Then another one. Then I close the bottle and put it away.

As I wait for the cough medicine to kick in, I open my

backpack and look at my books. I need to face my homework; it's building up already.

Twenty-five minutes later I hear Mom come up the stairs, but I act like I don't.

"I'm sorry about that." She deposits the quart of lo mein and a pair of chopsticks on my desk.

I don't look at her. She doesn't deserve it.

"Your paintings are safe." Mom puts the key to my studio on my desk. "But go see for yourself if you like." She walks away, her steps sounding more confident than she has in years.

I close my books and look out my window. My studio sits waiting. I know she's baiting me, egging me on, but also, maybe she's right. I have to face them someday, don't I?

I walk down the stairs. My legs feeling like jelly and the after-effects of the drugs from earlier are still in my system maybe fueling my bravery a little. But it's not like Mom faces things head-on either. I grab a flashlight from the kitchen drawer and play with the pink Converse sneaker on the key chain. The key feels good in my hands, like it's missed me.

I open the mudroom door, ignore the chill that hits me, and make my way to my studio. I head down the path, the flashlight shining ahead, though I could walk there with my eyes closed. When I get to the door, I stop. Do I really want to do this?

I put my key in the lock and jiggle the door. The door swells and sticks when it's damp, and it's been a very wet summer. I push the door open. Stale air hits me. The light from the moon shines in the room, making the sheets over the paintings look like ghosts.

I walk toward one, my hand stopping just short of pulling the sheet off, exposing it for what it is, when I hear Leah.

"Hey," she says. She's behind me, pressed against the wall, dressed in her black skinny jeans and Sean's school jersey, also black. When she steps in front of the window, the moonlight bounces off her soft, blond hair, making it glow. I can't help feeling like someone punched the air out of me as I look at her. My fingers go to my mouth. I want to believe she's really here so badly. I want to. I want to. I want to.

She puts her arm around me and pulls me away from the paintings. She nods toward the covered canvases. "Maybe we should start with something else first. Something easier. Like the montage on my computer."

"The one I'm not in?" I ask, trying to keep my voice from sounding whiny.

"You're on my computer," she says. "It's not like you're not on there at all."

My eyes trail down her arm that's draped over me—the one that can't really be there. I don't trust my voice, but it's the only one I have. "It's not the same."

She covers my hand with hers, which is more energy than flesh. She turns my hand over, exposing the screen of my cell phone. I watch as she navigates till she gets on the Internet and her Dropbox. She opens a photo album with her and me in it. Our fingers stretch a photo till it fills the face of my phone. We were modeling her clothes and posing. I wore the red mini; she wore the blue one. It was two weeks before the party. She let me try on her life that day and then, at the party, her friends.

"Remember these?" she asks. Leah looks at me. "You were always with me. Even when I didn't act like that."

I don't want to argue with her—it doesn't seem right to argue with a ghost—but she's wrong. I'm not with her, not the way I wanted to be. I was always in a back file. Never up front—like she was for me.

"You don't understand. Everything had to be perfect," she says. "I was doing what you do, Allie. I was painting a picture. That's all."

"And I messed that up?"

"No. You just weren't part of that particular...composition."

Since when did she use art terms in conversation? I turn away.

"Give me your cell again." She puts her hand out.

"What?"

"Just give it to me."

Part of me waits for it to drop on the floor—proof that she's not here with me—but it doesn't. She pushes the buttons to unlock my phone since she knows the password. Because she set it. She holds up the face for me to see. My wallpaper, a picture of Emery and me on the first day of school. "See, I'm not on yours."

"That's different."

"But you're the wallpaper on my phone. Just the two of us, remember?"

I do. She took it three days before she killed herself. Three days. I blink back tears. How could everything have been so normal three days before? How could she have been so normal?

"Remember the picture? Our picture?"

Of course I remember. I remember every single time Leah decided to be nice to me. It was a close-up of me and her, arms around each other, her telling me something funny, me laughing.

"Then show me. Where's your phone?" I ask.

"I can't."

"You won't."

My phone vibrates in her hands. "Hey, who's Nick?"

I put my hand out. Just like her to read my messages. No boundaries. Except when it came to her secrets. Hers were important. Not mine. I shake my head. I am so stupid.

"I feel so out of your life," she says.

She is, because she left it.

"But I'm back now, and I want to stay as long as I can."

As long as she can? She just got here and she's already talking about leaving? Anger blazes through me. "We had a deal. You were supposed to tell me."

"I didn't want you involved. I wanted you safe. And if you'd kept quiet, if you'd just kept your head, they'd never have known you were supposed to be involved."

Is she kidding? I fire my words at her, launch them like missiles. "A pact. It was a suicide pact. That means we agreed we wouldn't do it without talking with the other one. You were never supposed to do it without me."

"I changed my mind."

"Why?"

She sighs. "You wouldn't understand."

"You didn't even try to make me."

Leah shakes her head. I can tell she's trying not to cry. And she's right. What's the point of beating this dead horse? She did it. It's over. There are no do-overs in suicide. I put my hands over my face. I don't know why, but I don't want her to see me cry—like she doesn't deserve to since she left me.

"Let's not talk about this," Leah says. "Let's talk about the art. You want me to help find your colors? Your concentration?"

I nod.

"Okay. Then let's think. Why don't you use the paintings? My paintings?"

"I can't. It's too hard…"

"Okay, then you just have to figure out something else you love that you'd want to paint twelve times. Although, compared to me, they'd all pale, wouldn't they? Hey, that's funny…pale… because, you know…"

I stiffen.

"What's the matter?"

"It's not funny. You being dead is not funny."

"I'm sorry. I was just trying for a little levity. Get it? Levity…"

I walk to the door, then turn to face her. "Can you tell me why?"

"It doesn't matter."

"To me it does. It matters a lot."

Leah walks over to the wall and looks out the window. She traces a drop of condensation with her finger. "It all seems so stupid now. I was mixed up. It was stupid. I was stupid."

"Was it that guy? The secret one?"

"There's no secret guy. There used to be when I was stupid and thought love was the only thing that mattered. God, I was an idiot."

"What happened to him?"

She looks at the ceiling. "Nothing happened to him. It's what happened to me. I changed."

"Why?"

She looks straight at me. "You have to ask? You were there. You saw. Everyone acts as if love fixes all. But that's bullshit. Love kills more than it saves."

My breath leaves me. I don't want to finish the Cape memory. I don't want to see how it went down, but I know what she means. I do. "What about Vanessa? Was she why?" I ask.

Her eyes go to slits. "You're worried about all the wrong things—why you're not on my computer, why I did it, if those nasty little rumors are true. I don't need to answer to you."

First pain, then heat—then hate. Just like Dad, she slays me. She storms over to me but stops when she sees my hands. She takes them in hers. Her face softens. She points to my finger-nails, now painted Essie Mint Candy Apple. "Awww, pretty Cape colors."

I shake my head and let my tears race down my cheeks. Cape colors.

She moves my hair behind my ears. "Forget about me. Go on

with your life." She shows me her nails, the polish some color I don't even remember the name of, now peeling. "I'm last year's colors. And I always will be. I'll never change." Tears run down her face, leaving angry red, raised marks in their path. "And now I'm stuck here." She looks around. "In this dark studio you never even visit anymore."

I admit, that makes me feel a little guilty.

"I don't want you to go. I want you with me," I tell her.

"Find your art. Soon. Or Dad's going to get rid of me." Her eyes crawl over the shrouded paintings.

"I know. I'm trying."

Her hands fall on my arms. "Listen, I know you don't understand why I left you, and I'm sorry about that. But you can save me now. Isn't that good?"

"What if I can't?"

"You have to try." Leah puts her face so close to mine, I can smell the cherry Chap on her lips. "It's the only way."

I feel in my pocket—the second pill from my rescue dose already in there.

"It doesn't have to be just those. It could be other ones too. Art is something you have to sacrifice for. I did—for dance."

I think about the diet pills. And the pills she didn't take but should have. I think about what Piper said about finding my art. "I'm worried…"

"Just try it once. See if it works. Then maybe your art will come back on its own."

"Okay."

"Good. Now let's get you to sleep."

She gets in front of me and takes my hand, leads me through the door, back through the house, and up the stairs to my room. When I get there, Max and Emery are waiting. I think it's cool they keep showing up together for me.

"Hey," I say.

"Where were you?" Max asks.

"In my studio."

"That's great, Al," Emery says. "How'd it go?"

"Good." I smile.

Em jumps on my bed, her book for AP lit in hand. "This totally sucks. You're so lucky you're not taking this."

"Yeah, who's going to write my essays?" Max asks.

I lower myself onto the bed next to Em and close my eyes.

"Good night, Allie," Leah whispers.

"Good night," I whisper back—only Max and Em think I'm talking to them.

CHAPTER 9

A rt class. I've dreaded this all day.

"Hey," Nick calls, his hands shoved in his pockets, his gaze fixed on the scene in front of him.

"What's up?" I ask, but by the time I make it to the back of the room, I realize what he's looking at, and then all I'm thinking about are the three easels set up like executioner's rifles, locked and loaded. I touch the pill I stole from Mom that's stashed in my pocket.

"Ugh. We're doing this now?" I ask.

"Apparently." Nick groans. "Piper seems cool with it."

I look at her arranging her paints, a smile on her face, and I can't help but wonder if she indulged a little before class. She turns to face me, as if she read my mind. She winks, and I guess I've got my answer. It's what all the greats do apparently. Who am I to question it?

"Okay, how are my best students doing?" Mr. Kispert asks as he comes to join us. "I was thinking that today you don't have to work on your concentration—unless you want to. Feel free to just paint. Sometimes when you're trying too hard to find your idea, you just need to throw paint on the canvas and get things going."

He looks at me when he says this, and once again, I want to disappear.

I open my backpack and take out my Gatorade. My fingers go into my pocket again, where the Xanax lives—an Indian summer–orange oval. I remember thinking it looked like a malformed SweeTart when I took it out of Mom's bottle. The one she thinks is so cleverly hidden in her underwear drawer.

Something screams at me not to do this. Dr. Applegate saying she believed I didn't want to do it. Mom in the car: *Don't leave me, Allie. Stay.* Leah begging me to bring her back. I honestly don't know who to listen to.

I look at the paints in front of me, and it's like I've become color illiterate. I dab some red. Yellow. White. Black. Blue. Straight from the tube, they look like fingerpaints—bright and brash and ugly. I take my brush and start to mix them.

Nick looks at me and smiles, then goes back to his painting. He's mixed a dandelion, a cocoa, and an acid-washed moss. The colors are perfect and subtle. He's painting a baseball field, which is sort of brilliant, because it is the most basic thing he could paint. Everyone knows a baseball field. Especially him. But there are ten thousand ways to paint them and almost none of them are wrong.

"Wow," I say, and he blushes.

"Kid stuff really, but I gotta get my painting arm warm."

I smile. Nick is now mixing baseball and painting as adeptly as he's mixing his paint and that makes me wish I could find my art as easily as he always does.

I stare at my palette. I want to see what he sees. I just don't. I can't. I feel the presence of someone next to me. Is Leah here?

Piper's voice—not Leah's—says, "I remember what you wore that night."

Nick steps closer, and Piper holds up her hand. He tries to shake her off, but she doesn't listen.

She leans over me and mixes a perfect Venetian red—like the dress I wore to the party. She steps away. I see Nick out of the corner of my eye, watching me as I stare at the beginning of the end—that red dress.

"Tap into the pain if you have to, Allie. Art bleeds it out of you."

I mix the Egyptian-blue color, the dress Leah wore, my hand shaking as I do. I keep saying I want answers. I keep asking Leah. Why can't I just make myself remember? Fill in the blanks? I look at the colors, loud and accusing. Leah looked amazing that night, even better than usual. She shined when we walked into the party. My eyes close as I glimpse that memory.

"Come on," Leah had said, pushing me onto the stage. Her stage. "This is going to be your night, the one you'll always remember."

She was right about that. I will never forget that night—the parts that aren't pushed away by my damaged psyche or buried by my drunken blackout. The little pill in my pocket calls to me. Would it help unlock me? I shoot Nick a smile and then twist to grab my backpack and my Gatorade.

My heart beats fast as I slip the pill between my lips and swallow it with the thought that I'm going to end up just like my sister.

"It's not the worst thing in the world," Nick says, making me feel like he's gotten inside of my head. He points to the canvas and says, "You'll get it. You always do."

Nick goes back to working on his field. Piper is working at her painting. She's doing a portrait of a girl leaning against a window. It's mostly grays and blues, and it's kind of brilliant. That just leaves me and my blank canvas.

What's the easiest thing to paint? *Still life.* The words come to me. Not from Leah but from my mind, like it's taking over for me in this chess match. Still life. Still alive. Leah. It always comes back to her. But at least it's something I can work with. I start to sketch flowers in a vase, taking a top-down perspective. I am really just playing with angles, but it makes the flowers look like they're being slaughtered. Mr. Kispert says art is about choices. Am I making the right ones?

The headphones are snug in my ears, and the pill starts to kick in. My head starts to feel warm, in a tingly sort of way. And the pressure that's built up in my temples and neck and shoulders lessens. In truth, I loosen. And I get why Mom takes this stuff.

I turn up the music and try to create without thinking. I stop looking at the lines I've drawn and reach inside me for the colors. The red goes on the canvas.

We walk into the party. I see her friends. They were all smiling and toasting me with those red Solo cups that smelled like beer that had already gone sour. I turned away from the cups, and Jason handed me a strawberry daiquiri because he said it tasted better than beer.

Egyptian blue explodes on the canvas. I see Leah and Sean taking me home. Both of them are pissed, not just about me but at each other.

I paint one flower, jet-black for when I found her. She's dead.

"I'm sorry," Leah whispers in my ear.

For once I don't want to hear her voice with her excuses. And it's not just because I'm in school or was supposed to have a say in this. It's because I'm trying hard to get that last image of her out of my mind. I don't want to remember Leah with her colors bleeding out of her.

I blink. And she's there, standing next to my painting.

She looks at it and then back at me. "I like it. It's strong."

I wish I could get her to leave, but I know she won't. So I ignore her and let everything spill from inside me onto the canvas. And just this once, I don't care if it's right. Or if it's okay. Or if it's enough.

But when I'm done with my paint rapture, I'm scared. Because I think I might be insane—with the colors I chose and the emotion I unleashed. So I dip my smallest brush and add a tiny magenta outline and a few lines for accents, hoping a little bright can save this painting. Hoping a little Happy can fix it. So no one will see how fucked up it is.

Mr. Kispert stands behind me. A crowd follows him. My stomach tightens. "The colors…"

"I know. They're different…"

"They're powerful. Evocative." Instead of being a peaceful still life, my flowers look like baby vultures, mouths opened, reaching for their next meal. "I love the perspective. Stunning."

Leah crosses her arms over her chest and beams. "You painted my colors."

She may be right. They're definitely not mine.

Nick looks at my canvas, shakes his head, and smiles. "I told you. You're amazing."

I try to see what they see. The colors may be powerful, but they're stains from a wound. The only controlled element is that outline—one skinny purple line where I tried to rein it all in. I shake my head. I shouldn't have listened to Leah. I've made a mess of this. It's sloppy. Leah used to call me that—sloppy seconds.

I remember one day in my room last spring.

"It's perfect," she said as she typed it. All one word, lowercase letters. Now my new password for the new computer Dad got me.

"It's a play on words," she said. "Get it? You're second in the family *and* you're sloppy." She laughed so hard, she cried. I remember I did too. Everyone was all in when Leah was happy.

And now, I stand here in front of a painting that's more hers than mine. My head starts spinning, and I get dizzy. I'm that purple line, holding everything together. I wonder how long I can keep this up without letting my crazy explode.

Leah chews on her fingernail. "I know what you're thinking. You think you're crazy, but you're not. You're just sad. Trust me, I know the difference."

Maybe she's right. Maybe I'm just sad. But what's the

difference between sad and depressed? What makes her a suicide and me suicidal? I mean, if that's what I am.

"You never wanted to do it. I knew that."

I close my eyes and try not to think about how I wasn't strong
enough or committed enough or good enough to make a pact
with Leah. How I lied to her the whole time.

Mr. Kispert nods at my newest creation. "Great work. Okay,
everyone, let's clean up. Bell's going to ring."

I meet Nick at the big sink. "You're very talented," he says.

I turn to him. Get dizzy. My hand reaches for the edge of the
sink for support.

He cocks his head. "You okay, Allie?"

"I'm fine." I avoid his eyes. I'm feeling all strung-out and raw,
and I don't exactly need his attention right now.

"Call you later?" he asks.

"Definitely," I say, making my head move in exactly one
north-south movement.

I stagger to the bathroom, hoping not to run into Emery or
Max or Mr. Hicks on the way. When I get there, my eyes are
glassy and bloodshot. I pull out my cell. Two hours till lunch.
Not that I'm hungry. But I'm not exactly sure how I'll make
it through honors U.S. history and honors biology—the two
roadblocks that stand in my way. I lean over the sink and throw
water on my face. When I lift my head, Leah's there.

I jump. "Shit, Leah, you scared me." I look around to check
that we're alone.

"No one's here. We're good."

"I need a way to get through this," I tell her.

Leah looks at me and nods. "Don't skip classes. That's a rookie mistake."

"So how am I going to do this?"

"You got any NoDoz? Any caffeine at all?"

"Excedrin. That has caffeine, right?" I paw through my purse, my fingers raking for the pills I should have in there.

"Take two and get your ass to class. Before you're late. Also, do not start getting detentions. The key is not to draw any extra attention to yourself. Got it?"

I want to ask her if she thinks that's the best plan, considering: a pill to bring me down, another to wake me up. Like Alice in Wonderland, I'm stuck. When does it stop?

"You gotta get moving," she whispers.

I take one last look over my shoulder as I go. She's slumped against the wall.

Leah aims her gaze at me. "It's hard to be dead."

I leave the bathroom, the door banging behind me.

CHAPTER 10

I'm sitting at my desk trying to concentrate, but I just can't do it. I close my English lit book and pick up my phone. 6:45. It vibrates in my hand. I almost drop it.

Nick.

Sophie texted me a few minutes ago. She wants to go for a walk.

I smile. She doesn't have opposable thumbs. How did she text?

Her cute little nose?

This time I laugh out loud. I guess if she took the time to text you, she must really want to meet up. Ten minutes?

Deal.

My phone goes in my pocket, and I walk into my bathroom to check my look. Not too bad, definitely less strung-out than before. I'm glad. Nick shouldn't see me all rehab-ready.

I'm walking out of my room when I hear a tapping behind me. Max. He used to climb in my window before we had cells—or other people to date. I rush to open it for him.

"Hi, beautiful."

"You haven't done this in a long time."

"I have to talk to you."

I move out of the way, letting him climb into my room, even though his words freeze me, remind me of last spring. "What's up?"

"Can I talk to you? I—"

"I'm going to meet Nick. I'm late."

The muscles in Max's jaw tighten. "Please."

He sits on my bed. I join him, knowing I probably shouldn't. Max puts his hand on my thigh, making me self-conscious. Where is Mom? How long until I'm supposed to meet Nick? And more importantly, what does Max want?

"I know I've blown it with you."

I shake my head. Why is he doing this? Why now?

"I know I have."

I hold his stare so he can tell I mean what I say. "We're fine, Max."

He looks down at his hands, and I sigh. The cocoa butter he uses to heal his swimmer's skin relaxes me. I love that smell.

"Allie," he starts. "I wish… I wish…" He looks up at me; the misery in his eyes makes me want to end whatever pain he's feeling. "I can't stop thinking about you."

"Max, please…"

"You know how I feel about you, right?" He puts his hand on my face, and I cover his with my own. He puts his lips on mine. My heart races. He kisses me. Soft. Sweet. Sincere. I kiss him back. Of course I do, but then I remember how it ended with Max and me last time. And I wonder what this whole play is about now. I pull away, winded, confused. He looks me in the eyes, and I swear I see tears. My gut clenches. There's no reason for Max to be crying.

"I've done some things I wish I could take back."

Is he talking about last spring?

"I was so worried about you. I still am. I need to know, was the pact because of me? Was that why you were going to do it?" Max asks.

I actually thought he wanted to be with me. This is just his guilt talking. My face heats. I can't look at him. "No. It wasn't you."

His fingers trace my cheek. "I never wanted to hurt you."

"It wasn't you."

His eyes plead with me, and that makes me feel powerful, like all I have to do is find something he needs so I can give it to him. "What's really going on now, Max?" I ask. "What are you trying to tell me?"

The silence spreads between us. He takes my hand. "You remember Terry's party?" he asks.

"Don't," I say. "Tell me why you're here now. What's going on?"

He inches closer until his hand is on my thigh, and I can barely breathe. "It was ridiculously hot that day," he continues.

He leans in until I feel his breath on my neck. "Max...don't. I mean it."

"Someone started a water balloon fight."

I try not to give in to the pull of Max. Of the story of us. But it's hard, especially when he's doing this. "You mean *you* started it."

He gives me a lecherous smile. "Because I wanted to see you wet."

I smile back even though I know it's not the truth. I remember. He wanted to see Kelly Starks wet. He was chasing her then.

He reaches up and tucks a piece of hair behind my ear. "And then Billy Sullivan came after you, remember?"

"You nailed him with a shaving cream bomb. My hero." I laugh even though I don't want to.

"And…"

"And he chased you. You were caught; you had nowhere to go." I take over the story, not caring that Max has won. "So you flipped over the fence like it was nothing."

"And…" Max whispers, his face so close to mine now I can smell the gum he's chewing.

"And I knew I had to meet you," I finish.

"I know I haven't always been who you want me to be. But that doesn't mean I don't love you. I do. You know I do. You've always been mine, Allie. No matter what happened before or happens now. It's always been you."

I'm outside my body, yelling at myself to be happy. These are the words I've been dying to hear. And now he's saying them. But the thing is, I know it hasn't always been me. Most times, it's been other girls. The fun ones. The ones he didn't care about like he cared about me. Supposedly. But the ones he chose over me. Every single time.

"Please, Allie. Don't you want to try?"

I let my fingers trace his cheek, his stubble rough under my touch, making this moment feel so real. I understand what he means. He is mine. I am his. In the most important ways. I know that's insane. I know I'm being stupid and gullible and just plain weak, but I can't help it when it comes to Max. Then I remember—those are the same words he used last spring. Right before he left me.

He leans in like he's about to kiss me, then stops. "Text him." Max puts his hand in my pocket and pulls out my phone. "Or I'll do it."

I grab for my cell, which he is holding out of my reach. "Tell Mr. Baseball you're mine."

It hits me like a punch to the heart. That's what this is really about. "Are you kidding me?" I try to catch my breath. I stand. Turn to face him. "You don't want me until someone else does?"

He staggers toward me. "You're mine. Tell him you're mine and always will be."

I'm so disgusted by him. "Yours when you're not drunk? Yours in the light of day? Yours all the time, not just for a day or a week or a month until you get all claustrophobic and want someone new?"

"No. That's wrong. I was worried I would hurt you." He makes a motion with his hands. "I'm not a good boyfriend. I know that. Don't you think I know that? Don't you think I'd take back all of it if I could? Everything I've done? Don't you think I know I shouldn't have pushed you?"

"More like you shouldn't have replaced me the minute I wasn't ready."

Max licks his lips. Shakes his head. "I was scared. I knew I'd hurt you."

"Then why did you start to begin with?"

"I couldn't help it. I loved you. Love you."

"You have no idea what that word means. You are a player and you always will be."

"Not with you, Allie."

"No. Because this time I'm the one who's walking away."

I grab my phone and head for the stairs, not caring that Mom's in the kitchen, overhearing this dramatic little scene play out. *Max doesn't want me. Max doesn't want me.* I repeat that horrible chorus in my head till I know—even if I don't believe—that I'm being stupid. Max doesn't want me. He just wants Nick not to have me.

"Sophie!" I make it all the way downstairs and grab her leash and sweater.

"Come on, Allie…" Max holds his arms out to me.

Sophie comes, her nails making a clicking sound on the floor as she trots to me. I bend down and put her sweater and leash on.

"One day, we're going to be together for real. One day when we're through with all the other people, when we're ready to just be together, we will."

I burst out the door and leave Max standing there with his "one days" and his stupid, horrible, mean plays. Leah told me I was starstruck when it came to him, that I needed to grow up. She'd be happy to see that I'm finally on board.

CHAPTER 11

The day is gray, like my mood, and I'm glad. I walk into Mr. Kispert's room, the headache on the edge of my temples. Migraines used to just happen for me. Now they are a promise tucked into the back of my eyes, feeding on the sadness and the anger, taking over my head like an invading army.

I grab two Excedrin and a bottle of water from my backpack. Maybe this will be enough to hold the headache off for real. Piper is already staring at her easel. Nick's is prepped and ready for him. Mine is empty. I wonder if Mr. Kispert just ran out of time or if he's finally getting the message.

Today is a block day, some stupid freshman and sophomore school-wide testing makes us all go to half our classes but stay for double the time. Block days in art usually mean a crap ton of creating. I better get started. The supply closet door is closed but not locked. Mr. Kispert walks in the room, just as I turn the handle.

"Wait." He holds up his hand. "I've got something special for you."

His words create pebbles of worry inside my stomach. Nick follows on his heels, two large canvas grocery bags in his hands.

Mr. Kispert drags a table next to my empty easel. He nods at

Nick, who pours the contents of one of the bags into a messy pile. Rocks. Twigs. Shells. Pine cones. Leaves. Nick smiles at me like the hero he thinks he is. He sweeps the debris off the other side of the table. On that side, he pours nail polish bottles, lipsticks, crayons, markers, Post-it notes, those plastic Easter eggs, and candy of all different shapes and sizes and colors.

I cross my arms so I will take up less space. All that's missing are the cough medicine bottles and the pills. I'm glad no one understands what these colors really mean to me. It's like Mr. Kispert mined the world for every scrap of my guilt, like he somehow knew these were the colors that are responsible for my dangerous choices, then filled the table in front of me with the evidence. And now he wants me to paint. Excellent.

"I've been thinking, Allie." Mr. Kispert stands back, hands shoved in his pockets, jingling his keys. "Maybe we need to look at 2-D versus 3-D." He winks at me. "Today could be a play day for you."

Piper and Nick don't need one of Mr. Kispert's art interventions. I'm the only one with a table. But I also can't help but see the art here. I step forward. I reach for the shells and the rocks and the leaves first. Then I look at the candy and the polish and the lipsticks. It's all here, staring at me, and I know this is really about which I choose: real or fake. Paper or plastic. I open a bag of Skittles and let the candy pour out. I stare at them and know they represent Max, Leah, me. That night.

I open the root beer candies and the Nerds and the M&M's. I gather and group and arrange, and when I feel like I have a good enough idea of what I'm doing, I see that Mr. Kispert has already loaded my easel and started a palette for me. I take the brush and start to paint the colors. Candy as splatter pattern. Leah's. Feelings as sugar or pills or stupid drinks in the blender. Dresses and expectations. And at the center of it all, Max.

He could have come to that party. Some of the swimmers were there. He could have saved me from the blush-pink puddle that spilled from between my legs after I was with Jason because I had to grow up. He could have been the one with me, but he was somewhere else, with someone else. And now, after all the pills and the paint and the stupid, stupid choices, I have nothing left but gray feelings for him. So I paint those too. I paint the blue and the ice and the cold, and I hope that will bring the numb I really need. Like when I went into the cold water with Leah at the Cape. I paint prison gray and ash white and end it with a touch of black.

Mr. Kispert sees me cleaning up and takes that as an invitation to check on my painting. I glance at him from the sink. He's nodding. The knots in my stomach soften. He puts his hand on his face and looks at it from another angle. More nods. I can't help but smile as the water washes away the colors I just chose.

Piper holds her brushes in the water with mine. She leans against me, her tiny frame adding weight to my recently built fortress, the one I built with my brushes to protect myself from Max and all the bad. "Really great work today."

I close my eyes and think about the picture I just painted. For once, I agree that I've accomplished something. I just hope my new-found strength can stand up to the real world, when I actually have to see Max. That it doesn't get washed away like makeup after a good cry. Or a castle made of sand.

———•———

Everyone is excited about the pep rally. I get it. But I'm not part of that crowd anymore. Mr. Hicks is standing in the hallway. He calls me to him. "You don't have to go, Allie. Nobody expects you to." He looks straight at me, like he gets me.

"I'll be sitting with friends," I offer.

"Well, in case you change your mind, here's an excuse slip." He hands me a pass with my name already on it. "And I'd like you to come see me on Monday. Let's look at your classes and see how you're doing. Okay?"

"Sure," I say even though I have no intentions of going to see him. I slip the pass into my pocket and push out into the packed hallways with my head down so low, I almost don't see Max walk by, his arm draped around Tracy Summers's shoulders.

Max leans into Tracy and whispers something in her ear. She laughs. Pain flows through my blood. Max looks at me—just a quick glance—then he looks away. Max is mad. No question. But it's not like he has a right. He did this to us. He did. I'm just the one left behind on our battlefield, checking for survivors.

My cell vibrates, and for the five seconds it takes to pull it out and see who is calling, I let myself believe it's Max asking me to forgive him. But when I look at the phone, I've got a missed call from Nick. I steady myself and slow my heart.

I try not to get annoyed. It's not Nick's fault he's not Max. Nick texts.

Sit with me?

I blink back disappointment tears, pissed at myself for letting this happen. I have to be stronger than this. I have to stop being so weak. So I type back, glad it's easy to fake peppy in a text. Sure

I think about the bottle of Delsym still stashed in my back-pack promising a little Numb. It's not like I left it in there on purpose, but it's there, and maybe I can get through the pep rally with a dose of liquid anesthesia.

I start walking down the hall, counting the steps till I can get to my bunker—thirty steps, twenty-five, twenty, eighteen. At ten, I look up and see John Strickland coming straight for me. Two of his boys are walking with him but stop as he makes contact.

"Hey, Allie." He grabs my arm.

My heart speeds. I shove my hands in my pockets, try to get a little smaller. Without asking, he puts something in the top pocket of my jean jacket.

"Don't thank me. Least I could do. You look like you could use a little pick-me-up."

I look down, my face painted humiliation red. And then he's gone before I can say anything back. I put my hand over the lump in my pocket, shamed and curious at the same time.

Five more steps and I'm in the bathroom. I pull his stash out of my pocket and spill the contents into my hand like the candy on the art table. Pills. Four. Two small white ones with an M stamped on them and two small green ones. And a note: *Green gets you loose. White wakes you up. Take one of each.* Now I definitely feel like Alice in Wonderland. Should I take them?

I wonder if Piper uses John Strickland's pills, if Leah did. He said I could use a pick-me-up. John Strickland should know. It's kind of his job.

I stare in the mirror. Do I want to do this? Do I trust him? *No.* The answer is no. I shove the bag back into my pocket and leave the bathroom. I walk to my locker, trying hard to avoid the chaos in the halls, as what's left of the student body empties out into the courtyard. I put my books away and look at myself in the makeup mirror. John Strickland was right. I do look worn down.

My eyes go to all the pictures Emery and Max taped to the inside of my locker before school started. There are tons of Emery and me, and Max and me, and Leah and me. My fingers trace the one of Leah and me on the Cape when we were twelve and ten—a happy Cape memory. Before Mom and Dad waged their war full-time. Because the thing is, I do remember when they only had sporadic skirmishes.

I close my eyes. Maybe Mr. Hicks is right. Maybe I shouldn't put myself through this. Maybe I should go to the art room and paint. I pull the bag out of my pocket and push the pills around. Maybe I should take just one? I remember how it felt when I first took Mom's Xanax. At first it was okay. And it did sort of help. One part of a pill can't hurt. I could use a little life in me. I bite the white one in half and swallow it without a drink.

Voices build up in my brain, accusing me of being stupid and weak and out of control. I push the heel of my hand into my eye socket and pray they stop. I've done it now. Worrying about it won't help any. I'm wondering when I'll feel the effects of my new friend's little white pill and almost jump out of my skin when I see Leah leaning against the locker behind me. She's wearing her dance team uniform, the blue one with the silver wave outlined in sequins.

"I used to love pep rallies," she says.

I look around at the empty halls and whisper to her, "What are you doing here? You can't be here."

"You think you can handle John Strickland without my help?" She laughs. "Hardly."

Boundaries. I need them. I turn my back to her. She moves into the mirror so that when I lean in, her image rises before me. I face her. "Why are you here? Really?"

"I'm here to help you, of course."

"Help me what?"

My cell vibrates. Where r u?

"Help you figure this out."

"Nick's waiting. I gotta go," I say.

"Go ahead. I'll catch up." Leah's like Dad. You can never win.

I slam my locker closed and walk away, texting Nick as I go, but I have to lean against another bank of lockers, because all of a sudden, the hallway feels like it's tipped. On my way, I text.

"You brought me back for a reason." Leah appears next to me

as I walk-jog to catch up. "I'm pretty sure it wasn't to watch you make stupid mistakes, was it?"

I wave her off. My heart is beating jackrabbit fast, and I can't tell if it's because of that little white pill or that my sister's ghost won't behave.

I see Nick ahead of me, a sea of people separating us. My eyes feel a little out of sync with the rest of me, like they're moving faster than I am.

Nick tries to maneuver through the crowd and gets swept in the wrong direction, making me think about how he's mixed. Is he more jock than artist? Or more artist than jock? And more importantly, can I trust him?

"Stop thinking. You always overthink things," Leah says. "Just have fun. You're allowed to have fun, you know?"

Am I allowed to have fun? Aren't I supposed to be dead too?

Leah shakes her head. "You never wanted to, remember? You said you didn't."

"You coming?" Nick's appeared by my side. He reaches for my hand. I jog a little to catch up, trying to stop thinking so much. I try to just enjoy being with Nick. But it's hard because whatever is in this little white pill is making me feel like all I want to do is think.

"Hey, Allie." Cassie Lindberg smiles, her arm around Billy Crandall's waist. Shortstop Billy. Hotshot. Pretty boy. Cassie's long, tri-dyed curls fall around her face, her eyes huge. I nod.

"Come on, the team's sitting here." Nick drags me up the stands.

Great. Now I'm sitting with the team. That means we're high school official.

I try to slow him down so maybe the feeling part of my brain can catch up, but he's on a mission. He's going to take me higher—higher than this pill.

We climb past the soccer team. The swimmers are next. Max looks at me, a tight expression on his face. No Tracy for the moment and no seat saved for her. My heart warms. Maybe I was wrong about him. Then Tracy climbs past Nick and me, and Max scoots over for her. For *her*. I wrap my arm around Nick, glad to have some cover. I don't feel anything—but smug. And powerful. Like Leah.

The cheerleaders start shooting shirts into the crowd. One sails over our heads. Pat Mendez pushes forward, knocking Matthew Cronan and Billy Whitehead out of the way to get one. The senior football players stand at the top of the bleachers, waiting to rain down on us.

The announcer calls, "Sean Cunningham, running back, all-county three years, most yards rushing in Prince William County, all-state last two years." The crowd erupts.

Leah's Sean. I swallow hard. Leah reappears in time to shoot a death stare at him.

I think about the last time I saw him with Leah. At the party. Leah was crying. Sean was pissed. Six hours before she killed herself, she and Sean were fighting.

"It had nothing to do with it," Leah says. "He was a jerk but not worth dying over."

"Dave Wilson, three years' all-state offensive lineman," the faceless voice continues.

Sean and Dave rumble down the steps, making them shake. The announcer calls out the next name and launches Scott Horseman. I realize Jason comes after him. I look up, and sure enough, he's standing there, huge head and square shoulders. I shudder. What was I thinking sleeping with him?

"You were thinking you should get it over with. You closed your eyes and picked," Leah says.

I was thinking if I were the kind of girl who did, Max would want me, pick me. Nick pulls me higher. I feel like I'm flying. Or falling. It seems like we've been climbing forever. My heart races. The walls close in. I can't breathe. Maybe I was wrong to trust baseball player Nick. What sport you play says a lot about you—like which pill you take or which bottle you drink.

Nick finds our place on the bleachers and motions for me to sit. He leans in. "You okay?"

"Dizzy. Headache."

I reach for a Gatorade chaser and slip on my sunglasses, my eyes shut, as I slump against Nick's shoulder. He sighs, his arm slung around me.

"I can't believe I'm missing this." I open my eyes. Leah is sitting next to me. Her voice is sad, like a little kid's. "I should be on the field. That's my team." She's chewing on her fingernail, something she never did when she was alive. Leah puts her chin in her hand, which is balanced on her knee. "It's hard to see everyone move on. Like I wasn't even here."

Sean walks onto the field, approaches Leah's ex-bestie Brittney, and puts his arm around her, smooth and easy.

Leah groans. "I should have concentrated on my dancing. Like you should with your art."

Nick slides me close to him so Colin, the pitcher, and his girlfriend, Vanessa, can sit next to me, taking Leah's place, and I wonder where she's gone until she pops up behind me.

"Bitch!" Leah hisses over my shoulder.

Vanessa smiles at me, but I know it's just for show. She and I don't exactly have love for each other. Especially after that night.

Whatever is in that little pill ramps up as the dancers take the field to do their routine. My head starts spinning. Sweat beads on my forehead and chest despite the breezy September air. I feel a flush running from my stomach up to the top of my head. My ears start humming. But it all feels good. Better than Mom's stuff. This pill makes me feel like I can do anything.

Jennifer Skelton from the dance team takes the microphone. "Hi, all!" she says. "I'd like to announce this year's Robert Frost Senior High Dance Team."

Then it hits me: Leah's with me. In front of all these people. But for some reason, I don't care. I feel good and strong and like I could tell Nick and he'd totally understand.

"Don't be a dork, Allie." Leah laughs in my face. "He'll think you're insane."

Says my dead sister's ghost. That sort of cracks me up. But she's probably right. Still, I'm flying, and it feels so good to, well, feel good.

"This part's fun. Just be ready for the crash," she says. "John Strickland's pills always end with a crash."

I look at her. John Strickland? How does she know him? A weird sliver of a memory lurks in the back of my mind. From a really long time ago.

"Hey," Nick breathes in my ear. "You doing all right?"

I smile. My lips stretch like soft butter on rough bread. Nick looks at me, his brow furrowed. Another shirt rockets into the stands. I reach out as if I could catch one up here.

"You want a shirt?" Nick asks. "I'll be right back."

I watch him climb down the bleachers toward Pat Mendez. He taps Pat on the arm and then points to me. Pat slaps hands with him and gives him the shirt. Nick turns to me, holding it over his head like a prize, smiling as if he'd just won a trophy. I can't help but smile back.

"Hey," Max calls from behind me, making me wonder when he came up here and why. "You already got him running your errands?" He nods at Nick and laughs. "Not exactly an Iron Man, is he?"

Anger speeds through me. Ugly rage. What gives him the right? "Go back to your seat, Max," I say. It's all I can do to keep from lunging to smack him. He sits behind me. For some reason, all I can think about is how it took me this long to realize what a jerk he is—and how much I'd like to wipe that smug look off his face. He pulls back as if I were really going to hit him. As if. Except I catch my hand in my peripheral vision. It somehow flew up in the air without my knowledge. I'm officially on autopilot-bitch mode.

"And as team captain, Katie Krueger." The crowd cheers.

"She always hated me." Leah pouts.

I want to smack her too. Why can't she stop talking to me? Doesn't she think it's hard enough to get through this without her constantly talking? And Vanessa sitting next to me. And Max, acting like he has a right to be mad I'm sitting with Nick.

My heart starts beating so hard, I wonder if anyone else can hear it. It's thundering in my ears. I think about the pill I took. I'm starting to think the white one by itself was a bad idea. My head feels fuzzy and woozy. I have scratchy eyes. I'm edgy and exposed. I'm raw.

"You're losing it," Leah warns.

I want to scream at her to stop. Stop telling me things that make me crazy. Stop talking to me around other people. Stop with the warnings.

The world starts spinning. I put my hands to my head, pushing the glasses flush against my forehead. I stand to see where Nick is, why he isn't back yet. I'm ridiculously thirsty. Gatorade. I take a gulp, but some spills, and I have to wipe my mouth with my hand. I fumble, and it falls. All over Vanessa.

"What the…" she screams. She turns to look at me. "Do you see what you did? You are such a freak!"

I stand. "I'm sorry." I go to wipe her off with my bare hands.

She looks at me like I'm insane. "What are you doing? Don't touch me." She pushes me.

I start to fall. Hands reach out and grab me, yanking me backward. I am so dizzy, I think I'm going to puke. "I got you, baby." His voice, crackly and beautiful and breathtakingly familiar. Max.

My body responds to his touch and his voice and his feel, but my heart just gets harder. He's always doing this. Coming so close and then never coming through. Except with the Tracys and Marcies and Barbaras. The fun girls. Never with me. Even though I'm sure he knows by now that I'm as fun as any one of them. I did it. Didn't he get the memo?

With the stunning clarity that this pill brings, I realize I don't need his help anymore. "Don't touch me!"

"What's wrong?" Emery is suddenly right behind him and I start to get annoyed that they seem to always be together.

I want to tell him it's not me. It's the pill. Leah hijacked my painting the other day; now John Strickland's drug has my mind. I look like Allie but think like Leah. Then again, I want to tell him that I'm over him. That I painted all his pain out of me and need to steer clear of him at least until the paint dries and sets.

"Allie, look, I'm sorry about last night. I'm sorry about today. About everything. I'm worried about you," Max says.

Just like that, Max gets inside me, and I can't have that. Sure, he's here to be the hero, but where will he be tomorrow? Or the next day? Where was he that night? I stare him down. "I'm *fine*."

"You're not fine. Let me help you." He shoots Emery a look, and that makes me want to scream. A look that judges me as weak and needy—again. I need to change that perception. I need to rearrange the composition. So I shove him hard. So hard that even his one hundred and eighty pounds of all-state athlete is moved, and he has to grab Billy's shoulder to keep himself from falling down the bleachers.

He brushes his shirt off, then scowls before he walks away. And I'm glad. I can almost hear a bell ringing, signaling that I won the round. I want to throw my hands over my head and celebrate my victory, but part of me knows that's wrong. I am messed up. I have messed up. I am losing it for real.

Nick comes back, the T-shirt he got for me hanging limp in his hand. "You okay?"

I try to calm my heart that's beating like mad right now, like a wild thing.

"Something you want to tell me about you and Max? You guys a thing?" He hooks his thumb toward the space Max just vacated.

"No. We're nothing."

Nick looks at me for a long time. I wonder if he's more worried about the Max-and-me thing or how weird I'm acting. Does he suspect I'm high? If he knew, for real, what would he think?

"You look a little...."

"I can't do this right now." I stomp down the stairs, hoping not to fall.

"Wait up, Allie," Emery calls.

And then she has her hand around my arm, helping me even when I don't want to be helped.

When we get to the bottom, I shake loose of her. She grabs for me. "Allie, what's wrong with you?"

"Can you leave me alone? Can you do that?"

"I'll drive you home," she says.

"Why can't you listen to me? Leave me alone. Both of you. Leave me alone."

"No. You need help." Her eyes peer into mine. "Are you high?"

I hold up my finger. "Don't you dare!"

"You can't do that." She points at me. "You have to stop. All the drugs. Everything. You're scaring me."

"Don't you lecture me when you were her *supplier*."

Her face pales. "I didn't. She didn't OD on weed." She turns and walks back toward the pep rally, spinning around to shout a final "I can't believe you said that."

I walk past the baseball practice field. John Strickland is standing there, looking at me, or at least I think he is. His eyes are hidden behind sunglasses.

Nick's steps make me turn. "Hey, Allie, wait!"

"This was a mistake. I'm sorry," I start. "I just…"

He nods toward the parking lot. "Can I give you a ride home?"

I'm pacing. I know I look crazy, but I can't help it. It's like my legs can't stay still. "I think I'm gonna walk. It calms me down. This was a mistake." I look back at the stadium. "Leah and pep rallies. You know?" My hand goes over my stomach.

He nods. "I'm sorry."

"It's okay. I should have said something. I've gotta go. Okay?"

Nick looks worried. "Okay. We still on for tonight?"

"Definitely."

"You sure I can't drive you home?"

"No. I'm going to be fine. Really."

"Okay." He hooks his finger over his shoulder. "Then I'm gonna head back. I think they're going to shave Coach's head in a few. Don't want to miss that."

"Go," I say.

He trots off, and John Strickland takes his sunglasses off and looks straight at me. His stare makes me nervous, so I turn around to see Leah standing behind me. "I miss boyfriends," she says.

CHAPTER 12

I'm glad I set my alarm or I would've totally slept through my date. My head feels fuzzy and my body feels all leaden. I push up on my arms and fight the dizzy that descends. I better get going. Nick will be here in an hour. I go to the bathroom, my legs still wobbly. I splash water on my face. I'm a mess.

My hair's a wreck. It's been ages since I got it cut, so it's all one length, one color, and pin-straight. Like me, it's lifeless. My skin is whiter than white, as if I'm a ghost myself. The John Strickland drugs have put bags under my eyes. Great.

Leah pops into my head. "Maybe if you took it like he told you? You didn't listen." I guess she's riding the residual medicinal wave for as long as she can. Good for her.

But I don't get it. Why is she defending him? I want to yell at her. Shouldn't she be worried about me? Shouldn't she want me to stay away from the things that could hurt me? *I* was her little sister; shouldn't she care? At all?

"Stop being such a drama queen," she says, walking out of my bathroom and into my room. "I'm not saying you have to go all Amy Winehouse. Just take enough to find your art without Kispert's pathetic little interventions. And me."

I think about telling her she *is* with me, that I don't need the drugs to keep her. I think about telling her how scared I am about all this, but Leah doesn't like weakness. Leah was never scared. She was fierce. A warrior.

Until she killed herself.

I find her standing by my closet, hair down, straight and shiny, dark glasses on, plaid shirt, and dark jeans. Her college-girl look. She's got a sugar-free Rockstar, which she holds out to me.

"You need a little pick-me-up for tonight," she explains.

I grab it and take a swig, wondering if everyone in my life is getting blurred together because now she's using John-Strickland words.

"I don't get the feeling Nick's into the drug thing, do you?" she asks as she rifles through my closet, holding up a short black skirt and a belted shirt over it. "You're going to need to be careful with him."

"Was thinking of taking it easy with all that anyway." I push past her and pull out an oversized shirt with black leggings instead.

"Really?" she asks, and I wonder if she is talking about my decision to go clean or my outfit choice.

"You don't like?" I look at the clothes in my hand, thrust them back in the closet, and push hangers aside, searching for something else I feel like wearing.

"I don't think that's smart," Leah says. "This is going to be a very hard year for you. I'm just saying."

I lay my clothes on the bed and head back to the bathroom, partly to get away from her, partly to get ready. I try not to listen to the words repeating in my brain. *This is going to be a hard year.* Thanks to her. And now she's pushing me. Like usual.

Leah comes in the bathroom, stands behind me. I can feel her there, watching me, waiting for me to do what she tells me. To obey. And that makes me want to do the opposite. I don't have to do everything she says.

Leah quiets her voice. "Nick doesn't need to know everything about you. You need to set some boundaries."

I shake my head. This is nuts. *She's* talking to me about boundaries? I pour three dots of Clinique Alabaster foundation on the back of my hand and use a makeup brush to paint my face.

Leah leans forward. "Want me to do it?"

I nod.

She picks up Peach in a Pinch blush and brushes it on me. A wicked smile on her face, she takes her price: a tiny little pinch on my arm. "Sorry, couldn't help it," she laughs. And it feels like old times, just Leah and me.

"Come on." She pulls me by the hand and walks to my dresser, opens my drawers, and starts going through my underwear.

I push her out of the way. "I can do this myself!" I pull out a pair of baby-blue bikinis.

"Nice choice." Leah hands me the matching bra. "It says you're nice while you're being naughty."

"Haven't exactly decided about that yet."

"Why the hell not? Cherry popped means good to go. Don't hold back now, Al. Go get yourself some."

I move away from her and put my underwear on, thinking about what Leah said. Is she right? Just because I did it with Jason, does that mean everyone expects it? Every time? Does Nick?

"I know you're trying to go clean and all, but you could use a little something to relax you." She pulls a prescription bottle out of her pocket.

I stare at what she's brought. She couldn't have. But she did. It's the bottle of Valium she used. Or an exact replica. The label on the prescription bottle is torn at the edges. Leah liked to peel the labels off things.

I walk forward, pick it up. The name is still legible, despite Leah's tinkering. Mom's name. Karen Blackmore. The *K* almost completely gone. And the *more* just two letters: *MO*. I always wondered if she did that right before she took them. Did she play the I-will-stop-if game? Of course she did, and if I hadn't been so out of it that night, I would have woken up. I would have texted her. Talked to her. I would have stopped her.

"Look, I had to take a lot of pills and drink a lot of wine to die. It's not like one or two would do. You know this. You remember. You saw."

My head starts swimming, and I start shaking. I don't want to remember. I'd do anything to forget. "How could you bring these here?"

"To show you. It's not easy to kill yourself. You have to want to. It takes work to swallow all those pills. A few at a time. You're not addicted like Mom is. Or crazy like I was."

"You weren't crazy; you were just sad," I say.

"You were always so starstruck, Baby Sister," she says, but she smiles when she does, like she was glad I was struck by her star. "It's pretty intense to do what I did."

She opens the bottle and pours the pills into her hand, which is cupped and ready to receive. Robin's-egg blue. Oval. When I look at them, I see the splatter pattern they made by her body: some half-dissolved and puked back up, others whole that never made it into her. Chills spread through me. Bile rises. I run for the toilet, make it just in time.

Leah's there, waiting when I come up for air. She hands me a towel.

"You've got to grow up. We're not talking about losing your virginity. This isn't baby stuff. I know it's hard. I know you're scared. But this is for real. If you let me go, I'm gone. End of story. You have to stop pretending you're like me. You aren't. You're just sad. A pill or two won't hurt you like they hurt me. You are titanium."

I start to cry. She puts her arms around me. "I won't take those pills."

"Not these." She puts her hand on my arm. "But you might want to take a little something. You're going to see Max. You have to be strong or he'll kill you—for real. That's what love does."

I stand there, dumbstruck. Mute. Leah always ruled me when she was alive. How can she still be ruling me now? I

124

need to stand up to her. I know I do. But she's right. About Max at least.

"Why don't you wear my tall black boots? They'd be perfect with this." She hands me my plaid miniskirt and tight, black scoop-neck sweater.

It feels a little wrong to borrow her things now. Sort of like stealing from the dead. Isn't that a little low?

"Don't be a dork. It would be wrong not to. You're going to look amazing. Come on."

She goes into the hall, and I follow. I open her door. It squeaks just a little, and I jump. She laughs.

"They're over here."

I reach into her closet and bring the boots to her window seat, where I sit and put them on. Leah pulls on my hands and stands me in front of the mirror. Standing behind me, she plays with my hair. "You think up or down?"

"Down."

"Definitely." She picks up a brush and runs it through my hair. "You look great."

"You think?"

"I do."

I smile. Because wearing her things and having Leah say I look good and having her take care of me feels as good as any pill does. And I'm so happy and distracted by Leah being so sweet, I almost don't feel her slip the little package into the front pocket of my skirt. I put my hand over it.

"Shhhh," she says.

"Leah—"

"Don't worry. It's not the blue pills. Just the leftovers of John Strickland's little present. Only if you need. Only if you want to. Just to make sure you're solid."

I put my hand over hers. But inside, I wonder. Because her promise sounds like when she said she'd only come to me when I wanted her. That didn't exactly pan out, did it?

The doorbell rings, startling me. Crap. Better get downstairs before Mom catches me in here.

Just as I make it out the door, Leah calls me back. "Allie?"

"What?"

"I miss dates."

I start to tell her I'm sorry, but she's already gone. She said it was hard to be dead. And I guess that must be true. It must be hard to watch everyone else go on when you're stuck in last year's colors with no dates or parties or pep rallies. I wonder: If she could take it back, would she?

I hear Mom open the door, Sophie at her heels, woofing and circling. I watch as Nick bends to pet her. He stands and extends his hand to Mom, like the stand-up guy he is.

"Nice to meet you, Mrs. Blackmore," he says, his voice carrying all the way up the stairs.

Mom calls, "Allie?"

"Be right down."

I race into my bathroom and finish my makeup in record time. Mom with Nick makes me feel all panicky and exposed. I grab my purse and throw the makeup and some gum in it. I pull John Strickland's package out of my pocket and throw that in too. Just in case. I race down the stairs, taking them two at a time.

"You look amazing," Nick says.

He looks clean-cut good, wearing a long-sleeved collared shirt and jeans that are so crisp they look as if they've been ironed. Like Dad's. That reminds me of what Leah said. Nick probably wouldn't be okay with me using. I think she's right about that.

"Midnight. No later," Mom says as if she'll actually pay attention.

I push Nick out the door. He holds the car door open for me, then slides into the driver's side. Nick leans over, grabs my hand. "You ready?" I nod. He puts the car in reverse, and we leave. "We're gonna meet a few people. That okay?"

"Um, sure." I'd rather it just be the two of us, but it's not like I can complain. When we pull into the Pizza Inn, where the baseball team and football team go, I realize art isn't about a team. Art is private and personal. Art doesn't make you hang in a restaurant with people you don't know and probably won't like. All of a sudden, I'm thinking Nick's ball playing is bringing down his average. With me at least.

My stomach tightens. Can I do this? Do I even want to?

We go inside, Nick's hand on my back, steady and sure, guiding me. In my head, I'm dragging my feet, putting on the brakes. I move next to him, using his body as a shield so I can scan the faces in front of me. Nick steers me toward the tables of baseball players, where Vanessa and Colin sit. I smile, but it feels dry and plastic.

Vanessa makes a face at me. Colin comes forward and slaps hands with Nick.

"How ya doin', man?"

"Golden," Nick answers back. His hand envelopes mine, but it feels like a life vest that's filled with holes.

Cassie and Billy arrive, and Cassie's all full of energy and smiles. "Hey, Allie," she says. "I need to go to the bathroom. Wanna join?"

"Um, sure." I pull away from Nick, who leans in to kiss me—quick and sweet and obviously for show.

"Nick's so cute. I mean, you two are really cute together…" Cassie babbles. I'm impressed. She talks faster than I think. Even on the little white pills.

We pass a couple freshmen giggling on their way out of the bathroom. I hit the stall. Cassie goes to the mirror. I smell pot. Emery's vice. When I come out, Cassie's standing at the mirror, fluffing her hair and holding a joint.

I look at Cassie's fingers and the climbing smoke. She notices my stare. "Oh my God, you want some?" She holds it out to me.

"Um, no. That's okay. I'm good."

"You sure? It's just a little, you know. Very mild stuff really." She takes a puff, then tries to hand it to me.

"Aren't you worried about someone coming in?"

She shrugs. "I know the owners. They're totally cool. I do it all the time here. No prob. Here, have some."

I wanted to be clean tonight. But that was before Nick brought me here. Besides, what could it hurt? It's the mild stuff. Like Cassie said. No big deal. It's not like John Strickland drugs or Mom drugs or even over-the-counter drugs. Emery does it all the time. Cassie hands it to me.

I put it to my lips and draw it in. The smoke goes down my throat into my lungs, and I start coughing, my throat spasms, and tears spring to my eyes. Cassie hits me on the back. Vanessa walks in, sees me choking, and rolls her eyes.

She pushes the stall open. "Maybe you should stick to pills."

"Don't worry about her. She's such a bitch."

I nod. Cassie breathes into my face. Her breath smells sweet from the pot. She takes some, then hands it to me again.

"You might need a little help to get through tonight," Cassie says. "First dates suck."

She's right. I take some more. This time I don't cough. This time the smoke fills my lungs and mellows my head. I start to feel loose. I start to forget about how I failed Leah. How I didn't wake up. How I didn't hear her. How I completely let her down. But then I realize Nick will smell it on me. He'll know. I can't win.

"Hey, you got any perfume?" I ask.

Cassie rifles through her purse and takes out two bottles. One perfume and the other breath spray. "Holy crap." Cassie giggles. "We've been in here forever. The boys are going to think we're up to something." She winks at me as she collects her stuff.

By the time we leave the bathroom, the number of people in the restaurant and the level of noise has tripled. The place is hopping, but thanks to the weed, I'm feeling all warm and fuzzy. And hungry. Really hungry.

We make it back to the baseball players' table, and Nick opens his arm for me to crawl in.

"Hey, thought I lost you." He nibbles on my neck. My skin hums. I lean in closer to him, wanting a little more. His breath is a warm wind on my neck.

"I'm starving." I try not to laugh, but everything seems so funny and good now, and maybe I can relax a little.

Cassie grabs a fry off Billy's plate, teasing him with it, and he wraps himself around her so there's no space between them. Her pupils are so big, they're almost completely black. I look in them. Starstruck again.

"Perfect timing," Nick says as a waitress comes bearing our pizza like a prize.

The pizza tastes better than anything I've ever tasted before. It's warm and cheesy and salty. Just plain delicious. I try to eat dainty and cute, like you're supposed to on a date, but my stomach is growling, and I have to almost sit on my hands to keep from shoving it in as fast as I can.

Nick gets up to fill our sodas. I smile at him. Because at this point, I'm actually having a good time.

Then Max and Tracy walk in. His arm is draped around her, and she looks like she's showing off a new pet. My stomach drops. He slaps hands with some of the other swimmers. My heart drops.

Nick may be a cool artist. He may be an okay baseball player.

He could be Picasso or Monet or Andy Warhol for that matter, and it still wouldn't matter. Because he's not Max.

Nick returns and puts the sodas on the table and winds his arm around me, pulling me close. I feel his body, tight and fit, and try to pretend it's broad and hard like Max's. *Anybody would be happy to be dating Nick Larsons.* That's my new mantra, and I swear that I'm a believer. With the right kind of drugs or drink, I could make this work. People will see us together and know I'm not broken.

I turn to Nick, paste a huge smile on my face, and lean my body against his. His smile lets me know he's buying it. I give him my attention and the best mood I can fake. Chemical-induced happy is better than no happy at all.

"Hey, wanna go somewhere else?" Nick smells like black licorice and spearmint: yummy and cool. He puts his drink down, pulls my hair back, and his lips brush my neck, waking my skin.

"Sure."

"I'll be right back. Just gotta make a pit stop." He kisses me long and sweet like a promise of things to come.

"Okay."

"I like Nick." Leah pops up across from me, blocking my view of Max. "He's cute even if he is wound way too tight. Maybe it's the baseball pants."

I want to tell her she has to leave. I want to tell her to get out of my head, but I can't. Not in front of everyone. Instead, I take a drink of my Coke and try to ignore her.

She leans forward. "By the way, you're doing very well with Max too. He can't stop looking at you."

I sputter on my Coke, sending a spray out of my mouth.

"You okay?" Cassie comes around to pat me on the back, leaving my view of Max completely unobstructed. He's laughing with his friends. Tracy heads toward the bathroom.

Max catches me looking at him and stands, obviously taking this as a signal to come over.

"Uh-oh, here comes trouble," Leah says.

I didn't need her warning. I saw this one a mile away. With Tracy out of the way, he has room for me. I feel bruised. All over. The pain is so severe, I consider taking that little green pill.

I feel Max's arm go around me, his touch unleashing a tsunami of emotion. My body wants to reach for his, but I know I can't. Even if we were here alone, he wouldn't choose me—not only me. "You having a good time?" he asks.

I shrug out from under his arm. "Yeah."

"Hey." He looks right into me, like he can see all my bad parts and doesn't care. His voice is low and shaky. I've gotten to him. He puts his hand on my arm. "We okay?" he asks.

"Sure." I look into his eyes, and I wish he would take my face into his hands and tell me he wants me again. Just me. But he's here with Tracy. I'm with Nick.

"I'm sorry. About…you know…"

"Me too. Pep rally wasn't the best idea."

He pulls me to him and kisses me on the top of my head. "Next time, I'll skip with you, okay?" Lie.

"Sure."

Tracy stops before going into the bathroom. Shoots us a look. Max follows my gaze and waves at her, giving her a wide smile that makes me feel like I could die. "Tracy's okay, you know, for a little fun?"

I want to scream at him. Fun? That's what this is all about?

He grabs my hand. "You know I love you. It's different between us."

I pull away. His eyes narrow. He's used to having it both ways. Max and his *one day we'll be together* crap. Not this day though. Today, he's with Tracy Summers. Because she's fun. I don't know what I see in him. Max is being a colossal jerk.

"Nick's coming. I've gotta go." I collect my things, my hair falling over my face.

"Don't be like that." He reaches for me. I evade his grasp. "You know how I feel about you."

"It's not fatal," I say as I brush by him.

I almost run smack into Nick on my way out. His gaze locks on Max. He knows Max got me riled up. Grabbing Nick by the neck, I pull him to me. My mouth opens, inviting him in. His urgency is the only thing I pay attention to.

"Let's get out of here," I whisper, needing to drown out the sad that starts in my heart and bleeds into my veins.

"You got it." Nick's voice is low and tight.

On our way out, I throw Leah an evil look. A stay-away-from-me-or-else death stare. I hope she listens. Because the last thing I need from her is advice on this next part.

———————•———————

Back Lake Park. At night. Cars are parked like islands in the dark. We take our place as Nick nudges the car into an abandoned corner. I want to get out and drink in the crisp air. But that's not what we came for. It's time for me to pay my bill. I may as well do this.

Nick reaches behind his seat and pulls out a bottle. Peach schnapps. He opens the cap and offers it to me. I take a swig. The first taste burns the back of my throat. But the next one goes down easy. I try to hand it back, but he waves it off. A few more and I'm good, all loose body and no mind, just the way I want to be.

"You're so pretty." He leans across the console and rubs up and down my arms, making me feel like I want to jump out of my skin.

The first kiss is soft, and I can tell he's holding back a little. I reach for him with my mouth, force him to kiss me the way I know he wants to. I hear him ache for me. And at this moment, my mind woozy from the pot and the drink, I want to give it to him. Even though he's not who I want, I do want him. At this moment.

"Allie, are you sure?"

I take his face in my hands, look into his not-blue eyes—and the wrong color makes me pause for a second. *Maybe I'll change my mind. Tell him no and we'll go home. I don't have to do this.* But I remember Max. He didn't choose me. Nick did. Does.

All I have to do is choose him back and I can have him. Right now. Should I? Is that what I want?

I nod, a huge smile spreading across my face. I want him to know I'm his. Right now. I want to be with him. I want to see what that does for him. I want to hear him want me, see it painted on his face. I want to know I'm the one he wants to be with.

He looks from my face, down my body, and back to my face. He smiles and pulls me to him, kissing me fiercely. My heart beats fast, and my body burns for him.

Nick pushes me backward, and I'm pressed against the door. His body leans against mine, his purpose clear. But it's okay. At this moment, I want Nick Larsons. His desire for me fills me, and I reach for him, my body matching every bit of heat he sends me. Every bit.

He pulls up my shirt. I unhook my bra. And it's good. I hear myself groaning. So I know it's good. I see his face, totally caught up in me. Me. I am everything he wants. Right now. I am it.

My skirt is down. I grab for his pants. I unzip them and reach in for him. My hand closes around the proof. He wants me. Really wants me.

"Allie, you're so hot," he whispers in my ear.

I push him away for a second.

"Hey," he whines. I sort of love that. I love the power I have over him right now. I am the queen of right now. Feeling for the first time in a really long time that I matter. That I'm enough. That I'm perfect—for Nick. At this moment.

"Did you bring anything?" I ask.

He fumbles for his jeans, his fingers clawing the pocket, and he pulls out a condom. It takes him a minute to open it. I hear the wrapper rip.

He suits up and pushes me back. Once he's inside, it doesn't take long. He doesn't have much more. I can't say I'm not disappointed. I wanted my reign to last longer than this.

"Sorry," he mutters into my hair, all tamed and happy.

"It's okay. It's fine." I'm really thinking Leah would get more. And I'm upset because I'm no longer out of my head. I'm all the way in it, wondering about Max. And Tracy. And the sad that I kept at bay as long as Nick was into me creeps back in like a mist.

"You sure?"

"I just...I need to get home." I hold up my phone, show him the face: 11:58.

"Oh, crap! It's late." He pulls on his jeans, tucks in his shirt, wipes the grin off his face in record time. I match his speed with my own. We pull into my driveway at 12:06.

"I had a great time tonight." Nick kisses me one last time. But it's not like before. He's had what he wanted; now he's over it. And I wonder, by giving him what he wanted, have I made him want me less? I get all panicky about that thought. Even though I didn't start out wanting Nick, I don't want him to end up not wanting me. God, I'm crazy. More than seeing my sister's ghost crazy. Worse than that, I'm twisted.

"Allie?"

"Yeah, me too," I manage. "Good night."

"You want me to walk you in?" He goes to get out of the car, but I wave him off.

It's getting harder and harder to smile at him. "I'm good." I head for the house. Part of me is angry. Really angry. And I know I don't have a reason to be. I made the choice. I did. Still, part of me blames him. For all of it. Because he couldn't keep the pain away more than a few minutes. Aren't I worth more than that?

I try not to shake as I walk in the door. But it's hard, because I gave myself away for so little. I let Nick have it all, and he didn't have the decency to last. God, I hate myself.

CHAPTER 13

I can't make the water hot enough. Or strong enough. Eventually, I give up and get out. Wrapped in a towel, combing my hair, I look in the mirror. I figure the devils be damned, let them come. I'm ready.

Leah appears behind me and starts rubbing my shoulders. I put my head in my hands and cry.

"It's okay, Allie. It's going to be okay."

"What am I going to do?"

Leah grabs a brush and starts working it through my hair. "You gotta get all the knots out," she says.

It feels so good to have her take care of me. Each stroke reminds me that I'm worthy. That she loves me. That I'm not disposable.

"Of course you're not. Don't be ridiculous, Allie. But honestly, it was your choice. And why the hell not get you some fun. Guys do it all the time."

She's right. It was my choice. So why do I feel so bad about it now? My teeth chatter. Leah appears with my fluffy, white bathrobe, wrapping me up. She takes my hand and leads me out of the bathroom. Sophie comes out of Mom's bedroom, her eyes squinty because we woke her.

"You wanna go in my room?" Leah asks.

I should say no. But I'm tired. "Yeah."

Leah props the pillows for me. I lay back.

"I just want something to matter, you know?"

It feels stupid to tell Leah these things. I worry she'll shoot me down, call me a dork, but she doesn't. She just holds my hand.

"I just think..." Tears fill my mouth. "That it should mean something. Maybe not everything. But something."

"So why'd you do it? Why'd you let him?"

Her question surprises me. I know she thinks I should be more casual about this stuff. Like she was. She never got weepy about guys. Leah was legendary.

Until she killed herself.

I put my arms over my head. "I don't know. It got confusing. I like Nick. I do. He's just not..."

"You have to get over Max. Maybe one day you two can be together. But not now. He's kind of a jerk now. No matter how you feel about him."

"You think that's why he doesn't want me? Because he wants to be a jerk? To be with every single girl he sees?"

"You're obsessed with the word 'why.' You need to stop. Why doesn't matter. It just is. Or isn't."

Sophie jumps up, climbs between us, and puts her head on my leg. I reach down, and she licks my hand. Tears course down my cheeks.

"It's not like Dad," she says. "I know you think that, but it's not."

"I want Max. He wants everyone else but me. Just like Mom and Dad. Only in this scenario, Nick wants me. It's algebra. Does that make me x—the thing to solve for?"

"Who knew your *cat* could be so mathy?" Leah's eyes point to my nether regions.

I laugh, then settle deeper in the pillows. "I hate that he's with her."

"We talking Max or Dad this time?"

"Both. I mean, I can't believe he left us for her. She's only five years older than you. Did you know that?"

Leah sighs. "Yes."

I sit up. "Is that why?"

She puts her hand on my arm. "No."

"It has to be. It's his fault, isn't it?"

"It's nobody's fault. Or it's just mine." She turns away.

I think about pressing her, but I know she won't budge. When Leah clams up, she's done. End of story. Like Dad. There's no moving her. Even though my head is screaming for more information. I relent and lie back down.

Leah rolls over onto her side, facing me, her head propped in her elbow. "Sometimes I pretend none of it happened. Sometimes I pretend I'm still here. You know? That I didn't take those pills or drink that wine."

"I pretend that all the time. I pretend you're still here. You know, full-time. Like before. When you were—"

"Real."

"You know what I mean."

"I do." She flops back. "But maybe I was never real. To Dad, I wasn't. Obviously. God, I'm so stupid. I actually thought he gave us those phones as a way to stay connected with him. If we needed him."

And I hate him. I don't know what happened the night Leah killed herself. Maybe I don't need to know. But I hate him. Full-on.

"You were more than real to me. You still are."

She laughs. "My baby sister. Starstruck as usual."

I look straight into her dark eyes, the chocolate brown I've always wanted, not just because they were prettier than mine were but also because they could hide secrets better than mine could.

"I know you don't want to talk about this, Leah, but I wish I knew—"

"It won't change anything."

"I know. But it would help. Knowing—"

"It wasn't his fault. I made so many mistakes, and I didn't know how to fix them. I wasn't strong like you are. You've always been much more solid than I am."

Her confession startles me. I'm not more solid. Just more obedient.

"I couldn't let you find out how fucked up I was."

I flash back to the night of the party. Her friends Brittney, Sean, Vanessa. Feral people. Something happened that night. Obviously. But what?

"Leah, where were you that night? Where did you go?"

"It's not important."

"Sean was looking for you. He was mad and couldn't find you. Even Jason helped look."

"Sean's not as great as he thinks. He didn't mean that much to me. I was done with him before that party. Well before. It just made it easier…to be all the way done. With him."

"I don't understand…"

She stands and leaves the room. When she comes back, she hands me the bottle of Delsym. "Shhhh, you should go to sleep. Just a little. It'll help you drift off. We gotta keep you moving. This is a very important year," she says, faking Dad's intonation and voice. I smirk. Then take it from her. She nods with encouragement. I take a drink and hand it back to her.

"I'll stay till you fall asleep. I'll watch over you."

I look at her ceiling. It's painted white with silver sparkles mixed in. When you look at it, it's like looking at the stars.

"I'm just so tired," I say.

"You need to rest," she says.

Maybe Leah's right.

"You need to get back to making art," Leah adds. "That's how both of us get to stay."

I think about how amazing it used to feel when I worked on a painting. Like the whole world faded away. I miss that. She's right. But I can't help feeling like maybe I can get there on my own again. Maybe I can find my colors. Mine. Not Leah's. But I'm not sure what that means for my sister. I feel responsible for her. Like she was for me all those years. When

I was tagalong. I close my eyes and hope tomorrow will be better than today. I can hope, can't I?

CHAPTER 14

I wake up in Leah's bedroom, covered with her blankets, heavy and soft. My phone is next to me, and I squint at it. Messages and texts wait for me, but Leah and Sophie are both gone. I prop myself on my elbows and look around. Leah's things remain as she left them, carefully arranged, clothes hanging neatly like little soldiers in her closet. She used to tell me that she liked to be able to see everything she owned, like a king surveying his land. I laughed at her being a king. But maybe she thought a queen would be powerless, like Mom. And me.

I push myself out of her bed, ignoring the massive headache from my overindulgence last night and trying to ignore the pain between my legs from my hookup with Nick. I lower my feet to the floor and go to Leah's desk. My fingers trail over the sea glass picture frames. Leah and Brittney. A close-up of Sophie. One of the two of us taken on our ski vacation in Vermont last year, Mom's last-ditch effort to keep Dad from leaving.

I loved that trip, even though Mom and Dad were fighting pretty much the whole time. Which left me and Leah on our own. Alone with Leah was always good. She could always find the fun.

"Let's pretend we're in college," she said as we got on the ski lift.

"Which one?" I asked.

"University of Boulder, where the snow is way finer than this, so fine it'd make you cry. Not like this broke-down, chewed-up slush we're skiing on."

Nothing was ever good enough for Leah. She wanted better clothes, better grades, and now, apparently, better snow. I always wondered if her standards were too high or if mine were too low.

"Now we need to make Dad pay, like, huge."

She was right. He needed to pay. So we made him. That weekend especially. He paid for everything and anything Leah wanted. That meant new ski clothes for her. I said mine were fine, but she made me buy a new ski hat and gloves anyway.

"He should be glad I don't buy a new set of skis," Leah joked, but her face was dead serious.

"I guess," I said, browsing the sale rack.

She turned to look at a pair of gloves, hot pink, to match the stripe on the new ski pants that were hanging over her arm. "You hear about his new 'get clean' program for Mom?" Leah asked.

"More than his raids on her stashes? Not that he'd find them all." I picked up a sweater from a table.

She slid in front of me. "He's making her take drug tests."

"What?"

"I heard them argue about it. He has a stash of them in their bathroom. A stockpile. And he made her pee in front of him. I heard it all."

"Oh my God." I couldn't believe it. Why would she let him? "You think Dad's going to leave her?"

"Are you kidding me? She should leave him. It's like he's trying to make her leave."

Emery comes bursting in the room, jolting me back to the present. "Hi. The wardens relax your restrictions? You're allowed in here now?"

"No. Mom up? We gotta get out of—"

"Relax. Let myself in." Emery holds up the key I gave her. "She didn't hear me."

"Oh." I get the picture. Mom crashed on the couch. Yeah.

We sit, cross-legged, looking around Leah's room.

"I'm sorry about the pep rally. I never should have said those things." Emery's gaze lands on Leah's ballet bar. "This year's show won't be the same without her. She was the best dancer."

It's true. Leah was the one everyone watched when she was on stage. She was it. The one. She was special.

Until she killed herself.

Tears run single file down Emery's face. I join her, but I cry sloppy. Not neat like a trained actress. I breathe out. Maybe it's time to change the subject.

"How was last night?" I ask. Big date with Michael Maddox.

"Whatever." Emery says.

"I'm sorry."

"It's cool. Like I need Michael Maddox. Plenty more where he came from."

"You wanna tell me what happened?"

"Nothing that a little retail therapy won't help. What about you and Mr. Baseball? He score?"

I smile but can't help how sad my face must look.

Emery puts her arms around me, and we go back to my room, where I pull on jeans and a T-shirt.

"He was there. With her. Wasn't he?" Emery asks.

God, I feel stupid. I try not to cry about Max. Stupid. He's not into me. Why do I care so much? Nick's totally into me. Why can't that be enough?

"You make it too easy for him. You need to start acting like you don't care about him. Let him see you happy with someone else."

"You're the actress, not me."

"It's time you start. It's what Leah would say if she were here."

But she's not. It's just me here, alone.

"You deserve to be happy. And if Max isn't making you happy, cut him loose."

I play with a strand of my hair.

"I know what'll cheer you up," Emery squeals. "Let's get you a haircut and some highlights."

I nod. Emery's right. There are healthier ways to numb my Max pain than to down pills, smoke weed, and sleep with guys. Retail therapy comes with a return policy, so very few regrets. That kind of works for me.

CHAPTER 15

Emery starts her car. "What do you feel like?"

"You choose." I sit back, my feet propped on the dashboard. She pushes them off.

I smile. It's good to argue about the usual with Em. I reach forward and play with the radio dial, tuning in my favorite station, which is playing "Bad Romance."

"Dork," Em says as she puts the car in reverse, looks in the mirror, and pulls out onto the street.

I take my cell out of my pocket, bracing myself for the worst.

Gnite. Sweet dreams. Nick texted last night at 12:22.

Morning. from him at 9:12.

Then U ok? at 9:36.

And U mad? at 9:54.

My shoulders tense. Nick. I should text him back. It's the nice thing to do. But what should I say? What says "noncommittal greeting without promising any future hookups"?

I finally decide on a simple Hi.

My phone jumps out of my hand. Like he was waiting for me to text.

How r u?

"Hey, watch it, asshole!" Emery shouts at the person who just took the parking spot she wanted.

I breathe out a big sigh. How am I? I suck. But it's not like I can say that.

Ok. U?

My phone vibrates again.

"Nick is really into you, isn't he?" Emery smiles at me like she's trying to talk me into Nick. "Won't leave you alone."

U free tnite?

I don't waste any time replying. Sorry.

Next time.

"He's cute. You should give him some play."

I want to tell her I'm not even sure if I'm into him. But how can I? When I've already let Nick think he's it for me. At least last night, in the moment.

"Let's get your hair cut," Emery says. "You'll feel loads better."

"Okay." I follow like the little lamb I am. Maybe I always have been. It's time to face facts. I'm not that strong. I'm easily led. Starstruck. Tagalong. Leah's dorky little sister who is too stupid to see what's right in front of her face.

Emery and I walk the mall.

"Love the blue highlights," she says, grabbing pieces of my hair. "You look more like yourself again."

I look at my reflection in the Forever 21 window. I almost think I see Leah standing behind me, but her image flickers and fades. Out of the corner of my eye, I see another reflection that makes me nervous. John Strickland. He doesn't seem to be a mall-troll kind of guy. What's he doing here?

"Wanna get a frappé?" Emery asks.

"Okay. I'll be right there." I point to the sign for the bathroom. She nods.

I duck into the hallway to the bathroom, wait to see if John follows. He doesn't. I breathe out and go inside. My image in the mirror shocks me. Emery's right, my hair looks like it used to: shiny, bouncy, and fun, but I wonder, does a makeover change anything? I'm looking for my colors. I'm pretty sure they don't come out of a box or a bottle. I'm pretty sure your colors come from inside you. Even still, I'm glad I've got my war paint back on. I can hide in my camo. Like Dad does.

"Is that how you see me?" I hear Leah ask again.

I shiver. I'm not sure I can keep this up. I'm not sure I can give her life. It may be hard to be dead, but it's also hard to be the one who lives.

When I get to the food court, I find Emery sitting at a round table with three coffees topped with whipped cream and chocolate drizzle.

Emery motions with her head. Beastie Brittney walks to the table, and I remember why I stopped coming to the mall. When Leah opted out of life, so did I. Now I'm wondering if I didn't come back a little too soon. I do not want this meeting. Not here. Not now.

"Allie. How are you?" Brittney kisses me on the cheek.

"Hi, Brittney," I mumble.

Emery shoots me an "I'm sorry" look.

Brittney slips into the seat across from me. Then she turns to Emery. "Can you give us a few?"

Emery looks to me for confirmation, and I nod.

"I've been meaning to call you..." Brittney says.

There's too much between us. Love. Hate. Sadness. One big emotional salad that neither one of us wants to dress. I pick up my coffee, draw a sip, and wait. Sitting across from her is hard. Like breathing. And living. Without Leah.

Brittney and Leah were always together. Always. I wonder what that feels like for her. Is it like some phantom limb where she imagines that Leah is still there? Does she still expect Leah to finish her sentences? Does she go to text her and then remember? Does she look for her calls on her phone? Like I do?

"Allie, I'm sorry. I just wanted to tell you that," Brittney finally manages, her eyes starting to fill.

"Sorry for what?" I stare at my drink, playing with the straw. Seeing Brittney cry is too much.

"For everything," she finishes.

"Okay." I say. I hoping that'll end it. Air cleared. All good. Kiss, kiss. We can move on. Brittney was never exactly deep anyway. This was probably a lot for her. I feel myself breathe out. It's over. Till it's not. Brittney can't let it go. Nobody's taught her to fold and run.

"I want you to know that Sean and I were never together when Leah was…"

"Alive?" *Is she kidding me?* I had no idea. It's all I can do not to throw my drink in her face.

My hand goes into my purse, the napkin that holds those little pills, my insurance policy, my John Strickland pills, promising relief. But I don't want to go down that road. I don't think it's the way to be. I know Leah said it would take a lot of pills to kill myself, but I do think the road starts with one or two. I hope to God I don't need this dose, but it's not looking good.

"Come on, Brittney. I'm not stupid. Neither was Leah."

"I mean it. We weren't. I mean, I always thought he was cute. But I would never. Never." She shakes her head as if to emphasize that point. I mean, no one could *possibly* lie while shaking their head, right? "Even after, it seemed wrong, a little."

"Look, Brittney, you date who you want. It's cool. Leah's gone. He's up for grabs. I get it." I draw a huge gulp of coffee, hoping to show how over it all I am.

"I know you're mad. I just wondered." She leans forward. I stay put. I'm not going to meet her halfway or a quarter of the way or *any* way. Not beastie Brittney. No way. Her voice lowered, she says, "Do you think Leah would mind, if she, you know, knew?"

"What do you think?" I snarl. "You were with him at the party, weren't you? That night?"

I remember Brittney texting me on the way back from the party. I had wondered why she wasn't texting Leah. Then my phone rang. It was her. I tried to hand it to Leah, but she batted it away. I had wondered what that meant. Leah and Brittney never fought. They were tight. As a drum.

"You okay, Leah?" I'd asked.

"I'm fine. Just rethinking my loyalties. I can be really stupid about people."

"I didn't mean for it to happen. It didn't mean anything." Brittney's lies fall out of her mouth like marbles spilling out of a jar. I hear each one ping as it hits the table.

"It must be hard for you," I say. "Wondering if…"

Brittney deflates. Her face sags. Her head bends. Mascara melts down her face, making her look like she's behind bars. And I love it. I love the power I have over her. Like Nick last night. Only better. Let her feel me. Allie the Terrible.

"It's horrible. I think about it all the time… If only…" She wipes away the black mascara, which just gets transferred to her fingers. Some marks are hard to wipe away.

I want to make her pay. Tell her we'll never know. I want to smack her across the face. This time, my rage can't be blamed on the pills or the drink. This time it's all me.

I shake my head, slip the pill out of my purse, hold it between my fingers, and bring it to my lips. But stop there. Something makes me stop. I'm not sure what. Maybe I'm just thinking the pain needs to stop.

I lean forward. Brittney looks up. Is this the truce she was hoping for? I'm not sure what I'm going to say until the words form in my mouth. "It wasn't you." I pause. "But it sure didn't help that you were a boyfriend-stealing bitch, did it?"

"You are right," Brittney says, misery coating every syllable. "You know what though?"

I raise my eyebrow. Too angry to speak.

"He's still not into me. He keeps wanting me to be…her. I think he really loved her. And he doesn't love me. Not like that."

Brittney's admission is stunning. I put the pill away and pick at the wrapper from the straw. Like Leah used to. Brittney's eyes zero in. She remembers too. Of course she does. They had been best friends since kindergarten. I make her pay in small amounts. Like ant bites. Not deadly all at once. But painful. And sharp.

"I know you don't believe me, but I miss her too. So much. And I would never have gone after Sean or been with him if I didn't think she had already moved on."

I look her over. She's skinny like me now. Her nails are trimmed but bare. It's like Leah's death spread like a disease. Or an atomic bomb.

"I believe you," I say, my voice small.

She reaches across the table and takes my hands. "Thank you." Her smile is weak, but it's sincere.

"Look, maybe you can help me." I twirl my cup around and take a sip. "Can you tell me why Vanessa said Leah wasn't going to be captain of the dance team?"

Brittney coughs. "Vanessa caught her doing something. Leah never told me what. I told her we could easily take that bitch down. But she said not to bother. It was over."

"What did she mean by that?"

Brittney's lips turn downward. "She was quitting the team."

"Why would she do that?"

"She just said that the little bitch finally got her way. But there was something else. Someone else. Leah was seeing someone else. She admitted that much," Brittney confides.

"Who?"

"She never told me."

Her secret love. "When did this start?" I ask.

"I don't know." Brittney dabs at her eyes with a tissue. "She was pissed at me that night because I told her it wasn't right. So she shut me out. Wouldn't tell me anything. I took her phone when she wasn't looking. We'd both used the same password for ages. But when I tried it, it wasn't the right one. Who changes their password all of a sudden?" She wipes more mascara off her face. "I told her it was stupid to give up Sean for some secret guy. I told her Sean was way better for her. So she got pissed. And just like that, after seven years of friendship, she cut me off."

Does she really want sympathy from me? Leah did change her password. We did it together. When Dad gave us the phones. It wasn't about what Brittney did. But Leah let her believe it was. Leah could be toxic. All this missing her and remembering and wanting her back doesn't change that.

"Look, I've gotta go. But I'm glad we talked. I miss her. Every day. I can't tell you how many times I've wished I had been a better friend. Really."

I stay silent. I'm sure she does wish that. But there's no going back, is there?

She nods and rises. When she's taken a few steps, I almost call to her. Almost. But my tongue is caught in my throat and the words shrivel and die.

"That looked interesting." I hear John Strickland's voice and turn, shocked to see him.

"Hi," I say. "We're friends all of a sudden?"

"May I?" he asks. "Brittney's such a bitch."

His smile is slow and completely captivating. His blond hair falls over his eyes, and he doesn't do anything to brush it away. But that's not what makes me interested in him. John Strickland is a little intoxicatingly dangerous. He swivels the chair around and sits on it backward. He leans forward, placing his hands together on the table in front of me.

I look at him and wait. John's not the kind of person you interrupt.

"You realize Brittney's full of shit, don't you?"

"Tell me how you really feel."

"Come to my house tonight. I'm having a party. And I'll tell you what I know." He reaches over the table and pulls my cell out of my hand without even asking. I stare at him as he unlocks my phone then programs his number and hands it back.

I almost ask him how he knows my password, but I'm too stunned by everything that's just happened so I stay silent.

"How to get me," he says. "Trust me. You'll want to hear what I have to tell you. And I won't hold back like that little bitch Brittney. I'll tell you everything I know. Scout's honor."

He stands. "Starts at eight. We'll be going all night. But if you want coherent conversation, you might wanna be there by nine. After that, no promises."

He leaves. And I breathe out.

Emery passes by him on her way back. "What was that about?" she asks.

"He says he knows something about Leah. And he'll tell me. Tonight. At his house. Party."

Emery's face screws up. "I'm coming with you."

"I was counting on it."

CHAPTER 16

Just by looking at his house, John Strickland's life looks normal. Suburban. Safe.

"You ready?" Emery asks.

"I guess."

We walk to the front door, and before we can knock, the door swings open as two guys from the football team leave. There's a sea of people blocking the entrance, and we have to push our way in. Loud music is playing, and my head gets overwhelmed by it all.

I recognize a girl with jet-black hair with a purple streak through it. I think her name is Trudy. She's backed against a wall, holding a bottle of wine and drinking from it like it's an exercise water bottle. James Everett, one of the lacrosse players, is leaning over her. He's kind of a dog. But Trudy doesn't seem to mind. She holds his face in her free hand, her silver bangle bracelets slide down her arm.

"Let's make this quick," Emery says.

What's got her so on edge? This is more her crowd than mine. I think about asking her, but with the music blaring, it's not like I'd be able to hear her answer. I look at her for direction, and Emery pulls me into what is supposed to be the living room but has become the dance floor with all the furniture removed.

"Hey, beautiful." Some guy I don't recognize grabs me by the hips and pulls me to him. I push him away. "What's wrong? I'm not your type?" Laughter erupts around him.

"Ass," I mutter under my breath.

Emery finds one of John's guys, a blond one, six feet tall. She leans in and brings his head toward her ear. He starts to argue. She pulls him to her again. He points.

"He's back here, second door on the right," she says as she pulls me through the mass of people, past the line for the bathroom, and to one of the bedrooms.

Emery pushes open the door. John Strickland is lying there, Tiffany Minor draped across his chest, her eyes closed almost entirely. He's smoking weed. The smell assaults me as I walk in. It's cloying and sweet and completely inviting.

John sees me and pushes Tiffany off him, handing the joint to Emery. She brings it to her mouth. "Thanks." She pulls hard and hands it back.

"No problem." He grabs my hand and leads me through the crowd and up the stairs. I don't ask where we're going. But when I get there, I know it's his bedroom. I start to get nervous. He laughs.

"Don't worry. I'm not going to do anything to you."

"Why am I here?"

He motions to the bed. I balk. He sits and pats the place next to him, then holds up his hands in mock surrender. "I'll be a complete gentleman, I promise."

I sit. He inhales, then offers the joint to me. I take it. It doesn't seem right not to. Impolite even.

"There are things about your sister that only I know."

I cough a little. Not sure if it's the pot or what he said that gets caught in my throat. "Why would you know about Leah?"

"You'd be surprised how much I know. About you too."

"Like what?"

"Like that pretty boy swimmer you're after is a complete ass and not worth your time."

"Why would you say—"

"And that clean-cut dork you're dating is too judgy for you."

He starts laughing—a horrible laugh that's fueled either by the drugs or my humiliation. My hand flies out—like it's not even part of me—to smack him across the face. He blocks me, grabbing my wrist. He holds on tight till the feeling goes completely out of my hand. When I let it go limp, he releases it. "Before you get all violent, I'll tell you something I've never told anyone but Leah. I loved her. I had a thing for her since we met."

"What?"

"I was her in-between guy. Whenever someone hurt her, whenever someone cheated on her, she came to see me. And I made her feel better. I was happy to."

I sit there looking at this guy's face and realize he's telling the truth. As much as he knew it to be at least. And I'm pissed at Leah again.

John Strickland hands the joint back to me. "Here, this'll take the edge off."

I take another hit. My head starts feeling woozy. My whole

body gets warm. He goes across the room and pulls out a stack of pictures, which he hands to me. They are of Leah and John Strickland together. All sorts of places. In the woods by a stream. Climbing a mountain. At the movies. In bed.

"This was after she caught Bruce Williams with Ashley Swain. The next set is when Jimmy Rollings turned out to be doing Darla Anfinson."

"I don't understand." I flip through the pictures. Leah without makeup, laughing, her hand held in front of her. Leah natural and with her guard down. He wasn't her in-between guy. He was her secret love. "How could I not know?"

"Nobody knew. It was between us."

He puts his hand out, and I give him the pictures. I rub my eyes. Her voice comes to me. When we were at the Cape that last time. She told me about him. *I'm myself. I don't have to keep proving myself. Being me is good enough.* I remember. But if she really felt that way about him, why did he call himself her in-between guy?

"She was so beautiful, wasn't she?" He looks up at me. I nod. "I always believed we'd be together in the end, you know? When all the high school bullshit was over."

I don't know what to say.

"You want to know about that night, the party?"

"Yes."

"She was here with me. She found out Sean was cheating on her. She couldn't face him. She left. But she was worried about you. I was going to send someone after you."

That's where she went.

"But she wanted to go. And on her way to get to you, she saw something that upset her. Even more than Sean cheating on her did."

"What?"

"I don't know exactly."

"It's my fault. It has to be. If she hadn't left to get me—"

"No. There was something tragic about Leah. She always said she felt doomed. Heavy. That's why she kept going all the time, dancing, working, playing. She couldn't not move or the heaviness got her."

I point to the pictures. "Not with you. She was quiet and still with you."

He rubs his hand over his stubble. "Obviously that wasn't enough."

"I think something happened with my dad. After she left you that night."

"Something was up. I should have known something was up." He lowers his head into his hands. "She told me to take care of you. She made me promise." He looks up at me through his fingers. "She told me she was leaving."

"Leaving? Where did she say she was going?"

"Well, she always planned to go to Chicago. I mean, we planned that. My uncle lives there, and he would have helped us. I was going to go to become a welder. She was going to dance at the Chicago Dance Conservatory. I was going to pay for her so she wouldn't have to count on your dad for anything. But I didn't think she meant she was going to…"

This news shocks me. My head feels like it's filled with cotton. Chicago? When? I start to get mad. Leah had so many secrets, and she didn't tell anyone all of them.

"I thought she was going to get a head start. I told her I'd bring her enough money, and she said okay, but I should have figured that's not what she meant. I guess I should have known." Misery leaks out of him and runs down his face.

"It's not your fault," I say. "It's mine. It's hers." And now I sound just like her.

He brings me to him, holds me against his brick wall of a body. He lets me cry. "Shh. It's not your fault."

He tips my face to his so gently, I can't believe it. He kisses me. Slow and long and hard. I feel him pour his feelings for Leah into me, and it feels good because I know we both miss her, and no one but us knows how bad that feels. Kissing him makes that feel less bad but also wrong, because I'm not Leah and he's not Nick. And even if I'm not in love with Nick, I think we're dating. Sort of. Isn't that what sleeping with him implies?

"We can't."

He shakes his head and smiles. "I'm sorry. I didn't mean. I…"

"It's okay."

"Look, if the pills I gave you didn't work for you, I have others. Some of these"—he reaches into his nightstand and grabs a Ziploc bag of unmarked pills: blue, red, orange—"are like taking candy."

"I don't know…"

"I'm not trying to push you to do this. God knows I have plenty of customers, and I won't take money from Leah's little sister. I just think this has to suck for you. I want to help if I can."

"I don't know."

He pulls out a small red one. "Ritalin to help you focus. I gave you Adderall at the pep rally, but maybe it was too strong to start with?"

I nod.

"This one is to take the edge off. Valium. This one is a Xanax. A very weak one. To bring you down. To take the edge off. I can keep you supplied. But you have to promise not to do what she did. I mean that. I can't have you doing that."

I nod.

"I can get you anything you need, but you can't let it get out that I'm giving these away. Leah was the one soft spot I had. Now she's gone, I'm back to being one hundred percent asshole."

He doesn't seem like an asshole, yet all the stories I've heard about him…like how he attacked a kid's car. "Last year," I say. "The crowbar. Whose car was it?"

He smirks. "One of Leah's disappointments."

I try to picture my warrior sister retreating to her warrior protector.

He shrugs. "When she told me, I wanted to take the crowbar to him. I told him that he better stay away from her. If he came near her again, no one would stop me."

It must have been nice to have him looking out for her when no one else did.

"But the damage was done. He'd already gotten Vanessa to set Leah up. She took a picture of Leah smoking weed and that was enough to get her kicked off the dance team."

My head swims.

"This is a lot to take in, I know. And none of it really matters anymore. What's done is done, and you have to move on. I know Leah wanted you to. She loved you."

I give him back the pictures. "She loved you too."

"Yeah. If only love were enough, like in those stupid-ass country songs."

I smile. "I better go. Thanks."

"Sure thing, Allie. If you ever need anything, I'm here for you. Crowbar at the ready."

I wave to him from the door. He is already rolling another joint. I almost ask him if he sees her too, but I don't. Crazy is not something you talk about, even with your dead sister's ex–secret love.

I find Emery talking to some guy in the living room, both of them drinking out of those stupid red Solo cups. "You done?" she shouts above the music.

I nod. We weave our way to the door, the pot and the info making me sway.

"What did you find out?" Em's eyes dart around, and I wonder what's making her so jumpy. She do more than a little weed?

"Just more pieces of the Leah puzzle."

"Spill," she says as she opens her car door and we both climb in.

"Let me ask you this: If Leah had been kicked off the dance team, would she still be able to audition for colleges?"

"I guess. It would make it harder, for sure. Senior year is the audition year, and she wouldn't have recommendations. She wouldn't have tape of roles she'd won. So the rumors are true?" she asks.

I swivel to face her. "What rumors?" I demand. No amount of pot can mellow the fire that's racing through me right now.

"About Leah being kicked off the team." Emery looks uncomfortable, like she wishes she hadn't brought this up.

That just makes me angrier. "You knew about that and didn't tell me?"

"I wasn't sure. Vanessa isn't exactly a reputable source, especially when it came to Leah."

"You should have told me."

Emery puts her head on the steering wheel and closes her eyes. She turns to me, one perfect tear running down her face. Emery cries cleaner than anyone I know. "I know. I felt like it was my fault."

She must mean because she gave her the weed. As Emery starts the car, I see Leah standing there in the street.

Her makeup is smudged as if she's been crying. "I miss John Strickland," she says.

CHAPTER 17

I wake up in my own room this time. My head is heavy, filled with all the things I've learned about Leah in the last few days and the remnants from the drugs I took to make those things feel less horrible.

Dr. Applegate is always talking about not holding in feelings like that's the real path to mental health. Leah kept more secrets than anyone I know. Look where that got her.

I lie back down and force myself to remember the rest of what happened on the Cape. We came back from the beach. It was cold and I shivered when the wind blew. Leah told me she had a secret love. When we turned the corner, we saw three cars parked in the driveway. Three was bad. Of course we recognized Dad's and Mom's. But the third one? A silver Kia sedan.

"Crap," Leah said.

"Who do you think—"

"I've seen that car before. At Dad's office."

"You know whose it is?"

Leah's face got cloudy. "Yeah. That new girl. Danielle. I saw Dad getting texts from her when he dropped me off at rehearsal last week."

"What's she doing here?"

Leah shot me a look. "I'm pretty sure it has nothing to do with business. Not work business anyway."

The front door slammed open. Danielle came running out, her hair messed up and her shirt untucked. She dropped her keys twice and barely got the front door to the Kia open before she backed out of the driveway.

"Shit," Leah said. Even ducking under our towels, I was pretty sure she saw us when we pulled away. Then it got to me. Why were we ashamed? Shouldn't Dad be? He was with her. When we were here. We could have walked in on them. "Come on," she said. "We can't stay out here forever."

The shouting that was coming from inside the house was loud enough to hear three houses away. The sound of glass being smashed made us pick up our pace. We had to get inside and stop whatever they were doing to each other.

"Get behind me," Leah said as she cracked opened the door.

Dad's legs. Those were the first things I saw. He was wearing his khaki shorts. Cape wear. No shirt. He was holding his shirt in front of him with his hands that were fending off plates that Mom was throwing at him.

"Stop it!" Leah called. "You have to stop."

Dad moved to block us, but Mom stopped throwing and started crying. She rushed to the bedroom.

Dad said, "We're leaving."

"No," Leah said. "We have to help her."

"She's crazy. Can't you see that?" Dad's hands were covered in scratches and tiny dots of blood that seeped out from where she'd gotten him with the plates. I couldn't stop staring at the blood.

"What's *she* doing here then, Dad?"

"I don't answer to you. But Danielle was on the Cape and was dropping off a file for me."

"Yeah, Dad. Not buying it."

I watched Leah and Dad, helpless. Their interaction was like the worst and most dangerous tennis match ever played. It made me wonder what exactly was in that text Leah saw.

Dad looked at me for support, but I just inched closer to Leah.

His eyes went to the floor. "I had no idea what she planned."

Was he talking about Danielle or Mom now?

"I never wanted to hurt you or your mom. It's not..." His eyes got teary. "She needs help. You know that right?"

"And doing your intern is your way of scaring her straight?" Leah's eyes stayed fixed on him the whole time. She didn't give him any wiggle room. I'm not sure now if that's what made him snap. Or if what Leah said next was. "We aren't going anywhere with you."

Dad looked at us, incredulous. "Really? You want to stay with *her*?" He pointed to the bedroom. "She's not a wife to me, and she's definitely not a mother to you. Not like what you deserve."

"Better than you," Leah said.

And just like that, she slew him. For a second he looked completely broken. Then he strode to the kitchen, where Mom had left her purse, opened it, and took out her wallet.

He pulled out the cash and credit cards. "See how you all do without me."

I didn't watch as Dad left. I couldn't. All I could think was how were we going to get home with no money. No credit cards. Mom was in the bedroom, completely distraught and useless. I remember I sat down. Glass from the broken plates jabbed at my legs, but I didn't care. He'd left us with *nothing*.

"Come on. You're freezing," Leah said. "Get changed. I have to go out for a little while. You watch Mom."

"I'm coming with you," I insisted.

"Then we have to get going." Leah talked to me the whole time I was changing. "It's going to be okay. We're going to be fine. I'll make sure."

"Okay," I said, but I didn't know how to do that when I felt like I was free-floating in space with no sign of the ground. I couldn't stop crying. And I was so cold. I'd never been that cold.

Leah pulled a sweatshirt over my head. She smoothed my hair down. "We can't be like Mom. We have to be stronger."

Then she went to Mom's purse and grabbed her bottle of pills. She poured one in her hand and took it to the counter. She took out a knife and cut it in half. Leah handed me one and put the other one in her mouth.

I didn't want to take it. I shook my head, but she said, "It's okay. Mom takes like two of these at a time."

I remember the sound of the cabinet opening and closing, the tap being turned on. She handed me a glass of water. I swallowed the pill. "Wait here," she said. She took the rest of the water and another pill into the bedroom.

I tried to listen to what Leah said to Mom, but I couldn't focus. When Leah emerged, she put the pills in her own purse. I knew she didn't want Mom to be left alone with a full bottle. We'd never talked about it before, but I knew. I may have been young and stupid, but I wasn't *that* stupid.

Dad hadn't stocked up yet, and there was nothing to eat at the house, so we walked the one and a half miles to the grocery store. Next door to it was a store that advertised the Best Price for Gold in big letters in the window.

"Wait here," Leah said.

"Don't." I pulled at her wrist. She was already fiddling with the clasp on the gold heart bracelet Dad gave her.

Her eyes were wild. "You think this matters? This is shit."

"No," I said. "It's yours."

"He thinks he can buy my love? He's wrong about that."

When she came out of the store, she looked different. Or maybe it was that pill I'd taken working. We bought peanut butter and jelly and bread and milk and a big bag of potato chips and a small spiral notebook with a tin can–colored gray cover. We stopped at the ice cream stand on the way back even though we were freezing. We each got a vanilla soft serve dipped in chocolate.

Leah talked to me the whole way home. I remember every word. "We are going to be fine. I promise."

"Even with Dad gone? We'll figure it out?"

"Definitely." She took another bite of her ice cream.

"Who's craziest: Dad for marrying Mom to begin with or Mom for staying?" I asked as someone drove a little too close to the grass we were walking on and Leah flashed them the finger.

"We are for letting them fuck with us. We're just pawns in their stupid, dirty little war. I'm sick of it. If I'm ever as miserable as they are, I'm getting out."

I nodded. I knew what she meant. But I started to cry.

"Shh. Come on. I don't mean now or anytime soon. I'm not going anywhere. I promise."

"Yet," I said.

"Okay, how about this? Since we both come from the same line of crazy, we could make a pact."

"A what?"

"A promise to each other. That if we ever wanted…we'd do it together."

I repeated what she said about going in the water earlier: "It's easier when you do it with someone."

"Exactly."

We were back at the house. Leah opened the front door, tiptoed around the broken plates on the floor, and walked in to see Mom. I put the groceries away. Except for the potato chips, which I brought out to the porch with me. Leah came out with a bottle of wine, a corkscrew, the notebook, and a pen.

I knew I wasn't feeling right with the pill in me, but I didn't say no to the wine. Being with Leah felt reassuring. An island of safe in a sea of danger. She showed me the front cover. "War colors."

"Yeah," I agreed and took a swig of wine.

"Perfect for our battle plan. First thing," she flipped it open to the first page, "is we make me the general."

"Hey!" I pretended to be annoyed.

"You'll make an excellent foot soldier *and* historian." She handed me the notebook and pen.

"I guess I could do that."

Leah's face got serious. She gestured with the wine bottle. "You know how Dad says crazy runs in the family?"

I nodded.

"He's right. But from both sides, not just Mom's. Dad's need to control every single thing and person, his need to be perfect, is so fucked up. He's sicker than Mom." She drank from the bottle, then looked me dead in the eye. "I mean, that's totally mental. He has to keep his kingdom, his dominion, his serfs in line; he'll totally lose his shit. Completely."

She was right. Of course she was. I started crying, but I knew what she meant. She handed me the bottle, and I drank and gave it back.

"The most important thing is we never do it alone. We tell each other."

I nodded. That made it sound okay. Like it wasn't even dangerous. "And we have to have iron-clad reasons. Sound ones. We need to agree, each of us. Because sometimes things seem worse than they are, so we need the other to verify."

I nodded and wrote it all down.

Leah put her hand over the book and put her face in front of mine. "The point is that we have each other and I never want to see you look like you did today—hopeless and powerless. Because you're not."

"We're not," I said. "We aren't hopeless, neither of us."

She nodded her head and took a drink. "We are not. But we do need to build an arsenal." She pulled the bottle of Mom's pills out of her pocket. I guess my eyes got a little wide because she said, "Relax. We'll just take a couple at a time. Mom won't miss them, and it'll get her to cut down. Win-win."

That's how the pact started. That night. And when we started it, I totally believed in it. But by the time we got up the next morning, Mom was awake and cleaning up, and I felt it a little less. Nobody talked about what had happened, so I let myself believe that nothing significant had. Leah sat in the back of the car with me and held my hand as Mom drove us home. I played with her silver ring and held onto the notebook that held our promises to each other. And in that time, our pact made me feel stronger, reassured me that Leah and I were on the same side, even if I didn't mean it deep down. I figured she didn't either.

CHAPTER 18

Nick isn't waiting for me when I get to English class. The bell rings. I go inside, glancing over my shoulder for him. He makes it in at the echo of the bell. Miss Lafrance looks up from her desk but nods once at him and goes back to talking with the students who are gathered around her.

"Hey," I say as he slides into his seat.

Head down, he ignores me.

"You okay?" I ask.

"All right, class, I want you to get out your essay on..."

"Holy crap! That was due today?" I whisper.

"You didn't do it?" His voice is icy.

"No. I forgot. You?"

He passes his paper to me, and I hand it to the person in front of me.

What's up? He couldn't be mad at me for not doing my paper. Could he?

A hand goes up. Shirley Counts. "Miss Lafrance," her sweet voice sing-songs.

"Yes, Miss Counts."

"I forgot mine."

"That's terrible," Miss Lafrance murmurs.

The class laughs.

"Turn it in tomorrow for ten points off. Ten points every day you're late. You're juniors; you know what's expected of you."

I pull out my cell and text Nick.

What's wrong?

The back of my neck starts to sweat. I have no idea why he's mad at me. I just know he is.

My phone vibrates. I hold it in my purse. It's a picture. But it's blurry at first while my cell downloads the image. It's a picture of John Strickland pulling me into his bedroom. Another text comes. A picture of me smoking weed. The third image is of John Strickland kissing me.

My heart beats so hard and fast that it feels like a herd of buffalo charging. The blood drains out of my face, and my ears are overwhelmed with sounds. Nick tapping his pencil on his desk. Jenny Berlin cracking her gum. Michael Flemming snorting from his allergies. David Hawthorn drumming his fingers against his leg, making the change in his pocket jangle. The sounds get louder and longer and more mixed together, and my vision narrows till it's like I'm in a tunnel.

In my haze Leah comes to me. "Lie to him; he'll believe."

What should I say? *I didn't kiss John Strickland? I didn't go to the party to see him like you think I did? I didn't really want to smoke the pot; it just seemed rude not to?* All the excuses pile up between us. My excuses, his hurt, layered like a chocolate cake. I bend my head and watch as my tears pour out of me, almost in slo-mo or something. *Splat.* They spill onto my open English book.

I text him. I can explain.

His reply comes back. Lightning fast.

Don't bother.

My throat feels like it's closing. I try not to choke on my sadness.

Leah reaches into my purse, taking my hand with her. She positions it on that green pill. The one that was supposed to loosen me. At least I tell myself it's Leah. But that's not right. It can't be. It has to be me. I know that.

I need a little something. Shouldn't I just own that? Why do I need to hide behind my sister's ghost? I slip the pill higher, holding it tight between my ring finger and my thumb. I swallow the little green pill and tell myself it's not too late with Nick. He might still believe in me. I wish I believed it.

The rest of the period goes by, and I'm practically floating on the ceiling by the time the bell rings. I don't try to stop Nick as he stuffs his books into his backpack. I couldn't if I wanted to anyway; my legs belong to someone else. Leah comes to me, this time for real, and leads me out of class.

"It's okay to skip just this once." She points me to the back exit. I take off toward the woods. I can't face anyone or anything. I shouldn't have to. When I get to the softball field, I lie down in a patch of grass and let the sun bake on me. The ground is cold and dewy. I put my hands over my head and fall asleep.

CHAPTER 19

I wait out back on the bleachers, next to the baseball field the girls' softball team uses.

It's not their season, so I'll be able to avoid everyone while keeping an eye on the parking lot.

I shake but not from the cold. I look at my phone. No more texts from Nick despite my pleading. And no answer from John Strickland either. I texted him an hour ago.

What's keeping Emery? I want to go home. I hug my arms around myself. When I see John Strickland walking straight for me, my heart pounds hard.

"Hey, Allie."

I climb down the bleachers. It's all I can do to keep from scratching his face raw. Or trying to before one of his powerful hands holds me immobile. Someone has to pay for the pictures.

"You called? You okay?"

My throat constricts as if he's holding it tight, squeezing all the life out of me. I can see it in the way he stands firm, his shoulders squared and his arms crossed. He's too much for me. He's way too much for me to handle. I should have realized he'd never help me. It's all business with him. Nick is bad for business. So he ended it for me. End of story.

I let the pot and the pain make me see him as something he isn't.

"You don't look happy to see me. What's up?" he asks, moving closer to me.

I smell the cinnamon gum he's chewing. He lifts his sunglasses so I can look into his eyes. The pupils are pinpoint tight, like my one-millimeter Staedtler drafting pen, the one I use to do my sketches. Coal black. "Tell me," he says. The smell of dead cigarettes mixed with the spicy gum comes off him in waves, triggering one of my headaches. I try not to gag. "You need something?"

A tear slides down my face. I hold out my cell. "Why?"

He takes the phone. The smile leaves his face. "I didn't."

"Sure you didn't. Nick just happened to get these pictures of me this morning. And you have no idea from who or why?"

"I swear I didn't. I have no idea."

"You don't have like a camera set up or something?"

"What the hell, Allie? I'm not like that. I don't take pictures of anyone who isn't willing or fully aware. Someone else did this. I'll find out who. You say Nick got these?"

"Yeah."

"How'd that go?"

"How do you think? He's not talking to me."

"If you forward them to me, I'll have someone look into it. I'll find out."

I nod and bat at the tears that run down my face.

John wipes them away. I hate how rough his hands feel, the

drag on my skin as his fingers scrape against it. I could ask him to leave and he would. But at this moment, I want his comfort. And I get a little why Leah would go to him—the hardest guy I know acting sweet and protective feels kind of amazing. He reaches into his pocket and takes out a small clear bag with a handful of small light-blue pills. I do a quick count. Five. Baby blue. Not robin's-egg blue. Thank God.

"Xanax," he says. "It'll help. But go easy with them."

Just the feel of the pills calms me a little. And now I have a tiny speck of hope wrapped in a huge justification. Today sucked. These could help. I breathe out.

"What are you going to do?" he asks. "About Nick."

"What can I do?"

"Lie to him. Tell him Emery brought you there. That I forced you. He'll believe you."

"You don't care?"

"Seriously?" he laughs.

"What about the drugs?"

"Tell him it was your first time."

I look into John Strickland's eyes. He slides his glasses back on and starts to walk away. He turns again. "You're going to get through this, Allie. You are stronger than you think."

Maybe with these I am. I take a blue pill out of the bag and swallow it.

"You're going to be fine."

He walks away. A moment or two later, Emery bursts out the back door of the school. Even from far away I can see her banging her keys against her legs, and it makes me wonder what the hell is eating her? She sees John Strickland and stops.

I close the gap between us. I want to get home as soon as possible. I can't be here anymore.

"Hey, I've gotta run an errand on the way home. That okay?" she asks as we walk to her car. Emery walks everywhere fast. Today, she's racing. I have to work to keep up, but I'm glad. The faster we leave, the sooner I can be home.

Emery checks her phone for messages. She frowns and throws her cell into her bag. She points her keys at her pastel blue VW bug and opens it. I turn the radio on. She puts the car in reverse and turns to look at me before pulling out.

"What's the matter?" I ask.

"Why are you hanging with John Strickland? He's bad news. You know that."

I chew on my fingernail and look out the window. Max is walking to his car.

"Maybe. But he's helping me."

His gym bag is over his shoulder, bouncing with each hurried step. His head is down, but his body is screaming mad, and he's missing practice. Not like him.

"Not what I heard. I heard Nick's pissed at you."

"I know." I pull out my phone to text him. But what could I say that would be different from the ten other texts I've sent him? And John's right. I'm a little over being judged by Mr. Clean.

Emery puts her hand over my phone. "What I don't get is why you spend all your time going after the wrong guy."

Rage fills me. "I'm not going after John Strickland. And if I were, it's my business. Not yours."

She continues. "Nick deserves an explanation. That's all I'm saying."

"You're supposed to be *my* friend, not Nick's. You're supposed to take *my* side."

"I know. I'm just worried about you. I like Nick. He's so much better for you than—"

"Than who?"

"Than John Strickland, who is suddenly your favorite person and also probably the reason you're getting high and taking pills. You're changing, Allie. This isn't like you."

Is she kidding? Of course I've changed. My sister killed herself. Did she think I'd still be the same after that?

I lean my head against the window. Why won't Nick let me talk to him? Why won't he give me the chance? I get so dizzy with all this that I have to close my eyes. I pretend I'm somewhere happy. Like our house on Cape Cod when Dad and Mom still liked each other.

A text comes in. I jump.

John Strickland, not Nick.

Found the guy who sent the pics. He's on the baseball team with Nick.

What are you going to do?

Make him pay.

I lean my head back and smile. Good, I text. Let him pay. Let everyone pay. I'm sick of being the only one.

"Is that Nick?" Emery asks.

"No."

"You seem sort of out of it. You okay?"

"I'm fine," I say again, even though each minute I spend with Emery makes me feel like I'm suffocating. Plus it's getting harder to keep it all from her. The lies are exhausting. Part of me wants to tell her the truth. But that's the weak part. Another part whispers that she'll never understand. That she'll ditch me when she sees how broken and stupid I am.

"Just gonna be a minute," Emery says. She gets out of the car and pulls her hood up against the rain that's starting. She disappears into Walgreens.

I settle into my seat and try to get those colors back, the Cape Cod colors. But every time I try to tune them in, they slip through my fingers.

My phone vibrates.

R we over? Nick.

I look at the text, run my fingers over it. He's the one who wouldn't talk to me. He's the one who got mad without even finding out my side of the story. I stare at it. What should I do? I delete it.

The phone rings. It's him. I want to answer. I do. But my mouth feels all weird and like I've been to the dentist. I don't want him to hear me this way.

"Don't answer it." Leah comes to me—too late.

"Hi." My voice is low and gravelly with the tiniest slur. "I just want to talk to you."

"You sound like Mom!" Leah yells.

I cover the phone with my hand so Nick won't hear her—and hang up on him by accident. I try to call him back, but my fingers feel impossibly big and can't work the buttons. I put the phone down. It's no use.

The phone rings. It's him again. I push the button to answer.

"Hi," I breathe again.

"You sound drunk. What's going on with you?"

"I'm just…"

"Call me when you can make sense," Nick says. And then he's gone.

"Leah?" I have a question I want to ask her, even more pressing than why she did it. I know Leah will tell me the truth. "Do I keep going after the wrong guys?"

Her eyes get sad. "Maybe. But that's kind of what everyone does. Until they go after the right ones."

"Did you love John Strickland?"

Her face scrunches up. "Love makes you weak. I was never weak."

Until she killed herself.

Lies. It hits me—Leah is lying. So stupid. Of course she is. She always did. She handed out little bits of truth wrapped in beautiful lies. She managed all the information. Even what she shared with me.

"I wanted you to look up to me," she explains.

"I did. You didn't have to lie."

"You wouldn't have understood."

"You didn't try."

"I wanted you to think I was perfect. Picture perfect."

"You didn't have to pose for me. I didn't need that."

Leah's face turns hard. "Oh no? You seemed to love it when I did. You lapped it up."

I want to yell at her, but I see Emery walking back to the car. Leah follows my gaze. "Get ready for the crash," she says, and I worry about her, because now her words are looping like a bad recording.

Emery opens the door and climbs back into the car, a little white bag in hand, her face pinched. I want to ask her what's wrong, but I can't. I'm exhausted.

We drive the rest of the way home without talking. Emery seems wigged, and I am just plain worn out. So is Leah. She rides in the backseat, her face cupped in her hand, her arm propped on the door. She looks as tired as I feel.

"Thanks," I say to Emery when she drops me off.

"I miss you, Allie." Emery looks like she's about to cry.

I come back, lean in her window.

"We'll talk soon. I just have a headache." My usual excuse.

"Yeah. Feel better." Emery waves as she pulls out of my driveway.

It occurs to me that I didn't even ask what was in the bag. I need to be a better friend.

Max climbs in my window as soon as I open the door to my room. He must have been watching for me. I swallow hard. This can't be good.

"Hi." He looks at me, sheepish, like I caught him doing something bad. Did I?

"What's up?" I ask, not really wanting to know. Knowing that this moment of suck, whatever it is, has been a long time coming.

"I need to talk to you." He looks at the floor. Not at me. Max always looks at me. "I have to tell you I'm sorry. But you're so mad all the time that I can't get to you."

"If I'm acting so bad, then why are you the one who's sorry?"

I sit down in front of my computer and put my head in my hand. The room is spinning. His voice is echoing, bouncing off the walls. I need him to stop talking. I need it all to stop.

He kneels on the floor beside me. "You know how I feel about you," he says.

I look at my hands that are trembling like Mom's now. "Do I?"

His phone vibrates. Out of the corner of my eye, I see him pull it out of his pocket and look at it.

"Whatever, Max. Why don't you go talk to whoever is texting you? Obviously they're more important than me."

"No one's more important than you." Tears slide out of his eyes. He braces his jaw. His hands go in his pockets. I've never seen Max actually cry. Whatever this is, it must be bad. "Oh God, Allie. She told you, didn't she?"

"What?" My head swivels, my stomach is suddenly cold like I've swallowed a ball of ice. Cold blood runs through my veins. Max makes my heart beat. He can make it stop too. Why do I give him so much power? Leah was right. I'm stupid when it comes to him.

"Allie, it was nothing…" Max backs up, runs his hand through his hair. I stay silent. I know who he's talking about—the only person who could hurt me more than Max. And now I bet I know what was in Emery's drugstore bag.

"I thought she was on the pill," I say. It's a guess, but I hope I'm wrong.

"She was. I mean, she is. She was late, and she was worried." Max looks at his hands. "I knew she'd tell you. I begged her not to. It was just that one time, and it didn't mean anything."

"When?"

He looks out the window. "Don't, Allie, it's not important."

I stumble across the room and start hitting him. My fists sink into his flesh over and over again, making a sickening sound. I want to beat him till it hurts as much as he hurt me. Even though that's not possible. I grab his arms and shake him. "Tell me," I growl.

"That night." He grabs my hands, tears running freely down his face now. "I'm so sorry."

"What night?" I whisper even though I know.

"The night you went out with your sister." The words come out almost unformed, like he doesn't want to touch them, like they taste bad in his mouth.

"She…she had an audition. She said she had an audition."

"She did. I went with her. Eric was supposed to read, but he got sick."

"Oh my God." My hand is over my mouth. This can't be happening. My legs buckle. I sit.

"It just sort of happened." He follows me to the ground.

I'm in a tunnel.

"She called me. I went to help." Max is still talking. I can hear the words, but none of it makes sense. Max and Emery. Together. "It was a rush to be up on stage like that. We went to a party after. We were drunk…"

Words float in and out of me. I am adrift.

"It was a mistake."

"Is she?" I look at him.

"Pregnant? No. That was her just now. She did the test. It's no."

I nod. The tears pour out of me fast and furious.

"Allie." He tries to put his hands on my face.

"Don't." I pull them off me.

"I'm so sorry."

"Don't." I get up.

"I… We…didn't mean for it to happen."

"Whatever. You're a free agent. So is she." The words sound distant. Like they're not mine. Max and Emery. Together. My world is ending.

"Don't push me away. I didn't mean it. I don't love her like—"

I turn to face him, my face wet and hot. "Don't. Don't ever say that to me again."

"Allie, please…"

"Get out of my room!" I point toward the door.

"Allie."

"Don't. Ever. Come. Back."

"Okay, I'll go. But I'm not giving up. You'll forgive me. You will."

The door closes, and I put my head in my hands and cry full-out. When I can't cry anymore, I grab my purse. I pull out the baggie John Strickland gave me at that party and the one he gave me today at school.

"Let me help you pick. I know these," Leah says.

She looks at me, her eyes now the exact same blue as mine. If I looked in the mirror, would I have her brown ones? Are we switching?

"God, I'm stupid," I say, hoping she'll disagree. Knowing she won't.

"Your friends were stupid. You were just too trusting." She rifles through the bag but must see me stare at her, because she says, "They're not the same. I wouldn't do that. I promised. These are powder blue. Baby blue. These won't hurt you. I swear."

I take the pill.

"I'll get you water."

I shake my head and swallow it dry. Don't need any.

Leah lies back on the bed. "I hate people. They totally suck. You need to be more like I was."

Before she killed herself.

"And I can't believe they *told* you. I mean, what was the point? If I didn't tell you, why would they?"

I sit straight up, despite the pills and the woozy and the numb. Somehow the message still gets through. The party. John Strickland's. Had to be. "How could you?"

Leah sits up too. "What did I do?"

"You knew. You knew and didn't tell me."

Leah's mouth gets firm, and her eyes turn to steel. Her jaw sets. "I couldn't."

"You didn't." For once, I match her.

"I was going through a lot." Her voice is buzz-saw sharp.

I get off the bed. I need to get away from her. As far as I can. "How would I know? It's not like you told me. You never told me the important things."

"You're too much. I killed myself. I *killed* myself. Doesn't that mean anything to you?"

"Are you kidding me?"

"I didn't mean it the way it sounded…"

"It means everything to me. It's the only thing I can think about. It's ruining my life. And my art. It's ruining me."

"I didn't mean…"

I stand. "Get out of here."

"No."

"No?"

"You heard me. I won't leave. You invited me here. Now deal with me."

"You said it was up to me. You said just when I wanted to see you."

She laughs. "I lied. I'm here because you brought me here. Remember that."

I look at her ring that I painted on my wall.

"Oh God, Allie. You can't be that dense, can you?"

"What are you talking about?"

"You think that's why I'm here? That graffiti? Hardly."

My head swims. My heart pounds. She can't mean…

"The paintings…"

I feel as if she slapped me across the face. Why am I always the last to know? I walk down the stairs, unsteady and fighting the dizzy and the sick. Black-and-white photographs of Leah and I that run the length of our staircase blur by me. I pass through the empty living room, choking on my pain. Sophie circles my legs, almost tripping me. I grab the key chain from the hook in the kitchen, knocking a set of keys to the floor. The sound they make reminds me of the Cape memory—everything crashing down.

I push the door open, Sophie on my heels, trying to keep up, her tiny paws slipping on the cold ground. I know I should help her. I know I should protect her, but I can't. The pain is screaming through my body. All I can think about is stopping the pain.

And the whole time I'm running, she's with me. Leah. She's my shadow, hugging me to her. I couldn't shake her if I wanted to. I should have known. I'm so stupid about people. When I get to my studio, I try to jam the key in the lock but miss. I try again.

"Let me." She grabs at the key.

I ignore her and shove it in the lock, twist, bump the door with my hip, and the two of us go flying inward. Once inside, I'm not sure I want to do this. Maybe I should go back upstairs, forget she said anything. Maybe I should just take another pill.

"You're going to have to face it one day," Leah says.

She's right. Like always. I creep toward the paintings, most of them covered with sheets, looking like burial sheaths. Just one is uncovered and I wonder when that happened. Who uncovered my past? It's the one with Leah in her ballet leotard. All black with pink tights. It was practically her uniform. So I tried to capture that mood.

"I'm so pink." Her voice comes from that memory, not from her ghost. This one memory is real. Not summoned. Or imagined. "Is that how you see me?"

I move forward, my hands tracing the painting. Leah standing straight, her back to me, the simple lines of her neck and back, the outline of her profile. She looked so sweet. And soft. And pink. All kinds of pink. *Innocence. Reverie. Blush. Bridal pink.* That painting was supposed to be a summation of all the Leahs—past, present, and future. Except now she isn't going to have one.

I move to the next canvas and pull the sheet down. It's Leah sitting on my window seat, wearing Sean's jersey over her skinny black jeans. I walk from one painting to the next, pulling the sheets off each of them.

Leah with Sophie in her lap, wearing her college-girl look, complete with violet glasses. I painted her hair shiny and honey blond with lowlights and highlights and everything so completely perfect, like she was. It's so real, I can almost smell the mango shampoo.

Leah in her dance uniform ready for the pep rally. These pictures are exactly how ghost-Leah looked when she came to me. All of those times. So it must be true. She's in my mind. Only in my mind. I was just remembering her. I sit down. I am crazy. Definitely.

Leah sits next to me. "Crazy runs in our family. You know that."

"You're not real?" I ask, hoping there's another explanation.

"Of course I'm real. To you, I'm real."

"Oh my God, oh my God, oh my God." I put my hands to my head. Press in. I need to make this stop. It's too much. I need to make it stop.

"This was how you brought me back. So what? You're grieving. It's not *that* crazy. It's not tragic crazy, kill-yourself crazy, like I was."

"But we had a deal. We had a pact. It *is* the same." I look at the pill bags in my hand.

Leah raises an eyebrow. "That's a good point, Allie. You know what Dr. Applegate would say if she were here?"

I shake my head.

"She'd say you need to take your pills." She takes the baggies from me and empties them into her palm.

I look at them and shake my head. "Not these. Not like this."

Leah's ghost that isn't really a ghost but really just me says, "The blue ones mellow you out. Take two."

I don't want to, but that makes sense. Mom always took two. Should I? No one answers. Of course they don't. Another test failed. I take two pills.

"You think I should take more? Is that the right thing?" I know it's crazy to ask advice from a ghost. Especially my sister's ghost. My eyes are swimmy and my mouth feels fuzzy. I'm not sure I could swallow more pills if I tried.

"It's about the colors, Allie. And the pills. And the choices. Which bottle, which pill, which color, which guy? The red one gets you up. Do you want to get up? The blue one gets you down. You already seem pretty down, so I'm thinking red."

I agree. At least I think I do. I'm not entirely sure. But honestly, why am I arguing? Leah's always right. Isn't she? Even imagined Leah?

"Good one, Al," she says.

I'm funny. Leah thinks I'm funny. And that feeling spreads through me, warming me, making me feel as if everything is going to be okay. Even though I can barely focus my eyes or feel my lips or fingers or anything. If Numb was what I was aiming for, I totally nailed it.

"You ready for a yellow one? A red? What color do you want, Al? You're the artist. What's your color?"

I look at her. And then at my paintings. I look at the pills in her hand. And I realize I have no fucking idea what my color is. I'm an artist who doesn't know her own palette. I start to laugh. Really laugh, because that's the funniest thing I've ever heard. I try to stand. My legs, guitar-string loose, won't hold me. So I sit.

My phone rings. I try to look at the number, but my eyes won't focus. I show it to Leah.

"Who's calling?" I laugh, because everything seems so completely hysterical.

Leah laughs with me. "Let me see." She squints at the phone. "Oh my God. Oh my God. You soooo don't want to answer this one."

"It's not…"

Leah nods. "It is."

"Max?"

"One and the same."

I take the phone from her.

"What are you going to do?"

"Hang up," I say, and I throw my phone against the wall, shattering it.

"Oh my God, Allie. You just killed your phone."

I giggle hysterically, bending forward, my body folding over completely.

"What's so funny?" Leah puts her face by mine. "Allie?"

I hold up the baggie that held the light-blue pills, which is now empty. "I think I killed myself too."

Fits of laughter come out of me and Leah till I can't tell who is laughing harder. Till I'm not laughing anymore—till I'm crying. Crying for my sister. Crying for myself. Crying because I never wanted to do this, and now I have. The room swims. I put my face on the floor of the studio, letting the cold seep into my skin, cooling my hot cheeks. My eyes close. I think about falling asleep and not coming back. The thought makes me a little bit happy and that makes me wonder when I switched with Leah, switched from the dopey little sister who didn't quite get it to the general in charge of this death mission.

"Allie?" Leah slaps my face. "Allie?" Her voice changes pitch. It's not her at all. It's Mom.

"Oh my God, Allie!" Mom screams. "No!" I hear her dial three numbers.

I pass out.

CHAPTER 20

The feeling of scratchy sheets under me and tape holding an IV in my arm, the sound of a monitor beeping, tell me all I need to know. I'm still here. I'm okay.

"Allie…" Mom's voice cuts through the cotton in my ears. "Thank God."

Guilt washes over me. What have I done? My eyes feel cemented closed. I try to open them, but I can't.

"Here," Mom says, patting my forehead with a wet washcloth. The water feels good. My eyes blink open. Her small voice and careful movements make me feel so sorry for her. It must have been awful finding me. Right after Leah. That must have sucked. And suddenly I wish I could take it all back. Tears slip out from under my eyelids.

"Oh, baby…" Mom cries as she wipes my cheeks. "Why?"

"I didn't mean it… I wasn't…"

I wish I could make her understand. I wish I could explain everything. But we're already on two opposing teams. She thinks I tried to kill myself. I didn't. I just tried to stop the pain. And it almost killed me. I know that sounds like a cop-out. But it's not. It's the truth. Straight up.

Dad's here. I scan my mother for her tells. Her hands are

steady, but her lips are droopy. That means she's taken just enough to deal with the situation but not enough so she can't drive home. Since Dad doesn't drive her anymore.

When he nears the bed, I see how much I've stripped his colors. He's white as a ghost and looks as if the air has gone completely out of him. Dad looks smaller. I've done that to him. He holds my hand. I fight the urge to pull it away. "Allie," he says, gruff voiced.

I never meant to hurt them.

"We are just so glad you're okay," Mom says.

I just wanted it to stop hurting.

"We just want to know why," Mom says.

"I didn't mean to…"

"You didn't mean to?" Dad repeats, anger creeping into his voice. "They said you had Valium and Xanax and Ritalin and all sorts of other drugs in your system. What were you doing? A science experiment?"

"David, don't." Mom puts her hand on his arm.

"Jesus." He gets up and walks away, parting the blinds and staring out into the parking lot as if he is completely wrapped up with what's happening out there.

Mom pours a glass of water from the mauve plastic pitcher on the side table. She holds up my head and twists the bendy straw so I can drink.

"It was an accident," I say.

"You don't take that much medication by accident," Dad says from his perch at the window.

This is the dad I know—angry and accusing and judging. Dad thinks he's so honest and upright. But he's not. He may be the biggest liar of all. He lied to Mom when he married her. And to us every time he seemed happy to be with us. He lied to Leah after one of her recitals, when he said she had been the best thing he'd ever seen. His new girlfriend is. He always puts her first.

He comes back to stand next to my bed, somewhere between deflated and demanding. And I'm not sure which side of him to trust.

"Thank God you're okay," he starts. Lie. "I love you so much." Lie. "I just wish I knew why you did this. With everything I've given you, a talented girl like you…" Finally how he really feels. I'm trapped. I can't breathe. I reach for Leah. Memories flood me. I see her as I painted her, the way she came to me. I can't believe she wasn't real.

"…don't know what I've done wrong. Your mother and I…" The pain hits me full-on. Leah is gone. Really gone.

"Stop. She's had enough," Mom says.

"I was just…" Dad's voice breaks. Lie.

I try not to listen to them. Try not to let them pull me under. I wish for the millionth time that Leah were here with me, deflecting her fair share. Sisters do that for each other. Until one of them bails.

"You're always just…" Mom says. Dad gets silent.

Images of the day invade in my thoughts, even though I don't want them. John Strickland. Max and Emery. Nick. Leah. My insanity. Everything explodes like the chaos of colors that Mr. Kispert said was my best work.

I close my eyes. Leah. She left more than a hole in my heart; she left one in my head too. She lived inside of me, and now that she's gone, what will fill in the missing parts?

Mom starts crying again.

"Karen, please." Dad's voice cracks.

"It was like finding her again." Mom sobs. "Sophie was barking at the back door. I followed her to the studio."

"Thank God you did, Karen, but you have to stop thinking about it, obsessing. It won't help." Dad says.

I remember finding Leah the morning after the party. She was mad at me. I had checked out, but I wanted to make up. Leah always had music playing or the TV blaring or was on the phone with Brittney. You could usually hear Leah from a mile away. That's how much life she gave off. But it was dead quiet that morning. I remember thinking she must have really been upset.

I walked in her room and saw her lying there, like she fell and couldn't get up. I could tell something was wrong. Pills, robin's-egg blue, formed a splatter pattern next to the bottle of wine she'd drunk from. Part of her lips were burgundy red—underneath the vomit that spilled from her. Some people might miss the burgundy. But I didn't. It's the color that stood out the most to me.

I knelt down next to her and saw she wasn't breathing. Her body was cold. So cold. My hands shook. She couldn't be dead.

She couldn't. She promised she wouldn't leave me. Nothing made sense, except she was so cold. I went to get the cover off her bed. I thought maybe if I could warm her up, it'd be okay, she'd be okay. "Please, please, please." I was screaming. "Leah, you have to get up. You have to!"

She didn't move. The air around me pressed on me, and I felt like I'd fallen down a hole. *Leah killed herself. Leah killed herself. Oh my God, she killed herself.* The words became real in my mind. *Leah killed herself. She really killed herself.* Then I remembered my training and thought, *I have to kill myself too.* I grabbed for the pills. They tasted like puke and death. I didn't care.

Mom rushed in. She put her hand over her mouth. Then she grabbed my arms and started shaking me.

"Oh my God!" Mom had screamed. "Oh my God!"

"No!" I shrieked. "She's okay. She's going to be okay." I don't remember scooping up the pills. They said I did, but I don't remember. "I was supposed to go with her. She promised me. She promised."

My mind had buried this memory deep so I wouldn't have to remember how much it hurt to find her. To know she was gone. Except I remember now. Fresh pain assaults me.

"Allie…" Mom sits next to me on the bed.

I lay my head on her shoulder and cry. The sobs feel good, like they're wringing the bad out of me. As if that's possible. After all that's happened. With Leah gone and me alone. With the betrayals and the lies. And the drugs. I cry till I feel cleaner.

I know there are still some drugs left in me. For now I feel better. A little.

"It's okay, honey," Mom says. Lie.

Mom lies to keep us moving. She is fine: lie. Dad still loves us: lie. I am good enough: lie. Each move is carefully negotiated. Each lie is designed. She plays an excellent game. I should be impressed. I'm not. I don't want to live like this anymore.

"Dad?" I ask even though I know he's gone.

"He can't deal. It's not okay, but he can't," Mom says. Truth. Finally.

Dad walked out. He can't stand weakness. It's worse than trying to kill yourself. He'd take tragic over lame any day. God, I hate him. Lie. My head hurts bad. I push my hands against my temples.

"Headache?" Mom asks.

"Yeah."

"I'm not sure you can take anything right now."

She means now that I'm a suicide attempt instead of just an addict. Labels mean something. Despite what it looks like, that label is a big fat lie. Despite the picture I painted for them, I did not want to kill myself. I'm completely sure of that. Mostly.

"My phone?"

"Honey, you smashed it." I can tell she wants to give me what I want. Like when I was four and screaming for her to buy me something I didn't really need. I can tell she wants to feel useful. "But I can get you another one. No problem."

My phone. Gone. It's stupid to be upset about it, but another

tie to Leah is gone. We had the same phones. Dad gave them
to us. Together.

"Allie?"

"I'm so tired. Going to go to sleep for a while." Lie. I turn over.

"Okay." She kisses my cheek. I wish she wouldn't. Because I
don't deserve it. She doesn't know about me. She doesn't know
I heard Leah up and moving around that night. That I didn't
think… She doesn't know I could have stopped her. If I'd just
gotten up and gone to her. If Mom knew, she'd hate me. Like
Dad does.

"I'll ask the nurse about something for your head," she says
as she leaves.

"Uh-huh," I mumble and pretend to be asleep. Just one more
lie piled on the heap.

"Oh, Allie? A psychiatrist is going to come in and see you.
Dr. Ziggler, I think." Sneaky-Mom timing.

CHAPTER 21

I hear the door open. A light switches on. A man walks over to my bed wearing green scrubs that make him look like a doctor. He is. Just not the kind who needs to wear scrubs. As one liar to another, I am offended by his weak attempt to make me believe he's more powerful than he is.

"Hi, Allie." He flips the page. Is he checking to see if he has my name right? How many suicide attempts could he have to deal with in one day? "I'm Dr. Ziggler."

I take in his colors. Gray hair. Blue eyes. Platinum wedding band.

He pulls up a chair. The noise of the legs being dragged against the tile floor makes me wince.

"Headache?" he asks.

I put my hand to my head, a movement so practiced I don't even have to try to fake it, and that's a relief. "Yeah," I manage.

"Hmmmm. You get those a lot?"

I wonder what this could possibly have to do with taking a bunch of pills. One doesn't lead to the other. Necessarily. I stay silent.

He clears his throat. "You get a lot of headaches, Allie?"

"Yes."

"And you take…" The rustling pages are like helicopter blades cutting into me. "Relpax, Topomax, Phenergan, Frova…"

"Not all at once." It's supposed to be a joke. I hope he laughs. He does, a little.

"Your tox screen from your stomach showed different sedatives and stimulants. That's just what you took yesterday." He flips another paper in my chart. "The blood tox screen, the other stuff you've taken within the last couple of months, showed additional recreational drugs, cough and cold medicines. So I guess I've got to ask, your headache meds not working?"

I stare at the wall.

"You want to tell me about it?" He lowers my chart and looks at me, like he's got all the time in the world. Like it doesn't matter that it's dark outside and he probably has a family to get home to or that he's ignoring the phone vibrating like mad in his pocket. He focuses on me. That almost makes it worse.

"I don't know what to say."

"I'm worried about you, Allie," Dr. Ziggler says, making me wish I were worthy of his concern. Because he's a good guy. I can tell. Even if he lied to me with the scrubs, he had his reasons.

"I'm good," I say.

He laughs.

"Considering, I mean."

"I'm not sure I believe that." He puts his left foot on his right knee and lets it bounce a little.

I stare, because even though it's a little gesture, it says he's confident and nice. If he played baseball, he'd be a second base-man, I'm guessing.

"Allie…" Dr. Ziggler tries to get me back on subject.

"I didn't mean it. I didn't think… I wasn't trying…" I stare at the wall again, the tears wrenching themselves out of me, even though I try to keep them in. "Nobody believes me. But I really didn't."

"You seemed like you did." His voice is calm. "That was a lot of medicine to take if you didn't."

"I guess I did at the time. But I don't anymore," I offer. True.

"Can you tell me why?" he asks.

I shake my head.

"Do you know?" He persists.

"No." Lie.

"You want me to let you in on a little secret?" He leans forward.

"Okay," I say.

"I believe you."

He shouldn't. I'm lying. I know exactly why I did it. Every reason is lined up in my head like crayons in a box.

"Most people don't know why," he continues. "Even when the reasons seemed so clear at the time."

Maybe. When I was taking the pills, I didn't think about it. I just did it. But I had to know on some level, didn't I?

"The most important thing is to be honest. It's the only way to get better. Whatever is hurting you, we have to get it out of you. That's the only way to get better."

Maybe.

"So, will you try to let me help you. Will you do that?"

"Yes." Lie.

"Good. Because I want you to get better. There's no secret that's worth this." He holds up his hands to indicate my current address.

I stay silent.

"You're seeing Dr. Applegate, right?"

"Yes."

"I'd like you to stay here for a little while. Till you feel strong."

I wipe the tears from my face.

"Sometimes having someone you love die makes you feel so sad, you don't want to live anymore. It's understandable. I'd like to put you on something to make you feel better. Exchange all those other pills for just one. Will you let me do that?"

He makes this sound so personal. He's worried about me. Would I let him help me? I'm so beat-down tired that I almost believe him. Almost. Then I remember. He's lying too. He showed me the moment he walked in wearing scrubs, as if he were the kind of doctor who operates instead of just messes with your mind and hands out pills.

I think about Leah throwing away her pills because they made her fat. The same pills that made me feel drugged and tired and totally disconnected. Those are the pills he thinks will fix me. "I'll try," I lie.

The door opens. Mom slides in. Dr. Ziggler unfolds his leg and pushes himself out of the chair, extending his hand. "I'm Dr. Ziggler."

"Karen Blackmore," Mom replies.

"Allie and I were just talking about a few things."

Mom looks at me. Then back at him.

"I'd like to put Allie on an antidepressant."

Mom nods.

The door opens again. Dad's entrance is stronger than Mom's but quieter than his earlier one. Contrite Dad is on the scene now. He makes my stomach crawl, but he's not dangerous. Not like angry Dad.

Dr. Ziggler extends his hand again. "Mr. Blackmore?"

Dad nods.

"I'm Dr. Ziggler. I was just telling your wife…"

"Ex-wife," Mom chimes in. I want to crawl under the covers. Dad gives Dr. Ziggler an aggravated smile. Lie. They're still married. For now.

"I was just telling Karen that we'd like to put Allie on an antidepressant for starters. Time in our inpatient facility will allow me to monitor her to make certain she reaches therapeutic levels."

"No."

"No to the medicine or no to the inpatient stay?" Mom demands.

"No to the stay."

"Mr. Blackmore, I think you're making a mistake," Dr. Ziggler says.

Dad flashes his aggravated smile again. "Thank you for your help, but we can give Allie everything she needs at home."

"She needs a neutral place to heal," Dr. Ziggler insists. "She needs a break from whatever it is that made her feel compelled to take those pills."

"Don't worry, Doctor. We've already made some changes."

My stomach turns. I wonder what he means by that. With Dad it could be anything. He knows how to hurt you in the name of loving you. Just ask Mom.

"I'm not sure…" Dr. Ziggler tries.

"We'll follow through on all your recommendations. She wasn't taking her meds. We'll make sure she does now." Dad shoots Mom a look.

"We thought she was doing okay," Mom says.

"She has to stay in the hospital for two more days. That's the law. After that, the choice is yours. My recommendations will be on file in case you change your mind."

Dr. Ziggler moves to the bed and shakes my hand. "Pleasure meeting you, Allie. Please stay well." His crystal-blue eyes are so clear, I want to jump into them. I want him to take me with him. Away from Mom and Dad. But he's not my father. I wasn't that lucky.

I watch him leave the room, my hopes sinking with every squeak of his sneakers. I'm going home. With them. Back to whatever they've done to sanitize my house. I try not to cry.

"Allie, you okay with this? You want to come home, right?" Mom asks.

"Sure," I lie, and I'm surprised at how little effort that takes. I've been telling lies for so long now, I'm not sure I know the truth. Each lie I tell connects to the previous one. These are Jenga lies. I'm not sure which one will send the whole tower tumbling. So I protect all of them—until I can think straight enough to keep the tower standing.

"You're going to be fine, Allie," Mom says, slipping me a new cell she must have gotten while I was sleeping. Mom's always prepared. Always has her bribes ready. As if she knew Dad would win and she'd have to make it up to me somehow. *May as well benefit.* Leah's words come back to me from when we got the phones.

"We're going to take care of you," Dad says. Lie. "I love you, Allie." Big fat lie.

I'm surrounded by lies. I'm swimming in them. And with no backup—no pills, no Leah, no Nick. No Max or Emery. Something Dr. Ziggler said made me think. Maybe *they* are what's making me sick. Maybe it's not me. Maybe it's them. I'm so consumed with that thought, I don't hear the nurse come in.

"Open up, Allie. Time for your meds," she says.

Mom and Dad watch me. I obey and accept the pill, like taking communion. Only something about taking the medicine feels wrong. So I push it to the back of my mouth and trap it against my teeth. What makes these pills different than the ones that landed me here? One pill made me see Leah. A different pill will take her away. I feel like I'm in Alice in Wonderland again. The wrong Alice, definitely.

"Why don't you try to rest," the nurse suggests as she writes in my chart. "Best thing for you really."

I wonder how much she thinks she knows about me. I think of all the reasons I took those pills, all the things I told myself. I had to save my art. I had to save my sister. But those were lies. I was the one who wanted the pills. Me. Not Leah. Because she was never really there. Except in my mind.

"Visiting hours are over," the nurse says, her tone short. She adjusts my IV line and checks the numbers on the machine hooked up to me.

"Good night, Allie." Mom brushes my cheek with a quick kiss.

"See you tomorrow," Dad says from across the room. He opens the door and backs out.

As soon as they all leave, I cough the pill into my hand. I go to the bathroom, wrap it in toilet paper a few times, and flush. I know I should trust Dr. Ziggler. But I don't want to be numb anymore. Any kind of numb.

I turn off the light and go back to bed. The dark room makes me feel completely alone. I do the math. No more Emery. No more Max. No more Nick. No more Leah. Who else is left? No one. Just me.

I play with my new cell. It's just like my old one, but it has an orange plastic cover. Max's color. Figures. When it powers on, there's no picture of Em and me, just the general, factory-issue wallpaper. Maybe that's better. My contacts are loaded. I scroll through and block Max and Emery. That done, I think about Leah again. There's no trace of her on this phone. Are there traces of her in my mind? I heard her. I saw her. I felt her. She was so real to me. Only she wasn't.

I want Leah. Even if she's not real.

Before, the pills and the headaches were catalysts. Now I've got nothing but the pain. And it's not enough. I close my eyes and let myself fall asleep.

I dream about Leah. She's underwater and I can't get to her. I see her face, bloated and pale. Someone is pouring milk through a funnel into her ear. I hear people talking about her. About how they're going to miss her. She opens her eyes underwater and reaches out for me. Her hand grabs mine, and she pulls me under. I gasp awake.

I crawl out of bed and walk to the window. It's the middle of the night. But in the lamplight, I can still see trees, the parking lot, the glint of metal from the cars. It must have rained because the ground is wet. I don't remember hearing the rain. I missed it, like all the things Leah is missing now. I don't want to miss any of it. The parties, the pep rallies, laughing with friends. I've always been tethered to this world while Leah was the one who was floating—like if she couldn't live the way she wanted to, she'd rather die. That thought settles inside me. I know it's the truth.

I press my forehead against the window so I can feel the cold and the condensation. I would miss this too if I'd done it—the way the window feels after it's rained.

I crawl back to my bed and close my eyes.

My cell rings, an unknown number. I answer it before thinking. "Hello?"

"Allie?" John Strickland's voice.

I'm so surprised, I almost drop the phone.

"Allie, you there?"

"Yeah."

"I just heard. You okay?" His voice is soft.

"Yeah."

"I just… I need to know… Were they mine?"

I'm startled by his question. I feel all hollowed out and exposed. Dr. Ziggler said the road to recovery starts with coming clean, but it doesn't seem right to hurt him.

"No," I say. "They weren't."

"I always wondered about Leah, if she took mine, if that's how she did it."

"No. Mom's."

I hear him breathe out heavy. "Thanks. I mean, it doesn't change anything, but I always worried about that. Are you really okay?"

"Mostly. I didn't actually mean to."

He laughs a small, soft one. "Really?"

"Yeah."

"I'm glad you're okay. You have to remember that Leah wants you to be happy. She loved you very much."

"You too."

He laughs. "Yeah. Me too."

He hangs up, and I think about John Strickland's dangerous eyes. His pirate heart. I let his concern wrap around me, and it feels good, even if it's temporary. Even if it's borrowed from Leah, it still feels good.

I stash my phone under my pillow. My eyes feel heavy, and I let them close. I relax and start to drift, but just before I fall asleep, a hand brushes my cheek. The touch is light and leaves the tiniest scent for my beaten-down psyche to decipher: mango. My eyes won't open, so I must be dreaming. I guess dreaming's okay. Dreaming doesn't get you in trouble. Dreaming doesn't land you in the hospital with nurses and doctors writing notes in your chart that aren't true. Dreaming is a free pass. Better than a random pill.

Then I hear her. "Allie," she whispers, "I miss you."

This time I know she's not really here, but I don't care. Because accepting Leah as ghost or illusion feels like a gift, even if it's a lie.

CHAPTER 22

The ride home from the hospital is uncomfortably quiet. Dad tries to fill the empty space. He thumps the steering wheel, turns on the radio, and hums along. It's all I can do to not shriek at him. I watch the geography flash by—highway, then exit, then trees and medians. Then neighborhood, then driveway. My stomach feels as if I've swallowed a giant rock. I don't want to be here.

"Here we are," Dad says. "Why don't you take her in, and I'll bring her stuff?"

We walk in the house. Mom flips on the lights. Sophie runs to me. I pick her up.

"Hi, sweetie," I whisper into her furry face. "I missed you."

Mom starts sniffling. I feel bad. "You hungry?" she asks.

"No."

"You've got to eat," Dad says, setting down the small suitcase they packed with my things. He talked about cleaning things up for me. What did he mean? My flesh crawls. With Dad it could be anything. None of it good.

I turn from him and walk up the stairs.

"Leave her," Mom says.

My feet slow as I approach Leah's bedroom. Did Dad do

anything to her room? I turn the knob, holding my breath and hoping he left things as they were.

The first thing I notice is that her bed is made. I walk to it and pull the covers back. I sit on it. The space in her closet where her tall black boots should be waits expectantly, making me feel guilty for wearing them and messing up her things.

"Allie," Dad calls as he climbs the stairs. His footsteps are deliberate and strong, like always. Dad is dependable that way. His movements don't change, no matter what the circumstance. "You okay?"

I don't answer. I climb under the covers. I hear him open my door. He didn't even knock. Just walked in. God, I hate him.

"Allie?" he calls, now sounding frantic. And that makes me glad.

"Allie?" Mom's steps are worried like her voice. I feel bad—but not bad enough to answer.

Leah's door bursts open. "Allie, for God's sake. Didn't you hear us calling you?" Dad yells.

"Leave her alone," Mom says. "She's just gotten home."

"Yes, just gotten home and look where we've found her!" He points to me in my perch under Leah's covers.

Sophie runs in the room and starts barking, which snaps me out of it. I crawl out of Leah's bed and sit on the floor. Sophie gets in my lap and puts her paws on my shoulder. She kisses my face.

"I told you we should have—" Dad's go-to emotion: anger.

"That's enough. Let's leave her alone for a little."

"Allie," Dad ignores Mom. "I don't want you hanging around in here."

I look up from Sophie's face to stare daggers at him.

"I know you think I'm being mean, but it's for your own good."

I wonder what else he's done for my own good. I stay silent. It's my best play.

Thankfully, he leaves.

"I'll be downstairs if you need me." Mom retreats too.

I'm frozen. I can't breathe. It's too hard. The front door opens and closes. Something about Dad leaving makes me feel like I can move. Mom's steps hit the ground floor. I stand.

I get up and rifle through Leah's desk drawer. Her last tube of Chap rattles around, and without thinking, I shove it in my pocket.

I almost don't want to walk in my room. It has its own horrible memories waiting for me. The last time Max climbed in my window. Leah. The pills. Going to my studio and facing the paintings. I open the door and slip in, trying not to disturb the air around me. It's like I can hear Leah's ghost calling to me. I trace the lines of the flower I painted on the wall and window. The one she called graffiti.

From my window I can see my studio. Something tells me I should go there and look. The thought comes like Leah used to, like a little voice advising me. And the little voice is right. I need to see where my breakdown happened. I need to be where I meant to finish this.

My steps are stealthy as I make my way to the kitchen, where the key hangs on the hook. It's back in its place on the pink Converse key chain, hanging next to a random key that's been there forever, its ancestry stamped with Dad's old bank logo on it. I do the math. After they called the ambulance, after they cleaned up, someone actually put the key back. I get chills. Dad's work, definitely. He's all about order. Then I realize, when he was talking about cleaning up the house, he must have meant my studio. *My paintings.*

I slip out the back door, Sophie following. In the studio, my breath catches. It's worse than I thought. My paintings are gone. All of them. I bend over and clutch my stomach. My breath is gone.

I hear Mom approach, small steps that remind me how weak she is. She's stupid to come out here now. She should know better. This is not a good time to go on the offensive with me. All the emotions I've bottled up are now coursing through my veins, making me ready to explode. She should run for cover. But she's never been good at war games. Always playing the corpse. Except when Leah was. Or I am.

"How could you?" I fire.

She looks around the room. Her face is greenish gray. She knows it was wrong. Her silence makes it worse somehow. She could have stopped him. Did she even try? Or did she stay silent and stupid, like she is right now.

"Say something!" I scream.

"Allie…" Her voice is calm and quiet, making me shake even more.

"They were mine!"

"Don't get upset… Your father…"

"Don't. Don't bring him into this." I start pacing, then turn to face her.

She looks at her hands. She knows. But her refusal to speak is so controlling, like Dad in the hospital with the doctor. Like Leah when I pissed her off. I'm over all the controlling people in my life. I'm not doing it anymore.

I throw an easel over. *Crash.* "You had no right." I pick up a chair and launch it across the room. *Bang.*

She comes toward me, her arms outstretched. "He was scared, Allie. It's what he does when he gets scared."

Tears pour down my face. My throat feels like it's closing. This would be easier with a few pills. A bottle of something. I push my nails into my palms and sit, my back pushed against the wall, using it as support.

"I did those before…" It's no use explaining.

"I know."

"I miss her, Mom. I miss Leah. Every day."

"Of course you do." She comes closer. Does she think I want her near me? After what she did? After what they did? "Your father was worried about you."

"You promised you wouldn't let him take my paintings. Don't you remember? You promised."

"I didn't know."

"You didn't know what?"

"I didn't know he took them." She looks around the

graveyard Dad left behind. "Must have been when I was getting your phone. I didn't know." I look at Mom. She looks completely defeated.

"How come he still has a key to our house? If he left us, how come you still let him come and go like he has a right?"

"I didn't think… I wanted…"

"You never think with Dad. You let him run all over you. And us. I'm done with it. It's not right."

"I'll get your paintings back, I swear."

"Bottom line, Mom. I am not like you. I am not like Leah either. Because I'm not giving up on my life. Like you did. I'm not giving up on myself like she did."

"You were always stronger than she was. Always."

And just like that, her words take the wind out of my argument. It shouldn't matter what Mom thinks of me after all this. But it does.

"Your father and I knew that. We worried about her all the time."

"You worried about Leah?"

"Yes. Because she wasn't solid like you."

I slide to the floor and put my head on my knees. Mom tries to close the distance.

"How do you know he didn't throw them out? How do you know he didn't destroy them?"

She sits next to me. "I just do. I know where they are. I'll bring them back. Give me a few days. A week, tops."

"Let's get them now then!"

"I can't."

"You won't."

"I'll bring them back. I promise."

I put my head back down. I have nothing more to say to her. My voice has been stolen. Lost. Like my paintings. I wish I could believe her. But she's not strong like Dad. It's like playing the house. He'll win. He always does.

"I'm going to make the arrangements," she says as she gets up to go.

When I'm sure she's really gone, I pull it out of my pocket, Leah's cherry ChapStick. I bring it to my nose and call to my sister. Can I make her come to me? I close my eyes and smell the cherry, then coconut, then mango. The scents fill my head. I cover my nose so I can trap them there. So she can't escape.

I push my hands against my eyelids and will her image to appear. A starburst of white erupts inside my mind's eye. Miraculously, Leah steps out of it, all outline and movement. But just inside my mind this time. I know if I open my eyes, she'll be gone.

When I look toward the door, I see a silhouette. At first I think it might be Leah. But as she steps forward, I see who it is: Emery. Her olive skin is sallow looking. Her curls are a mess around her head. "Thought you might be here." Actress tears run down her face, perfect trails of pretend pain. She walks halfway across the room and stops. "I know you don't want to see me."

"You're right. I don't." I don't try to get up because my legs are too shaky to hold me.

"I'm so glad you're okay, Allie. You have no idea."

I look down.

"I know you're probably never going to forgive me. I don't blame you." She starts to cry harder now and messier.

I shouldn't let her get to me, but she does. The pain leaks out of my heart and onto my face. Emery. Why do I have to lose everyone? First Leah, then Max, then her.

"I'm so sorry, Allie. I'd do anything to take it back."

"You can't."

She sits on the ground. Her shoulders shake with her crying. She wipes her eyes with her hands, then wipes her hands on her jeans. She's left black smears on her favorite jeans.

"Look, Allie, I know we're never going to be the same…" She stops to get her breathing under control. "But I know where your dad put your paintings. I can help you get them back. I know that won't make up for anything…"—she sobs some more—"but at least it will make me feel like I've done something. Will you let me do that?"

I want my paintings back. Like I want Leah and Max and Emery back. I know I can't have everything, but I want some of it. I put Leah's Chap in my pocket and stand. "Yes."

"We need the key," Emery says. "It's a storage unit, and I saw them lock it."

I'm pretty sure I know where it is. Dad's compulsiveness isn't exactly helping him these days. He's telegraphing his moves.

CHAPTER 23

We walk together into the house like we have a million times before. Mom greets us in the kitchen. She smiles at Emery, small and hopeful. Sophie jumps on Em. She wipes her eyes and picks Sophie up, but it's cool because Mom would expect Em to be upset at a time like this.

"Oh, Emery. So good to see you." Mom gives her a hug.

"We're going out," I say.

"Okay. Not too late?" she asks, as if I have to give her permission.

My hand goes to the key rack. I put my studio key back on the hook and swipe Dad's key.

Mom rifles through her purse. "Here, you two can go out for dinner if you want." She pulls out her wallet and hands me sixty dollars. "You have your cell, right?"

I pull my phone out of my pocket and wave it at her as we head out.

"Okay. Allie?"

I slow.

"Be careful. Okay?"

I turn but don't want to see her shaking hands or her twitching eyes. I don't want to see the signs of her relief at not having to deal with me anymore tonight. This is what we do. This is one of our lies. She pretends I don't know, and I pretend I don't care. It's stupid and pointless, but we're stuck, looping. I just nod.

The cold air smacks me as Em and I walk to her car, the silence enveloping us. Emery turns the radio to my favorite station. It's a concession, definitely. She likes hip-hop and techno. I like alternative. We used to fight about it all the time. Her giving in is sort of sweet but also sad, because it just spotlights that we are tip-toeing around one another.

Green Day's "Good Riddance" starts playing. My eyes slide to take Emery in. She's sitting, straight backed. Sunglasses cover her eyes despite the gray day. Her nose is red. She drapes her hand across her mouth.

I remember the last time we heard this song together. It was the last day of school. The colors were so different then. Summer colors, all reds and blues and crisp whites. Anything was possible. We were going to be juniors.

I got in the car and flipped the station just as the song came on. Clearly I'd won the last round of station choices. She made a face and went to change it, but I put my hand over hers. "Please?" I asked. "It's perfect."

She laughed. "Okay, Allie. It kind of is."

"Hey, you got any mints?" I reached for the glove compartment door.

"No, wait!" she called out.

But it was too late. I opened the door and a small white bag fell by my feet.

"I was going to tell you," Emery said. "I swear."

I opened the bag and pulled out three packs of birth control pills. I held them up for her to see. "Tell me what? Or who? Or when?" I asked.

Emery reached for them. "It's no big deal."

I should have pushed her, but I was upset. She didn't trust me. She didn't tell me.

Looking back, that's when there started to be space between us. We became two different people—those who have and those who haven't. I was squarely in the haven't circle. She'd moved on.

The space grew after the party and her hookup with Max, no question. But it started with that first secret taking up space, like a cancer, strangling all the life around it. Dr. Ziggler was right about lies killing you.

I make myself focus on the present. "How do you know where my paintings are?"

"I watched the movers take them." She turns the wheel, navigates traffic, pointing her car in the direction of the industrial park. "I came to see if… I wanted to talk to your parents. I saw someone taking them."

My head feels like it's in a vice. "Just you?" I ask.

"No."

"Oh."

"Allie, when we heard, we both came. It wasn't planned."

The two of them together. Again.

"It's never going to happen again. I promise. Neither one of us wants it to."

The words kill me, as do the visions of the two of them together. I shake my head to clear them. I'm back to not caring about what happened with Emery and the mystery man. Because I already know what happened with her and Max. And it makes me sick.

"I know it was wrong," Emery pleads, "but we didn't mean for it to happen."

"I can't talk about this." I turn away.

"Okay." Emery nods her head repeatedly.

"Tell me about the paintings," I say to the window.

"I was waiting outside…to talk to your Mom or something, you know?"

"And…"

"I saw a moving truck pull up. Two men got out. One guy pulled a key chain out of his pocket. It had the pink Con on it." She stops. An actress pause for effect. "I recognized your studio key, so I knew they were there for your paintings. So we…"

"You and Max."

"Yes. We watched them load your paintings, then followed the truck to the storage place."

I put my head against the window. What I wouldn't give to go back to June. I'd make her tell me who she got the birth control to be with. We'd still be besties. I wouldn't have gone to the party. She wouldn't have gotten with Max. To think, all this misery might never have been if I had just been more persistent. Or if she had been more open. The lies are killing us. Slow and painful.

Emery pulls into the U-Store It facility and parks out front. "It's around the side, over there."

I get out of the car, shocked again by the cold, pulling my jacket around me. A gust of wind makes us bend forward and walk faster. I watch Emery's long legs and wish for the hundredth time that I was exotic looking like her. Even in the cold, she looks lean and strong and inviting. No wonder Max wanted her.

"You have the key?"

I reach in my pocket and hand it to Em.

She takes her gloves off to open the lock. As the lock slips open, I feel my heartbeat go crazy. I just hope they're here. That they're all here.

"Ready?"

I nod.

She lifts the bay door and stands back so I can go first. The light from outside is only enough see the sides of canvases and framed pictures stacked against the wall. They didn't throw them out. But something's wrong. There are too many. Almost double.

"Where is the…" Em says. Then a light switches on.

My eyes drift to the sides of the storage unit. Paintings are propped up against the walls, three to four deep. Oils. I kneel down. The first is a field of wildflowers. Whoever painted this used a similar palette to the one I used to use. Monet's palette: titanium white, cadmium yellow, viridian green, ultramarine, cobalt blue, crimson, and vermillion. My breath catches. I look at the tiny brushstrokes. The shadows are done in greens and purples. I could have painted these when my colors were pure.

"Who did these?" Emery lifts a picture of a vase of flowers on a table. Vermillion and dandelion and tangerine are the base for the colors in that one. "They're amazing."

I look at the bottom of the canvas. The name is scrawled but legible: Karen Crenshaw. Mom.

"Oh," Emery says. "Did you know?"

I lift another. "Had no idea." First pain, then heat, then numb. How could she keep this from us? From me especially? She was a whole other person. Someone I should know. But don't. Someone who understands how violated I feel to have my paintings taken, because someone took hers. Dad? Did he do this to her? Did she surrender them willingly or fight to keep them?

"I guess you can tell where you get your talent from."

"Well, I never thought it was from Dad."

"You want to take your pictures out of here?" Emery asks. "I could keep them for you if you want."

"That's okay. I guess they're safe here. I mean, with Mom's and all."

"Yeah."

"It's not that I don't trust you or want you to have them… It's just I'm not worried about them anymore."

"It's cool."

"Let's go," I say.

"Okay." Emery waits for me, then turns out the light. I

take one last look at the paintings as Emery starts to lower the door.

"Wait!" She stops. I run back in and grab one of Mom's small paintings. A tree on a blue background. It looks almost biblical. Somehow she made the colors look translucent, like stained glass. I run my fingers over it, tracing the leaves of the tree, the canopy. I'm not sure why I want it. I just do. Something of the other Mom that mine could have been. I nod to Emery, and she lowers and locks the door.

We rush back to the car, the wind having picked up and a drizzling rain making my cheeks burn, the picture cradled under my jacket.

"Emery," I say when she gets the car started. "Thanks."

"No problem."

"You think he made her give it up?" I ask.

"I don't know," she says. "Guys make you do awful things sometimes."

I think about that. It's true. But how is it true for Emery? Who made her do awful things? And what did he make her do?

"Emery," I start. "What's going on?"

She turns to me. Her mouth forms shapes, but she stops, and I get sad.

"You could…tell me anything. I mean, even after…"

"I know, Allie. But done is done."

If only it were. Sometimes done is only pushed down deep, waiting to be discovered. I could tell Emery that, but I'm not sure she'd believe me.

My cell vibrates.

R u ok? Nick.

Yes.

"Who's that?" Emery asks.

"Nick."

Can I see you?

Emery takes a jagged little breath. "Cool," she says.

BLP 10 mins?

Yes

"He wants to meet me at Back Lake Park. Can you drop me there?" I lean back and close my eyes. I don't open them again until I feel Emery's car crunch on the gravel entrance to the park. I'm worried about seeing him. Will he be mad still? I remember the last time I was here with him, just a week ago. It seems so much longer than that.

"Don't you want me to wait?" Em asks.

Nick's car pulls in.

"No. I'm fine."

"You going back to school on Monday?"

"Yeah. I think so."

"Do you want to ride with me?"

I open my door and slide out. I shake my head. "No."

"I wish I could go back in time and change things, Al. I really do." Tears cascade down her face. No clean actress tears, full-out ugly tears. Make-your-face-swell tears. I should be impressed.

"I know." I shut the door and turn away. "But you can't. No one can."

I walk to Nick's car, my feet feeling as if they're weighed down. I want to see him, but I don't want to have this conversation. He knows how much I screwed up. He tried to tell me. But I didn't listen. I wish I'd told him I wouldn't meet him. But that's ridiculous. I'll see him on Monday. May as well grow up and take my medicine.

I open the door to the passenger side, and Nick pulls me in and against him.

"Allie, I'm so glad you're okay. I was so worried." He takes my face in his hands and looks me over. "Are you all right?"

"Mostly," I say.

"I'm sorry about hanging up on you. I feel so bad about that—"

"It wasn't the reason…"

"I just—"

"Stop. It wasn't you. You were right."

"I should have come over to see you. I should have tried to help."

"You couldn't."

Nick leans back in his seat. "So what happens next?"

"They want me to take medication. You know, to make me less depressed."

He reaches out and holds my hand like Leah used to.

"Hey." Nick squeezes my hand. "It's okay."

"I'm scared to take their meds. I have no idea if it'll work."

"You should try. If you're having that hard a time of it, you should."

"I don't know. What if they change me?"

"Didn't the other stuff you were taking change you?"

I nod. He's right. Taking John Strickland's and Mom's meds did change me. Even the cough medicines did. "It's just that they seemed more manageable. More in my control. I knew they would wear off, and when they did, I'd still be the same underneath. I don't know if that makes sense; it's just how I felt."

"It does make sense, but if you're in charge of your doses, then you can take too much too. I've never had anything horrible happen to me. I've never lost anyone I loved. But when you went in the hospital…"

He cups my chin and pulls me to him. He kisses me. And I let him. Until I don't. I pull away.

"I can't. I need some time."

"I'm sorry. I shouldn't have."

He holds my hand again, and it feels good. Maybe this medicine would help me forget. Maybe it would be a way back for me?

Or maybe not.

Maybe it would dull the colors. Make me fat. Take the last of Leah from me. I hated that her ghost lorded over me. But at least she was here.

I grab my purse to pull out my lip gloss, and Mom's painting stares me in the face. I almost forgot about it. I hold it in front of me, careful with it as if it were made of glass.

"Hey, what's that?" Nick asks.

I hand it to him. And I start to get nervous. Which is weird because it's not like I painted this. But still, watching Nick assess my mother's art is scary. I want him to like it.

"This isn't yours?"

"No."

"The colors are similar to what you do, but the technique's different."

"It's my mom's."

"I didn't know she was an artist."

"Neither did I. Till earlier today."

"Wow. She was good. Really good. She still paint?"

"I've never seen her. So, no."

"Why would she stop?"

I try not to, but I start to cry. It's all too much. Why didn't I know about this? What made Mom stop? Suddenly all the things she lied about on a daily basis seem like nothing compared to this huge mountainous lie. How could she? Why would she? Why did she stop painting? Did the pills make her?

"I don't know. I wish I did," I say. True.

"I'm sorry. Hey, you hungry?"

As if cheesy pizza and an icy Coke would fix everything. I do the math. It's Sunday night. Not too many people out tonight.

"Yeah. Kind of."

"Let's go then." Nick starts his car. I don't know a lot about cars or care for that matter, but something about the sound of the Mustang's engine makes me feel protected by him.

———◇———

Mom walks into my bedroom. "Here, Allie, your pill." She puts it on my desk with a glass of water.

I look up from my book, *The Alchemist* for English. "Thanks."

"How are you doing?" she asks.

"Okay." I go back to reading.

"You nervous about going back to school tomorrow?"

"Yes," I say before I line up my defenses.

She sits on my bed. I want to crawl into her lap and tell her I know about her paintings. But I don't. My lips are numb, like my heart. And for some reason, I think about when she used to read to us when we were little. If I concentrate hard, I can hear her laugh—her laugh this time, not Leah's, but just as ghost-like and far away. I wonder what made her stop laughing and painting.

"Ask her." I hear Leah. It's like all of a sudden, she's become my intuition.

"Mom?" I decide to try an alternate route. A test. "Do you ever wish you hadn't married Dad?"

"Oh, Allie, of course not."

"Seriously, Mom, I want to know."

"If I hadn't married your father, I wouldn't have had you." She smooths the hair out of my eyes. I pull away. I don't want bullshit from her anymore. I want real. Even if I'm a liar, I want my mother to tell the truth.

"I'm serious, Allie. You and Leah are the best things I've done."

I let her words settle into me. Could she really mean that? I think about the paintings in the storage unit, and I want to understand why she stopped. I don't get how you could be so good at something, love it entirely, then lock it away in a storage unit. Does she ever visit her paintings? Does she wish she were painting now? I want to ask her these things. But I don't.

"I'm glad you saw Emery and Nick last night. You have such good friends. You always have. That's another thing I've always loved about you."

I hope she doesn't bring up Max.

"Have you seen Max yet? I thought for sure he'd be over."

And just like that, it hits me like a blow to the stomach.

"He has a big swim thing. He's been gone." Lie.

Her face relaxes. "Oh, I'm sure he'll be over as soon as he can."

"Yeah. Mom, I've gotta finish this."

Mom gets up, goes to my desk, grabs the pill and water. She hands them to me. I put the pill in the back of my mouth and secure it with my tongue. I'm getting good at not taking pills these days. I'm almost legend at it.

"Not too late," she says as she leaves my room.

Lying in my bed, looking out the window, I try not to think about Max. It shouldn't be about him anymore. But there's no escaping him. He's been in my life and my heart for so long, it's hard to flush him out completely. I would if I could, because just the mention of his name makes me feel as if I'm falling. I pull out my phone, go through a series of buttons, and unblock Max.

My phone vibrates.

I hope it's not Max. Lie.

Hi Nick.

I'm grateful. Lie. It's better this way. Lie. I don't want to see him again. Lie.

Hi Urself I type back.

My phone vibrates again. Then again. Then again. I see the backload of Max messages waiting for me. My finger hesitates over them. I could just click and see what he said. I could let his words take care of me. I could let Max take care of me. Instead, I surprise the shit out of myself and shift my attention to the new text that Nick just sent.

How r U?

Ok. Nervous about coming back.

I bet. But I'll be there for you. Piper will.

I pray he doesn't mention Emery or Max. Then, of all the timing, there's a knock at my window, and I know it's Max. My heart beats faster. I want him. I still want him. And he's there, perched on the roof under my window. All remorseful. Maybe I could have him now. Maybe I should let him in. He'd be mine at least for the moment. Would that be enough?

"Allie…" Max's voice cracks. Even his crackly voice makes me want him. Even if he's not good for me. Even if he breaks my heart.

My phone vibrates. Nick.

Srsly. Don't b nervous. U can do this. Piece of cake. Or cupcakes. Hey we could do cupcakes!

Max knocks on the window again. "Please…" I need to tune him out and walk away. Nick. He wants me. I'm not sure I want him, but he wants me. Me. I scroll through my Max messages. The ones I had blocked because I knew I wasn't strong enough to stand up to him. *He loves me. He's sorry.*

He'll change. He wants me. Except I know none of these words change anything.

Max doesn't leave. He waits for me on the ledge outside my window. He thinks I'll give in to him like I always do. I want to. He's my warrior when he's not off chasing some other girl. Should one night, one mistake, make that much of a difference?

"Just let me talk to you…" he pleads. "You won't answer my calls or texts. Don't send me away now."

I look at Max and wonder why I can't let him go. Why Nick can't be enough for me.

"Allie…"

I put my hands on the window. I see the pain in his eyes. But I can't stop it. I can't save him.

"Just open up, Allie. Let me see you for a minute. Please."

I wish I could help him, but how do I save Max without losing myself?

"Good-bye, Max. I can't be friends with you. It's killing me, and I'm not doing that anymore." True.

I walk straight into my bathroom and shut the door, open the medicine cabinet. Nothing. I drop to my knees and open the doors under the sink, reach to the back of the cabinet. My hand finds the back roll of the toilet paper stash. My heart races as I reach into the center of the rolls and my fingers find the bottle. I stand, bottle in hand, and turn from the mirror as I open the cough medicine, bringing the mouth of the bottle to my lips.

I close my eyes and drop the bottle in the sink. I don't want to do this anymore. My legs get rubbery, and I slide to the floor.

My phone vibrates.

Can't wait to see u tomorrow. Nick. I'm bringing some of my pictures to paint from. U want to also?

I nod my head, even though he can't see. Yeah. Pictures. He's right. I push off the floor and go back into my room. There's a small filing cabinet at the back of my closet with my pictures. All the ones I've taken over the years. I pull out the thick files and pour them on the floor in front of me until I'm buried in them. But being buried in my art feels pretty good.

I swear I almost hear Leah in my mind, laughing, saying "Good one, Al." But I know it's just my memory of her.

The first pictures are of our vacation at Cape Cod. I was twelve. She was thirteen going on fourteen. Almost all the poses are of her trying to show off her new boobs. I can hear her laughing.

"Don't be jealous of me because I'm beautiful," she said.

"You're messed up."

She sucked in her stomach and twirled. "This year's going to be the best!"

I remember thinking she was right. I had started to get good at painting. Dad built my studio. I took pictures of the rocks on the beach, the cedar shingles on the houses, the different colored flowers, huge and beautiful. In two months, they'd be gone. But the summer was theirs.

"You're such a dork! Take pictures of me. People are going to want to know one day what I was like. I need a record. You can keep me real."

That was the last time I remember us all being happy together. That vacation in Cape Cod. More snapshots. A piece of Leah's skirt as she twirls, the green-gray-blue cedar plank with parts of it chipped away and other parts weathered dark gray. One of the rocks on the beach, the water spraying up between them. A close-up of a huge hydrangea. The most optimistic flowers ever. And I know. This is the picture I'm going to paint in class tomorrow. The Cape Cod colors. The color of easy laughs and belief. The color of on the brink. And new paths. The color of hope. I curl up on my bed.

My cell rings.

Im sorry. Max.

I know he is. But just because he's sorry doesn't mean I have to let him get in the way of me and my art. I turn my phone off. And go to sleep.

"Good one, Al." Leah's voice is the last thing I hear as I drift off, making me smile.

CHAPTER 24

We pull up to Dr. Applegate's office.

I start to get ridiculously nervous. I start to sweat. I'm scared to see her. Like I'm all open and raw, and she'll be able to see through me. All the way through. And I have no idea what I'm going to do with that.

This time I catch the receptionist, iPod earbuds in, jamming out. I wonder what she's listening to. I almost ask her, but I don't. Just like I don't ask anything I really want to know.

"Simple Plan," she offers.

"Oh, cool."

"I know it's so old school, it's lame. But I like it."

"Me too."

She smiles at me. And for once I don't think judgy thoughts about her. Who knows why she keeps herself small? She might have her reasons.

"She'll be with you in a sec."

"Thanks."

Mom comes in from parking the car. "You want me to go in with you?"

"No."

"What are those pictures for?"

"Something for art class. I was just thinking of what to do with them."

"May I?"

I don't want to. When she didn't tell me about her paintings, she built a wall. Why should I be the one to scale it? She holds out her hand. It's like when she held my hand in the car. Maybe this could be like that. I give her my pictures and hold my breath.

"I remember these," she says. "Cape Cod. What are you going to do with these?"

"I don't know. I'm going to put them all together somehow." I reach out so we are holding the pictures together. "I was thinking I'd take some of the hydrangea, here, and put it with the cedar and the rocks. And Leah." I layer the pictures sort of how I see it in my head.

"That's going to be beautiful. Have you thought about the colors?"

Of course I have. It's all I've been thinking about. If I can find them. If they'll come back to me. Right now, all I've got are the ones in the pictures. I hope that's enough to help me find the colors underneath it all—the ones about the feelings.

"Dr. Applegate is ready for you," the receptionist says.

I walk in, my legs a little steadier, although I feel like it's a little surreal talking about my art with Mom, knowing she really gets what I'm trying to do.

"Hello, Allie." Dr. Applegate is wearing all black today. Pants with a cashmere sweater. There's a white rose pin on her sweater.

The stark white reminds me of her manly art. But on her, it's pretty. And I start to feel better about trusting her.

"I spoke with Dr. Ziggler."

"I figured."

"You had a rough weekend?"

"Yeah."

"He recommended you go on medication."

"I know."

"The same meds I want you to take. How do you feel about that?"

I start chewing on my nail. Should I tell her I don't want to take the medicine? I don't want to lie to her. I don't know. I'm stuck. I notice she's brought a light-blue lamp in. It sits on her desk. A smile sneaks onto my face.

"You like my lamp?" she asks.

"It's perfect. Just the right color."

"High praise from you. Now let's work on you. Tell me what you want."

I want my sister back. I want my art back. I want me back.

"Let's talk about the pills. Pros and cons."

I try to listen to her. Really listen. She thinks I should. Maybe she's right. I let her words wash over me like the colors used to. As I do, I picture Leah. What would she think? What would she do? And I realize, it doesn't matter what she would do. This is my life. My choice.

When she's done talking, I tell her, "No pills. Not yet. I want to try this without them."

"You realize that the best treatment for depression is a combination of medication and counseling?"

"I'm not depressed."

"I've got to keep recommending the medication for you, Allie. I think it's best."

I think about arguing, but it won't change anything. "Can we just do the relaxation exercises? They really help."

"Okay, Allie."

I close my eyes and listen to her voice, but truthfully, I'm already there. I almost expect to see Leah, but I don't. Surprisingly, I'm a little grateful. It's nice to be alone and quiet. I'm in the ocean. I look up and see a bright-blue sky with puffy, white clouds. I can almost feel the water, cool and silky on my skin. I feel the waves nudging my legs and holding me up. I'm floating and free.

Dr. Applegate's voice caresses my body like a massage. "Look around. I want you to remember what it looks like. I want you to remember what it feels like where you are now."

I go even deeper in my mind to that totally safe place where I'm in the water, the sun beating down on me, the sounds of the lazy waves filling my ears. I remember being here the last time I felt completely safe. And then I hear her. Just her laughter at first. From that day. The day we took the pictures. Swimming with Leah.

"Told you I'd help you find your colors," her voice comes to me. I hear her like she's right in front of me. Because she is. Her hair fans out in the water, like a lily pad floating there.

"So this is it. All that's left of me," Leah says. "Look how deep you have to go to find me."

"No pills," I say. "I can't. They almost killed me."

She turns and walks away. I watch her fade into the light. I feel bad. I should want to bring her back. Shouldn't I?

But this is my life.

My life doesn't have to be about military strategy, doesn't have to be about taking pills and bringing Leah back. It could be about finding my art and connecting to Mom. And forgiving Leah.

For killing herself.

———◇———

Mom stays silent on the way to school. We pull up front. I unhook my seat belt.

"No. It's okay," I say. "I don't need you to walk me in."

She hesitates, then shakes her head. She pulls out and drives around to the visitor parking spaces. "I'm going to anyway."

As I go to get out of the car, she puts her hand on my arm. "You sure about going back already?" she asks.

"I have to keep going." I pull the handle and open the door.

"Okay."

Mom puts her hand on my backpack and guides me to Student Services. Mrs. Williams, the secretary at the desk, nods at me. "Allie, so glad to see you."

"Hi," I say. It's hard to go back to school, where everyone knows how stupid I am.

"I have a note somewhere..." Mom rummages in her purse, which, as usual, is a huge mess.

She produces the hospital discharge papers. Mrs. Williams smiles at Mom, a small, understanding sort of smile. I am grateful to her for that. Mom could use a little understanding. She never got any from Dad. Or Leah. Or me. Mrs. Williams switches to her computer screen and adds *E* to all my absences: Excused. She returns the papers to Mom and fills out a yellow excused-absence slip for me to take to my teachers.

"We're in second period now, Allie, almost third," she says.

Mom hands me a Coke and a package of cheese peanut butter crackers, the kind she never lets us eat because she says it's junk food.

"Okay, thanks. Bye, Mom."

I make sure Mom's left the building before detouring. I've got no intentions of going to second. That's one lie I can live with. I shouldn't have to do everything hard, especially not U.S. history hard.

CHAPTER 25

I spend the rest of second period in the bathroom. I think I see John Strickland once on the way to art, but he doesn't seem to see me, and he disappears into the crowd. When I get to third period, Nick is there, waiting for me. He gives me a half-smile, as if he's checking the temperature of my mood and adjusting to it. Maybe I underestimated first basemen.

"Hi." I make my way across the room.

"You okay?" he asks as he wipes mascara from under my eye. Tiny flecks of black cling to his skin. I'm changing his colors. I don't want to be responsible for his when I can't even find mine.

"I'm a mess," I say.

"That's okay."

Nick's arm slung around my shoulder, I check out the setup of the room.

"So today, we paint?"

"Guess so." I fan out my pictures on the table. He reaches into his backpack and hands his to me. Then he picks mine up and looks at them, one at a time. The room starts to feel smaller, and I start to sweat. Will he think I'm stupid? That I picked something stupid to paint?

I flip through his two at a time. Baseball fields; diamonds;

bases, battered and worn. Up-close pitchers' mounds. I wonder where he's going with this. I drop two of his pictures and reach down to get them, worried I'll have them out of order when I hand them back. Order matters to him.

"Sorry." I give them back.

"It's fine." He flashes me a smile and then jogs to the cabinet, grabbing paints for his palette.

"Okay, let's get started," Mr. Kispert says as he walks in the room, making all the talking around us grind to a halt.

Piper bounces in, late but confident. She gives me an understanding look that feels nice coming from her. "Glad to have you back, Allie. Painting with Nick makes me feel like I'm painting in the guys' locker room."

Nick protests, but I laugh.

"The important thing..." Mr. Kispert walks to the back of the room and starts pacing like he's a general sending his freshman and sophomore troops into battle. "Is that you really throw yourself into this project. No pressure."

There's nervous laughter from the front of the room as the drawing and painting kids sketch.

"Little suck-ups," Nick grunts.

"Seriously." Piper starts sketching.

The next few minutes crawl by. I grab paints and try to assemble my palette, but nothing comes. I see flashes of colors, but I know they're straight from the pictures. Not from me. I figure it's a good enough place to start. I mix a reasonable iris blue. Then a periwinkle. And a cerulean. Mix in some snow white, whitewash, and three different shades of gray: argent, charcoal, and cedar grove. Leah's hair and her skirt are the same color: chocolate brown with fuchsia highlights. And black-blue lowlights. It's a representation of that day, the three pictures combined. But nothing about the emotions. Technique-wise, I'm fine. Emotionally, I'm screwed. I try not to panic. Maybe I can't do this clean?

My eyes slide to Nick, who is painting with work-shirt blue and baseball-mitt brown, field green, and rust. He's got one paintbrush in his teeth and another in his hand. He's leaning forward, his fingers clutching a slim brush. One spot of whitewash has made it on his face. He must feel my stare, because he looks at me.

He lifts his eyebrows like he's asking if I'm okay. I nod. I'm not okay. Not even close. I'm lost. And alone. And done.

"Time to wash up," Mr. Kispert announces.

Nick finishes his last few strokes and comes over, carrying his brushes. "You look upset." He looks at my painting. I wish he'd stop. Having him see my mess makes me feel like puking.

I point to my canvas. "It sucks."

"It doesn't suck. You're just starting. You'll get it."

"I'm sorry, it's just… I mean, obviously…"

Mr. Kispert comes over. "You guys working through lunch? No problem if you want to."

"Yeah. She is. Thanks," Nick says for me. "You just need to slow down and let it come to you. You've got the perspective right. Now you just have to work on the rest of—"

"The colors are wrong."

Piper steps in. "They're not wrong. They're just not all there. It's like I'm not sure how this painting is supposed to make me feel yet."

She's exactly right.

Nick puts his hand on my shoulder. "You use color to set the mood better than anyone I know. You'll get this."

I blush. It's nice that Nick gets my work, but he can't help me. If I'm going to be honest with myself, I wish I had some pharmaceutical backup. Because with the drugs, Leah came and lent me her colors. Even if they weren't mine, they were a direction. And right now I feel like I'm on the ragged edge, very close to losing it all.

"You're not used to being patient." He sits on the top of one of the tables. "It's always come so easy for you. Happens in baseball too. Sometimes you lose your rhythm. You just have to get it back."

Is he right? Have I taken art for granted this whole time? If I relax, will it come to me? I look at my painting. I look at the pictures I brought with me. I close my eyes and remember that day. Freedom. Possibilities. Hope. What's the color of hope? I've honestly got no idea.

He winks and backpedals out the door.

Piper stays for a moment longer. "Nick's right. You'll get it."

She leaves, and I know I should too. Because staying here, staring at this thing, isn't helping.

"You doing better, Allie?" Mr. Kispert sits at his desk, facing me, spooning yogurt into his mouth.

"Honestly?"

"You stay and work through lunch if you like."

I work on my painting, but the bell's about to ring for sixth period. I'm closer to what I want but not there.

I take my brushes back to the sink. As I'm washing them out, I look over and see Mr. Kispert looking at my work. My stomach tenses. I don't want him to know that I'm not good enough. But I also don't want him to tell me it's beautiful, because if he did that, I'd know that he was lying all the other times he said I was talented. I don't want Mr. Kispert to lie to me. In here, with my art, I'm all about truth.

"This is a good start," he says. "The colors are much closer than your first attempt."

I join him as he appraises my work.

"The blues and whites are fine. And the gray is perfect," he says.

My eyes scan each color as he names them.

"It seems as if you're missing some though."

"Yes," I say.

"I'm not sure which."

"I know."

"You need to figure out your point of view for this painting. What you want it to say."

I wonder if he's disappointed in me and my work. I hope he's not sorry he put me in this class.

"This is an excellent start."

I sigh, relieved. Maybe I can do this.

"You've got to get to class. I can't let you stay here all day." He goes to help some other students set up, passing Nick, who has returned.

"How do you feel about it now?" he asks, standing, his hands on his hips, studying my painting.

"Better. But not great. Do you ever worry you can't do this?"

"No. And neither should you. Art isn't something you can question. You need to know you're good. Even when you're stumbling. You need to believe it's going to come to you."

"I guess."

"Look, Allie, watching you get where you're going is half the fun. Your whiffs are better than most people's home runs. It's not a level playing field. It just isn't."

"Thanks."

"You're tough." He pulls me by my hand, away from my painting and out the door. "Can I give you a ride home?"

I stop. He does too. "Nick, I just can't right now. You know. I am just in a weird place…"

"It's okay. Friends can walk each other to class, can't they?"

———————◦———————

We pull up in front of my house. I keep going over my painting, trying to piece together what's already there and what needs to be added.

"See you tomorrow," Nick says.

"Thanks for the ride."

"Sure thing."

I walk up the steps to the front of my house. He toots the horn. I turn to wave. I just need some time alone to work this through. I find Mom waiting for me. This can't be good.

"Hi," I say, dropping my backpack on the floor.

"I want to talk to you."

This is bad. She never wants to talk.

"Okay, but I've got a ton of homework, so can we talk while I eat?" I try to walk by her into the kitchen, but she blocks my way, one hand pointing to the living room. What did I do? What lie will I have to explain?

"Allie, please sit down." She motions to the couch in the living room, the one we were never allowed to sit on. Dad's spot.

"You're scaring me," I say. True.

"I'm sorry. I'm not doing this well." She shifts her position and then gets up. "I need to get something."

I don't know what I'm so scared of. After all that's happened, what could she say that would make any of it worse?

A few moments later, Mom comes in holding her painting. The one I took. "I found this in your room."

First, I register fear. She knows. Then outrage. How did she find it? And finally, the worst feeling of all: loss—overpowering and strong. She hid the best part of herself from me.

"I guess…" she finally says. "I guess you found them."

"Guess so." I look down so I won't yell at her. That won't help. But I want to ask her how she could give it up. Instead I say, "It's beautiful."

Her face softens. Her eyes linger over the trees in the picture. She smiles, small but real. "It was always my favorite."

I stand. "Why did you stop painting, Mom?"

"I don't know. I just…"

"Just what? You were good. You were incredible."

"It may be hard for you to understand. Sometimes in life, you have to make choices. That's all."

I close the distance between us. I need to hear her explanation. My mom didn't have to be like this: deadened and broken. She could have been the way her paintings were: beautiful and alive. "So tell me," I say.

"It was a long time ago."

"Was it Dad? Did he make you?" *Sometimes guys make you do awful things*, Emery told me. And it's true.

"Dad had his reasons."

Fire builds inside me. He did it. I knew it. He's always doing things like this. And now I know he killed my mother.

"I was obsessed with it. I got carried away…" She rubs her hands on her legs.

"Of course you did. I saw how good you were." Does she think I wouldn't get that? I'm on her side. She's an artist. Like me. We get lost sometimes. It happens.

"You don't understand. It was too much. I couldn't paint and watch you two…"

The world closes in on me. It wasn't Dad who stopped her. It was me. And Leah. "What are you talking about, Mom?"

"It was so long ago. Why should we talk about it now?"

"Tell me." I need to know. I need to hear the truth. Did Leah and I kill Mom?

"I was painting. I was working on a scene. I was really into it. You were a year and a half old. Leah was almost three. You were sleeping in your crib. I guess you were crying, and I didn't hear you."

I nod to keep her going.

"Leah went to help you. She got you out of your crib." Mom lifts a hand to her forehead and rubs her brow. "And she couldn't find me. I was in the garage looking for one of my paints. I couldn't find it, and I needed that color. Just then."

Like me earlier today—sometimes when you're locked in, you can't pull yourself out. For anyone. Mom's telling the truth.

"It's okay, just say it."

"Leah took you outside."

"Oh, Mom…"

"I was crazy looking for you by the time your father came home. Jessica from down the street…" Mom makes a face. She used to call her *that Jessica* when she was talking to Dad. "She walked you back. She said she found you two in the street…"

"But we were okay."

"But you might not have been. Something could've happened to you, and it would have been my fault."

I see Mom's struggle, and I know what she's thinking. She's thinking she doesn't deserve us. But she's wrong. Everyone makes mistakes. She shouldn't have to pay forever for one mistake. "But we were okay," I say again.

"He told me I had to get a grip. Be a real mother to you two. He wasn't wrong. So I let him pack up my paintings and put them in storage."

"You know what, Mom? He's a bully." I can envision how that whole conversation went down. Dad scared. Then mad. Then nuclear. Dad did this. Mom screwed up, but he could have handled it a different way. Hired help. Gotten her a studio. Instead he killed her a little at a time. Because when you're an artist, every day you don't paint or sculpt or draw kills you.

"I didn't want you to know. Or to think I loved art more than I loved you two."

"We would never…"

"But you know, I think Leah remembered. After that, she always looked at me like she didn't trust me. Like she was waiting for me to screw up again."

"That was just the way Leah was."

"Maybe."

"Mom, whatever happened, you need to start painting again."

"You're not mad at me then?"

"For making a mistake, no. For giving up, yes."

Mom smiles a little.

"Can I ask you something? Why did Leah start going to Dr. Gates to begin with?"

Her face falls, and she shakes her head.

"No more lies, Mom. I need to know."

"Do you remember winter break two years ago? You went skiing with Emery's family for the week?"

I nod.

"That was her first attempt."

"What?" I sit down on the couch and put my head in my hands to stop the world from spinning around me. I know we talked about it, but I never thought she'd really do it, and I kind of thought she was doing it for me, like it was a sister thing. A bond or a promise, not a threat. How did I not know Leah was that sick?

"She begged us not to tell you."

"Why?" I mumble through my fingers.

"Why what?"

"Why did she try to do it?"

Mom sits beside me and slides her arm around me in a hug. "Leah was depressed. She wouldn't take her medication. And breaks were hard for her. It was like the minute she stopped dancing or working or studying, she got incredibly sad. Like, the minute she stopped moving, it took her over."

I lift my head. "I didn't have to go with Emery. I could have stayed home."

"Were you going to be her bodyguard her whole life? Leah didn't want that. Neither did we."

And once again, my whole world feels like it's crumbling. I didn't know. They didn't tell me. Leah lied to me. "How did she do it?"

"She took one of my bottles of Xanax. Took all the pills. We found her in time."

Anger covers me in a suit of armor. "So let me get this straight:

my sister tries to kill herself, and nobody thinks I deserve to know about it?"

"You're right. We should have told you. But Leah insisted. And we thought it was a good idea."

"Because suicide is contagious?"

Mom looks at me. "No. Of course not."

"And you kept the medication around after that? After all that?"

"No. I got a safe for it. I kept it locked up. And Dad bought drug test kits for her. For a while we made her take them."

I think about how stressed Mom and Dad were when I got back from the ski trip with Emery's family. I remember thinking Mom and Dad were stressed because of their marriage, but it was really about Leah. She was the one who told me Dad was making Mom take drug tests. When she was angry at Dad, it was because he saved her and was making her take drug tests rather than punishing him for what he did to Mom. Leah lied again. Why am I surprised? I need some truth to balance out the lies. My head needs a due north. So does my heart.

"How did Leah get the drugs this time? I saw the bottle. They were yours."

Mom sighs. "She picked them up at the pharmacy that night. Walgreens called and left a message on our machine that day. Maybe she heard it. Maybe she knew I'd seen my therapist the day before. I don't know. It was at the twenty-four-hour one. She picked them up that night. I never thought she'd do that. Went through the drive-through. They should've asked for her license to confirm it was me, but the guy working was new and didn't do that."

Leah always had a plan. She did. Our battle plan may have been bogus, but hers was always solid. Those pills plus the alcohol equals suicide.

"There is nothing you could have done to stop her," Mom says.

I stare at the painting on the coffee table. Mom's painting. She's right. I know she is, but the lies haven't helped either. I think of the biggest lie I told Leah and then Mom and Dad, and all of a sudden, I feel like a big fraud.

"I was never going to do it," I tell her.

"I know, honey."

"No. I mean, it was just something we talked about some-times. I mean, I know you know about it, but I only went along with it because I never thought she would either. I would have stopped her if I'd thought she was serious. And my 'attempt' wasn't that. I messed up. I was trying to stop the hurt, but I never wanted to kill myself."

We both sit there with the knowledge of all we wished we'd done and didn't, knowing none of it makes a difference now. None of that would bring Leah back. I need a change of con-versation. We all do.

"Did you ever get stuck? You know, when you were painting?"

"Of course. Everyone does. When you first start, it's so easy. You find what you need almost like magic. But as you get better, it gets harder."

I nod. That's exactly it.

"And you're going through a very hard year…"

I blink back tears. She's right. But that doesn't help.

"You know what I used to do when I was stuck?"

I shrug, not trusting my voice.

"Sometimes the canvas seemed too confining. So I'd paint on other surfaces."

I think about my room. Leah's ring. Maybe that's what I was doing. Trying to become unstuck.

"I drove my mother crazy. I painted on everything and anything—clothes, my wall, the bathroom counter."

"I can't imagine Grandma being okay with that."

"She was actually. She knew I had to get whatever I was working out out of me. You do too. Especially after Leah…"

"So I can paint on every surface in the house?"

"Everything but the dog."

"Won't that piss off Dad?"

She reaches in her pocket, pulls out a shiny new key, and puts it on the table. At first I don't believe what I'm seeing. She waits for her bombshell to register and then says, "He doesn't have a say in how we live our lives in this house. I'm going to make dinner. It'll be ready in an hour."

She leaves the room, and I'm almost tempted to clap, except I'm totally floored—in a good way. How I always felt after watching Leah dance. I want to stand and yell *brava*! But she's already gone. Cue the curtain. Karen Blackmore has left the stage.

The key looks like a magical object, as if it will open a doorway to another life, and it kind of will. If Mom can stand up to Dad, maybe I can stand to do something equally spectacular.

I go upstairs, my hand gripped around the key, feeling good. When I open the door, the replica of the ring I painted lights up with the sun sitting low on the horizon, just as it did the first time Leah came to me. I blink and rub my eyes. I know she's not coming. She never actually did. But that doesn't mean I can't tell our story. We were sisters with secrets, that's true, but we were sisters first and foremost.

I turn on my music and start to paint—small, big, and medium-sized flowers. All the same simple shape. Some I just outline and others I fill in. I try my best to match the colors of my memories of us together. I mix my palette to match the colors of Leah's favorite nail polishes, the ones I always borrowed. I'm a Pisa Work red for when we went to see *Scream 4*. Shatter Me for the time she and I went shopping for New Year's outfits. Hyacinth blue, my favorite Cape Cod color. When I'm finished with my creation, I stand back and look at what I've done. I'm happy with my new work in progress.

I'm just finishing up one of the flowers when my phone vibrates.

Hey. John Strickland. Can you meet me? I have something for you.

Why would he want to meet with me? Is meeting him really a good idea? But it's not like I can turn him down. He knew Leah even better than I did. If he wants to meet, I'm there.

Yes. Where?

I'm at the end of your street.

I race down the stairs. "Mom?"

She looks up from her cutting board. "Yeah?"

"I'll just be a few. Need to get some homework from a friend."

She pauses her chopping. "You want me to drive you?"

I give her a kiss on the cheek. "Nah. I'm good."

I walk down my street to his waiting Jeep. The beginnings of a cold drizzle are starting to fall. I pull my hood up and my jacket closed.

He puts his hand out the window and waves me over.

"Hey, Allie."

I walk over and lean in his window.

"Get in?" He nods to the passenger-side door. I almost hesitate. Who am I to get in a car alone with John Strickland? When I climb in next to him and shut the door, he says, "I want to give you something."

I put my hands up. "I'm not really doing that anymore…"

"I'm not talking pills, Allie. I'm never going to give you pills again. Seriously, don't ask. Not for you."

"So what…"

He reaches under the seat of his Jeep and hands me a small wooden box. It's red with blue-and-pink flowers carved into it. It seems familiar. Like I saw it a really long time ago. But I can't place it.

"It was hers. Leah's."

I'm suddenly transported back in time. My mind reaches for the memory, and it comes slowly, like pieces of a puzzle fitting together. She got it at one of the souvenir shops on the Cape when we were really little. It used to sit above her bed. One time when I was seven, I tried to look in it. And Leah grabbed it from me, protectively.

"Don't ever touch this. Ever."

"But what's in it?"

"My heart."

I pulled back.

"I could show you, but it's all bloody and still beating. Wanna see?" She chased me all over the house with it. I remember screaming the whole time. I didn't really believe her heart was in there. Not really. But now maybe I do.

My hands close around it.

"It's all I have left of her." He doesn't let go yet.

"I can't—"

"No. You should have it. Just, when you're done with it, if there's anything you don't want, can you give those things back?"

"You sure?"

"You answered something for me the other day—something that's been bothering me since she died. I needed to know if she took my pills. I'm glad she didn't." He leans forward and kisses me on the cheek. "Thank you," he whispers in my ear. I feel his stubble, rough and scratchy against my face. He releases the box and then leans back in his seat, pressing the heel of his hand into his eye. "I knew she was unhappy. I thought I was enough to help her."

I put my hand on his arm. "It's not your fault."

He brushes the hair off his face. "She gave me her phone." His voice is now choked up. "It's in the box."

"What?"

"Her phone. She gave it to me. Said I needed to keep it safe for her. That she didn't want to be tempted to answer Brittney or Sean's calls. She said she'd be back to get it the next day. But then…"

"I don't understand…"

"I should have known. She would have never given up her phone. I should have seen through what she was planning."

I look at him; his jaw is braced, misery on his face.

"It wasn't you. I…I was right next door. One room away… And…and I heard her. I heard her up but didn't do anything…"

He reaches out for me and holds me. "I wanted us to be together. I didn't want to be without her. I was better when she was with me."

I know exactly how he feels.

"We have to stop." I wipe my face. "We can't keep doing this. Leah did this. Not you. Not me."

"I know. I just miss her."

"Yeah."

We drive the three blocks to my house in silence. He parks out front.

"You're a sweetheart. I want you to know that," he says.

"Thanks for this." I show him the box. "Really."

"Some of it might be hard for you to see. I almost didn't give it to you because of that. But you have a right to know."

I reach forward and kiss him on the cheek, then rush out of the car to my front door. I turn and wave to him again. I want to be nice to him. He didn't have to give this to me. I know I should be grateful. Truthfully, I am. But more than that, I'm skating between scared to know and dying to find out.

———•———

Mom's on the phone when I come inside. I wonder to whom. She gives me a nod, then goes into her bedroom and shuts the door. I pick up Sophie and race up the stairs.

"Come here, girl. I could use a little company."

Once in my room, I lock the door and put on my music. Medium loud. Don't want Mom to come in to ask me to turn it down but loud enough that the rest of the house fades away. My hands shake.

I hold my breath and open the box and empty its contents till I'm covered in Leah's secrets. In addition to her cell, there are piles of pictures. And sticky notes and cards. The sticky notes are all different colors and sizes. One has a picture of a hand with the middle finger extended on it with the words *haha* written on it. Another says *Sorry I made you mad*. His writing. *You make me smile.* Hers. *Breaking up with U* with a tiny heart drawn next to it. Little bits of my sister and John Strickland. I pore over each one, trying to reconstruct the ghost of their relationship, one I didn't even know existed until after they were no longer a couple. I open the first card. It has two tiny hearts on the front.

You and Me written in her scrawly handwriting. *Xoxo, Leah.*

Another has a picture of a moose on the front. Inside, the

card read, *Moose be love*. And he wrote under it. *You know I do. Xoxo, 5gradecrush.* Glimpses of this boy who held my sister's heart are caught in these. I wonder if John Strickland put these in here to prove that Leah did love him. That he didn't make it up.

I leaf through the pictures. One of her posing in his bedroom. Sitting on his bed. Smiling. A totally free and easy and happy smile.

A picture of her from her fifth-grade class trip. She was standing in a group of girls. John on the sideline, looking over. On the back he wrote, *I've been into you for a long time.* Another one from that same trip. Leah on a tire swing. Posing for him.

There are a bunch of pressed and dried red and purple flowers, with leaves falling off them. A mate to the silver hoop earring he wears. A picture of Leah pointing to the silver ring on her finger and smiling broadly. The one she always wore. Was that ring from John?

He said he was her in-between guy. But looking at this, he was much more. I could see she felt safe with him. And I'm pretty sure that was not a feeling my sister experienced often.

My hand closes around her phone. John said he thought about not giving it to me.

I try to turn it on and it's dead. I climb off my bed and grab my charger. Plugged in, I power it up. The wallpaper picture of me and Leah takes my breath away. I keep going. I need to do this. The last text messages she exchanged were with Dad. My stomach drops. I get dizzy. I don't want to see those yet.

I can almost hear Leah's singsong voice, "Save the best for last."
I scroll down.

She texted 5grcrsh. I'm guessing John Strickland. Need u.

Him back to her: Where r u?

Her: Ill come to u.

Party going on. Come around back.

The next series of texts are from Brittney. After the party.

Tlk to me.

Please

Pick up

Before the party.

Whatcha wearing?

My hair sux

Mine 2

Urs never does

xoxoxo

I look at these texts, and something suddenly makes sense to me. Brittney wasn't her bestie. John was. Brittney was her cover. And I feel like laughing. Leah did have taste. Secretly. Scrolling down, I find another series of texts from an "unknown number."

Unknown: There's nothing I can do.

She wants me off the team.

I can't help you. Drugs mean automatic dismissal. Zero tolerance. But I won't send your file to anyone. I won't stop you from transferring.

That's the end of that conversation. But I picture Vanessa

at the party taunting me. "Ask your sister why she isn't on the team anymore. Ask her."

She meant because Leah was caught with drugs. I look at Brittney's texts, and I remember her saying that Leah reset her password to keep her out. But I remember that day that Leah set our passwords on our phones. Dad had just left. I was destroyed, and Leah wanted to help me. She was always doing that.

"IMSS," Leah had said, grabbing my phone.

"Stop, Leah. Give it to me," I said. "You are so messed up."

I grabbed hers. "Okay, then yours will be"—I laughed as I typed—"IMWF."

"What does that mean? I am white female? Dork!"

"No." I imitated her sharklike smile. "I am worst first."

I expected for her to be mad at me, but she just laughed. I remember I'd made her laugh.

"Okay, that fits. I *am* the worst."

I'd handed hers back to her and tried to take mine. She'd held on for an extra second.

"Promise not to change it though, Allie. Because that would be cheap." She'd looked right into me. "It'll be our thing. Between us. And I love you, even if you're sloppy."

"I love you, even though you're the worst." I nodded solemnly, despite having to work hard not to smile.

Her eyes teared up, and she hugged me hard for just a second. Then she pushed me away and got off my bed. "You should totally take my bed when I'm gone."

I thought she had meant when she went to college.

I scroll to the texts from John Strickland, one of their conversations a few days before she died.

Her: Lets really do it. Run away.

Him: I'm in. When?

Her: Im Srs.

Him: No ur not. What's wrong?

Her: Nothing.

Him: Tell me.

Her: I've messed everything up. I don't know that I can fix it.

Him: Then I will. Come over. Now.

Her: K.

I stand up. And pace. I piece together the puzzle of Leah's last few days. And it's pretty grim. So far, I've got that she wasn't going to be on the dance team anymore because of drugs and Vanessa. As horrible as that is, then she found out Sean was cheating on her with Brittney. And then the texts with Dad. Was he the last straw? And what exactly did he do that made her feel so hopeless?

John Strickland warned me that some of it would be hard to take. The *being kicked off the dance team* thing sucked. But I'm betting the Dad stuff is worse. Should I look? I sit back on my bed and chew my nail. I have to know. I open up her conversation with Dad.

I scroll to the begging of their conversation. The first message she sent him.

Dad? I need to talk.

What's up?

Can u talk?

Can't. In a meeting.

Please. I need to talk.

Text me what's wrong.

I need to get away. I need to start over.

Are you taking your meds?

It's not about the meds.

If you take your meds things will seem better. Take them. Then we'll talk. That's final.

The rage boils up inside me. Too much to contain. One of Dad's get-tough campaigns. Wow. How could he take a chance like that? What kind of father doesn't listen when he's previously suicidal daughter asks for help? Who puts conditions on helping her?

Almost an hour later.

Leah: I'll take my meds. Okay? Then can I come live with you?

I don't think that's a good idea.

Y not? Please.

He never answered her. I wonder why. I think back to that night in my bedroom. She said she found out that Dad was living with Danielle just before. So what's missing? My head spins. I have some guesses, but I have to know the whole picture.

I pull out my phone and dial John Strickland's number. Not the one he gave me. His personal line. The one he only gave to Leah.

He answers on the second ring. "Figured you'd call."

"Hate being predictable," I manage.

He laughs. "What's up?"

"You know why I'm calling."

"You sure you want to know?"

"Please."

"She went over to face him. To force her to deal with him. And found Danielle and him together."

"I figured. After she found them, did Dad talk with her?"

"Yes."

"What did he tell her?"

"He told her he was sorry, but Danielle said she couldn't live with them. In a year, she'd be leaving to go to college anyway. He'd help her in any other way possible. She should take her meds and go home and things would look better."

"God, I hate him."

"Get in line."

"You think he gets, for one second, what he did?"

"I don't care about your dad. I'm sorry. I don't care about him at all. I could have taken care of her. I would have. But for some reason, she wanted *him* to. Or she believed he should want to. And if he didn't want to, it was just more proof she wasn't worth it. How fucked up is that? It's like she had to pass all these tests…"

The tests. It takes me a second to catch my breath enough to say, "I've gotta go."

"What are you going to do?"

"Nothing bad."

"If you need to talk, call me. I'll keep my phone on."

"Thanks."

My head's swimming with too much pain and rage and information. I go into Leah's room. Her sacred space. All the sparkle was a show. The biggest role Leah played was herself.

Leah lied to me. All the times she said she was fine, she lied. All the nights she acted like she was okay, lies. She wasn't okay. She was losing herself. Bit by bit. And I didn't know. She kept me away from her on purpose so she could do what she had to do. She should have come to me instead of Dad. I would have helped her. I would have. But she didn't want my help. I was always just her backup plan.

I take the picture of us skiing and throw the frame as hard as I can. Sea glass explodes against the wall. I'm glad. I took something of hers and broke it. Like Dad broke her. And like she's breaking me now.

I pick up the picture of Leah and Brittney and launch it against the other wall. Shattering Leah's image feels great. She was never as perfect as I painted her.

I think about Dad. He chose Danielle over us. Not just over Mom. Over us too. Like we were a mistake he couldn't get away from.

"I hate how you treated us!" I scream at Dad. And to Leah, "I was never good enough for you. I hate you for leaving me!"

I throw more picture frames, relishing the sound they make as they break. I hate Leah. Lie.

My heart beat slows, and I start to wind down, collapsing next to the heap I've made. I push the debris away and pull out the picture of Leah and me on the ski trip.

"Let's pretend we're in college," she had said as we got on the ski lift. Her voice reaches across time and echoes in my ears. I cut my finger on the fractured glass. The blood leaks out of me and onto the picture.

"Shit!" I say to the empty room. I try to get a grip. "Did you think I wasn't strong enough to kill myself? You think I would have chickened out? You don't know me. You don't know."

For the first time in a long time, I think about my emergency stash of pills. The one Leah collected for us to use if we needed. Our arsenal.

My whole body is screaming with pain. Not just my heart or my head. I am a mess of heartbreak. Raw and raging and out of control. I need a getting-over-Max Help. I need a forgiving-Mom Help. I need a missing-Leah Help. I need something. Anything.

I stand, grab my phone and Leah's, and head downstairs.

I take Gatorade from the fridge. Anger pours from me in waves. I put on my boots and my jacket. Sophie follows me. "You stay here this time."

She puts her head on her paws and whines. I can't have her see me like this.

I grab my studio key and go out the door. I pull my hood up and brace against the rain. The twenty seconds it takes to make it to my studio leave my face feeling pinpricked. The path is slick, but I keep going. I need to get this out of me.

I jam my key in the lock and push open the door with my hip. I open the first cabinet and stick my arm all the way back until I find the baggie I'm looking for. A stash she made me promise not to ever take without her. Some of Mom's pills but also John Strickland's gifts. The ones she didn't take that night. Maybe because they weren't enough. Maybe because she didn't want John to feel guilty that she killed herself with his stuff.

I spill the contents into my hand. Twelve pills. But is this what I want? My hand shakes. I think about the choices in front of me. Pills or pain? Art or life?

I look at the empty easels, waiting for my decision. What's it going to be? I take my phone out and almost will it to jump to life. Play the game again. If someone calls, I won't do this. If anyone texts, I won't. But the phone stays silent. I've got to decide this for myself.

"Oh, fuck!" I say to no one in particular. So I change the game. If there are canvases in the other cabinets, I'll paint it out. My hand shakes as I check the first one. Empty. Shit. The next one is the same. Last door. Please be there. Please. I close my eyes and open it. I'm shaking and sweating. Please. When I open my eyes, I can't believe it. Four empty canvases are there, waiting. Four. Thank God. I shove the pills in my pocket and take two of the canvases out and throw them on the easels. I have art to make.

I open the drawers and grab a handful of paints and brushes. I start to mix. This one's going to be Dad's painting. As I paint, the pain seeps out of me and onto the canvas. Every stroke of the brush, every decision, takes some pain away.

Dad's palette starts with the camouflage colors—army green, gray, khaki, and black. I grab a size-twelve brush and paint a rose opening. The camo colors spill from the flower and across the painting from the top-left corner through the middle of the painting. I dribble bloodred throughout. In the bottom-right corner of the canvas, I paint robin's-egg blue ovals. Some complete, some distorted. To the left of the blue ovals is a pool of burgundy. Around the top border and wrapping around the right side, I write *I don't think that's a good idea* in charcoal and ebony.

I pull out another canvas and put it on the easel—another round in the chamber. I paint tiny strokes of Leah's colors: purple, powder blue, canary yellow, silver, gold. Then I add Dad's colors—charcoal, ebony, army green, gray, khaki—in lines. Leah's reasons. Each stroke an accusation. War games. Death. Betrayal. Each one displayed for the world to see. How Dad ran out on us, how he broke Leah. And Mom. But how he didn't break me. In the corner of this one, in tiny baby blue letters, I paint *That's not a good idea.*

When I'm done, I sit and look at what I've made, my hands shaking. I pull my phone out. I take close-up pictures of the letters and then back up and show the full view of each painting. I send a copy of each to Dad. And then to John Strickland. Exhausted, I turn out the lights and lock the door. I walk across our yard and back into my house. I open the cabinet and return the pills. That's when I see Mom's note on the counter.

Let Sophie out earlier. Just go to sleep when you're done. Your paintings will be coming home tomorrow. XOXO, Mom.

I pick up Sophie and walk upstairs. When I get to my room, I collapse in bed, fully clothed. I'm about to fall asleep when my phone lights up.

They're beautiful. Like you! John Strickland's text reads.

Gnite. Sweet dreams.

I put the phone under my pillow and close my eyes. I'm beat-down tired, and I could use some sweet dreams. When I'm almost all the way out, I see her. Leah. I'm sure she's just part of my dream. But I don't care. She's sitting in the grass, the sun a halo behind her head. She's clapping her hands for me. The last thing I see before I'm out is an explosion of sweetheart-rose pink.

CHAPTER 26

I sit in the waiting room, restless, my paintings by my side.
The receptionist opens the door for me. I slide past her and take my place on Dr. Applegate's couch. She comes in from the other side of the office, closing a door behind her. I wonder what's behind that door. But Dr. Applegate isn't required to hand over her secrets. That's my gig.

"Good morning, Allie," she says.

"Hi."

"How are you feeling?" she asks before turning to see that I've brought a little show-and-tell.

I shift in my seat. How am I feeling? Pretty freakin' crappy. And raw. And used up. All in all, I feel pretty much done. "I'm fine," I say.

"Fine?" she asks, her eyes resting on my display.

"Yes. Fine," I insist.

"What have you brought me?" she asks.

"Just did them last night." I hold each one carefully by the edges.

"May I?" she asks.

"Yes."

She walks over and picks up the camo-rose picture. She

holds it up and examines it. Then she walks to the light by the window and turns it so she can see every bit of it. I should be nervous. I usually am. But these paintings are good. I know that. And more than that, they are exactly what I envisioned when I painted them.

"Do you have a name for this one?"

"*Downfall.*"

She turns to me and flashes a bright smile. "I love this. It's very complex. These words. I'm assuming they are important."

I nod.

"Do you want to tell me what they mean?"

"No."

She extends her hand so we can switch paintings. Her face screws up. Finally she says, "This one feels as if it's about pain. A driving rain kind of pain. Relentless. Unyielding. I want to look away, but I can't. Because it draws me in. Is that right?"

My throat closes. I can barely get the word out. "Yes."

"These are excellent. Do you have a title for the second one?"

"*Reign.*"

"Like rain from the sky or the other kind?"

"The other kind."

"They're very powerful."

"Thanks."

"How would you say these compare to the ones you did of Leah?"

"I wouldn't."

"Your art has changed. That's normal, considering."

I look at my painting. My art *has* changed, but is it for the better?

"I mean, you could have gone darker with your art. You didn't. You got more connected to it. You got closer."

There's part of me that believes this, that thought this before she even said it, but I've always got those doubts about my art. I mean, when you are so close to it, how can you really know? "It's true. Think about the Leah pictures. Besides the pink one, can you tell me about the others?"

"There was one with her wearing her skinny black jeans and Sean's jersey."

"And what perspective was that painted from?"

"From the front."

"And below or above?"

"She was sitting on the window seat in my room."

"Where were you?"

"I was on the floor."

"Why?"

"It's just how we set it up."

"We?"

"Leah and me."

"But I thought you were the artist."

"I am… I was…" I squirm in my seat. All of a sudden, I'm feeling overwhelmed, remembering how I let her manipulate me. How I always let her decide.

"But this painting, the rose one, who set that one up?"

I look at it. "Nobody did."

"You had to. You were the artist, right?"

"I didn't." I stand and pick up the painting. "It just…came to me."

"It came to you? Why? When you were painting it, were you worrying what people would think of it?"

"No."

"Did you worry about what Leah would think when you were done painting her?"

"Yes."

"All the pictures of her? Did you worry each time what she'd think?"

"Yes."

"How about other paintings you did? Before Leah's. Did you worry what people, your art teacher, you parents, the judges at the contest, the other art students would think?"

"Yes."

"But not these, right?"

"Right."

"Because your art has changed. It's matured."

Guilt invades me. Isn't it wrong to benefit from this? How can I get better because Leah died? I'm the one who gets to live. I'm the one who gets to paint. Why? I close my eyes.

"Your art is deepening. That's good. That helps you. But I think it's important to think about how you view your art and yourself."

My head starts to pound. My hands go to it. The pain I tapped into when I painted these wants its payment.

"Think back to the first Leah painting. The pink one. Can you think of a word that describes Leah in that painting?"

Tears drip down my cheek. "Flawless. Leah was flawless."

"Flawless. And you?"

"I don't know…"

"If she were flawless, then that makes you…"

"I don't know."

"You do. If Leah was flawless, you were…"

"Not. Okay? You happy? I was not like her."

"What does that mean?"

"Perfect. I wasn't perfect. Not like she was." My face starts to heat. My breathing gets tight. I shift in my seat. I don't want to talk about Leah like this. Have Dr. Applegate dissect her.

Dr. Applegate softens her voice. "You think Leah was perfect?"

I stay silent. She can't make me testify against Leah. She can't.

"Allie, do you think Leah was perfect?"

"No. I guess not, okay?" I push the heel of my palm into my eye. "I mean, perfect people don't kill themselves, do they?"

"They don't?"

Leah wasn't perfect. She wasn't. But she was the best I had. And way better than I will ever be. Wasn't she?

"Allie?"

"No, perfect people don't kill themselves," I say again.

"No, Allie, they don't. But to be fair to Leah, nobody's perfect. Even if that's how you painted her, she still wasn't. Do you know why you always compare yourself to her?"

I shake my head.

"I think you see yourself as reflections of each other."

"I guess."

"But it doesn't have to be like that. You both could be power-ful. You could both be wrong. She doesn't have to be the way you painted her. It could be different."

I sit silent. Is she right? Did I take make myself smaller just so Leah could shine more? Was that because Leah expected it? Or did I just paint myself that way? Isn't this what sisters did for each other?

"Tell me what you thought of the pact," Dr. Applegate says. "What it meant to you."

"I don't know."

"Come on, Allie."

I grit my teeth against the barrage of questions I know will come now that Dr. Applegate is in her rhythm. But part of me thinks it's time to do this. Or at least that I'm tired of having to keep it all in. "It was a promise."

"A promise of what?"

"Like a safety net."

"If it were a safety net, why don't you think Leah used it?"

I look out the window. A few leaves on the tree have already started to turn. My stomach twists. Everything changes. Everything. There's no stopping it.

"Allie, this isn't a rhetorical question. I need you to answer. Why don't you think Leah came to you about the pact?"

"Because she didn't trust me. Because I wasn't strong enough or good enough or just plain *enough*."

Dr. Applegate shakes her head. "I'm pretty sure that's not it."

I stay silent. Dr. Applegate can speculate all she likes, but how will I ever know the real answer? No one will. Leah took that secret with her.

"You keep telling me you're not depressed, and I agree—you're not. But Leah was. She told Dr. Gates that sometimes it felt like she was drowning, even though she wasn't in the water."

I nod. That's true. I know it is. There were times when Leah would get so dark, no one could reach her. She'd hide away in her room until she was feeling better. I remember sitting, my back against the door, waiting. When I was little, I'd slip notes under for her, but I'd stopped that long before she killed herself because I knew when Leah was like that, you just had to wait it out.

"She said sometimes that the darkness was so heavy, she couldn't see a way out of it. That's why I think she did it. For some reason, whatever happened at the end, Leah didn't see a way for it to get better. She couldn't find her way out of her darkness, and she didn't tell you for two reasons."

I lean forward, my hands on my knees. I know Dr. Applegate is guessing, but maybe she's on to something. Maybe, just maybe, she can help me with this. "What reasons?" I ask.

"One, she didn't want you to stop her. Two, she didn't want you to follow her."

Her words light a fire inside me. Could she be right? Could it be that simple? I lean my head back and close my eyes. What I wouldn't give to know the truth.

"Okay, Allie, why don't you relax?"

I nod, too tired to fight her or her treatments. I let myself go. For once my mind doesn't seek out the memories. This time I go back to that happy place in my mind I went last time we did this exercise. The ocean. The colors. Cool and clean and beautiful. Me. Alone. Until I'm not. Leah finds me. I don't look for her, but she finds me anyway. And at first I don't really want to see her.

She's walking into the ocean, her hair curled at the ends like the mortician did for her funeral. Like she wore in the production of *Beauty and the Beast*.

I almost don't want her to go too deep into the water. I don't want her curls to be swallowed by the waves, but I don't say anything. I watch her walk all the way in, the water now almost up to her neck, her hair trailing in the sea. I think she's going to be mad at me for not bringing her back. I'm sure she's going to say something mean. I can't take that right now. If Leah is sharp with me, I'm going to shatter.

Instead, she reaches out for me. She looks soft, like she did in the pictures with John Strickland. "I'm sorry, Allie. For everything." She starts to cry.

Her nails are perfect, the French manicure Dad sprung for so she would be perfect in her casket. Her silver ring shines on her delicate hand.

I point to it. "John's?" I ask.

She nods.

Leah bobs in the water in time to the slowly churning waves.

283

I bob too. It's what you do when you're this far out. "I know you're mad, but I didn't want you to know how sick I was."

"I wouldn't have cared."

"But I would've. I was your big sister. I wanted you to think I was perfect."

My mouth goes dry. "You said it wasn't Dad, but it was."

"It wasn't only him. He was one of the reasons. He was going to be my way out. If I could live with him, I could go to Southside. The dance coach there, Colleen Dimarco, loved me. It would all be fine. I felt better than I had in days. The pressure lifted. You know?"

I nod.

"And I got all excited. You were going to the party with me. I wanted to make that night special for you. My baby sister was growing up. I thought you wanted that."

"I did." Lie.

"And we had a good day together, didn't we? We had fun. A great last day."

"We got ready together," I say.

"You wanted to go to the party that night," Leah adds. "Because Max was out with someone. You didn't know who, but he was going on a date. Remember? And you had decided you were ready to do it, to show him you were ready, that you could be fun too."

I'm dizzy. My ears are ringing. She's right. He came over just before I left, smelling like my favorite body spray: menthol and something spicy. I loved that smell. It made me want to press my body against his. That body spray made me want to act on feelings I always pretended weren't there. My face burns. He had put the cologne on for Emery.

Leah looked in the mirror, holding a blue minidress to her body. "Hey, what do you think about this one? You can wear the red one; it makes you look eighteen at least."

I had taken the dress from her hands, mine shaking. Leah was trusting me with her clothes and her friends. She walked to her desk and opened the top drawer. She pulled out a crumpled-up napkin. She opened it. Inside were two little blue pills. She held them up.

"You might need a little help loosening up tonight. Take one now and then one right before, you know." Leah smirked. "If you need."

A lump forms in the back of my throat, the same size and shape as the pill I took from her. I needed some power. Max had taken all I had, and I couldn't embarrass Leah. She said the pills made her more fun. I figured if she could do it, I could. I remember. I wanted to be fun. Like Leah and Emery. Like the girls Max liked.

"Not bad," she called as she held up her phone and took a picture. "You look sophisticated."

I remember being so happy. Leah thought I looked good. Not baby-sister good. Sophisticated good.

"We got to the party, and right away you started drinking." She continues, "I thought it was cool. That you'd be okay. You chose Jason, and he was all in. I told you to take it easy. I went to find Sean."

I see it happen in my mind, like I'm there again. Jason flirting with me, handing me that frozen drink. I started to believe it was going to be okay. My mind got all loose. Jason leaned into me, his eyes focused just on me. On me. His hand played with the top of my dress.

"You're so pretty, Allie."

I smiled and leaned in to kiss him. And it felt good. I remember I wanted to. Mostly. But I was scared too. So I drank some more. Sophisticated, fun girls don't chicken out. I had to do this.

"You want to go somewhere more private?" he asked.

"Okay."

He led me to one of the back bedrooms. I remember his friends whistling a little as we passed by. He turned off the light, leaving just the glow from the fish tank to illuminate our way to the bed. He started kissing me.

"Shouldn't we lock the door?" I asked.

"Oh, okay. Be right back." He got up, and I took the other pill out of my purse and bit it in half. I swallowed the pill with a big drink. "No luck. No lock. It's fine. Nobody's going to disturb us."

Only he was wrong. After we were done, the door flew open. The lights went on. I heard laughter. A bunch of football players and Vanessa stood there. My face was hot. They came forward and tried to bump fists with Jason, who was trying his best to shield me. Instead, they slapped each other's hands. The sounds echoed in my head.

Jason looked at me like he wasn't sure what to do. I tried to cover up, but my body wasn't working right. It felt wet between my legs. I looked down. There was a little circle of blood. Blush pink. I was surprised how pink it was. I reached for my clothes.

"Cherry popped," someone laughed.

I wanted to puke. I was a joke. A party foul.

"Get out of here!" Jason yelled.

"Relax," a voice said. One I recognized. Vanessa. She snapped a picture on her cell.

When I was dressed, I went to find Leah. I just wanted to go home. But when I got out to the party, I couldn't find her.

Where are u? I texted Leah.

I pushed past people, not even paying attention to who they were. My legs were rubbery. The sounds of the party were ridiculously loud in my head, making me feel like I was being bombarded. Vanessa approached me. I tried to move past her.

"Two Blackmore girls crash in one night. Does it get any better than this?" She smiled sharply. Sharklike. Then she said, "Ask Leah why she's not on the team anymore. Ask her."

Hands came up behind me. Jason. "You okay?"

I twirled around. "I need to find Leah."

"I'll help." My mind shifts back to here and now. With Leah.

"Leah, where were you? I was looking all over for you. After Jason. After… I wanted to…"

"I went to find Sean while you were with Jason. He was…he was with Brittney. I caught them."

I lean forward. "I'm so sorry, Leah."

"She always wanted him. And she was jealous of me. So I

decided. I wasn't going to let Dad sleaze out of this. I needed to get away. He owed me. I went to see him." She stops. Her face filled with a combination of hate and agony. "You know how that went."

"You could have told me. You *should* have told me."

Leah brushes the hair away from her face. "I know. I'm sorry."

"You were in the other room. Just down the hall from mine. Right down the hall. Do you know how many times I've wished I'd gone in to see you that night? That I'd been able to stop you?"

"I'm sorry."

"Did you know how many times John has wished he could have figured out what you were going to do?"

"I wasn't entirely sure."

"What?"

"I didn't know I was going to do it. I was still deciding. John made me feel better. He said he'd take me away somewhere. He had plenty of money saved. He'd go clean. He'd go to college if I wanted that. Did you know he's really smart? He could do it too. He had enough money saved to do that. We'd have been fine."

"So why didn't you? Why did you do it?"

"It's so stupid really. It's all mixed up. He was walking me to my car. I was going back to the party to get you when I saw them."

"Who?"

"Max and Em. Together."

It's like being punched in the stomach. She saw them. She knew. I want to cry. "It was bad enough that Brittney betrayed me. She was never that deep or loyal to begin with. But Max. And Em. It shook me. I'd talked you into getting with Jason… to grow up for Max. It was as if the rest of the world fell away… and I thought about John, really thought about him. I didn't want that life with him. I know that sounds awful. I loved him. But I knew one day, I'd hurt him the way Max hurt you. And the way Dad hurt Mom. And how Dad hurt me. And I couldn't do that. Not to him."

"Don't you think killing yourself hurt him? Don't you think it hurt me too?"

"The thing is, at that time, nothing seemed real. It was like being Alice in Wonderland. Or performing on stage. Everything seemed distorted. When I got home, I just said to myself, 'Maybe I'll do this.' I never fully decided. I thought, *If I don't get caught picking up the pills at the pharmacy, maybe I'll do it.* And I thought, *If I don't get caught getting the wine, I'll do it. And if Sean doesn't come find me, I'll do it.* It was like a series of tests I kept failing. And when I finally took all the tests, when I'd used up all my chances, I sat at my computer and made it all look like it was okay."

"I heard you that night. I thought I heard you moving around, but I didn't get up. I was mad at you. You left me and didn't tell me where you went, and I had been humiliated."

"I'm sorry."

"And then when I found you…it was the worst thing because

I saw the label was peeled, and I knew that whole time you sat there peeling the label, you were thinking about it. And if I hadn't been mad at you, I'd have gotten up and found you... and stopped you. It's like I killed you. Like I'm responsible too."

She puts her hands on me. "No. I did it. I killed myself."

"But I should have known. I'm such a bad sister."

"No." She pulls me to her, her arms wrapping around my neck. "I didn't want you to know."

"I should have asked you... I should have taken care of you."

Leah hugs me hard and then looks straight into my eyes, hers blazing. "Listen to me. I'm the big sister. Not you. I didn't tell you, end of story."

"How can you say that? After everything?"

"Because I love you, Allie. You're my little sister, and I love you. And sometimes the truth is the thing you don't say, even if you want to."

"But—"

"If I had to do it all over again, I wouldn't have done it. I would have been stronger. I would have turned Vanessa in for the conniving little bitch she was. I would have switched schools. I would have told Brittney what a freak she was. I would have broken up with Sean, and I would have dated John Strickland publicly. Because part of the space between us was how secretive we were. I would have told Dad I was pissed at him and made Mom wake up. I would have ruled the world. I should have. But I was never as strong as you are."

"Now I know you're lying," I say, my voice salty.

"I'm not. You always had your own sense about you. You were an original. I envied you."

I look at Leah's eyes and see her browns mix with my blues, like the reflections we are.

"I left you a present." She looks at her ring finger now empty. "You have to find it. Like you found me here."

"Are you leaving? Now?"

"I have to. But I love the new paintings," she whispers in my ear. "They're about me, right?"

I nod.

"Is that how you see me?"

The question from months ago becomes tangled with the now and I wonder for the umpteenth time if I'm crazy. Isn't it crazy to still think she's with me? After all that's happened? Is it insane to believe she's real?

She reaches her hand out to touch my cheek. "What if you made it about you? The Cape Cod paintings?"

The words swirl together in my mind, like tubes of paint being squeezed onto the same palette. I hear her soft laugh, and I realize that no matter who I have in my life, no matter how close, they will never be as close as Leah and me. Evil Leah, harsh Leah, funny Leah, perfect Leah, the one I never knew—all those Leahs were connected to me and my life, my history, my family. Only Leah knew what it was like to survive our mess of a family. Only she didn't. I did. Maybe that means something.

"Okay, Allie, it's time to come back," Dr. Applegate says.

"Don't go. I'm not ready..." I say.

Leah comes closer to me, one hand on either side of my face. She kisses my cheek and then she's gone, leaving behind the slightest scent of mango. I put my hands over my face, trying to capture her essence, but I know that when I open my eyes, she'll be gone.

"Okay, Allie?" Dr. Applegate's voice forces my attention back to the room.

I nod. Open my eyes.

"I want you to think about how you see yourself this weekend. Because if you only see yourself in relation to Leah, you're going to be lost. You have to see yourself as your own person or it's going to make it harder for you to let her go."

I can't talk. Leah's gone. Again. And Dr. Applegate's talking to me like everything's cool. How can she not know that I'm still that foot soldier, marching to everyone else's orders?

"If you had to describe yourself in one word, one that did not involve Leah, what would it be?"

I shake my head.

"You don't have to answer. Just think to yourself."

I almost laugh. Almost. I don't even know how to think for myself. I realize I've only been the negative space in Leah's life this whole time. I have to stop. My life deserves a canvas, and I get to paint it.

———————•———————

We drive to school, quiet. Mom drops me off in the front. "Have a good day," she says as I put my hand on the door handle.

I'm grateful she didn't decide to walk me in this time. I need a little space. I look at my cell as her car pulls away.

We're still in second period. I can't deal with U.S. history. Good thing it's not AP, even though I'm pretty sure I'll be failing it this semester anyway. I bypass the front of the building, loop around the side, and make my way to the bleachers behind the school. I try not to think about the last time John Strickland found me here. That seems like so long ago. So many things have changed since then.

My phone rings. Dad's number. My heart speeds up. I shouldn't have sent him that picture last night. I let it go to voice mail. It rings again. Him again. I hit ignore again. Another voice mail.

I take a few deep breaths, then put the phone on speaker and listen to him yell at me. "I know what you think. I know you blame me. I didn't know. Don't be like this."

My hands shake, and I hit delete. In the next message, he's calmer. "I'm so sorry. You can't know how sorry. I would do anything to bring her back. Anything. I love you both so much. I know I've screwed it up, but I didn't realize." Pause. "I should have. Maybe we can go to breakfast this weekend. Just you and me. Call me back."

I stare at the phone. I believe he regrets not being there for Leah. I'm sure he does. I believe he didn't realize how precarious she was. I don't want to speak with him now but maybe later. I stretch out in the sun and let it bake me. The warmth feels good, and I'm at peace for the first time in months.

I reach into my backpack and pull out my sketchbook and pastels. I start experimenting with the colors, trying to find what's missing in my Cape Cod painting, when Piper and Nick approach. His confident walk, rust-colored hair, and sweet smile warm me, like the sun is. I feel myself lighten.

"You guys skipping?" I ask.

"I was in the art room and saw you out here. Met this guy in the hall and dragged him with."

Nick smiles. "Didn't take much dragging."

I look at Nick and wonder if I'm changing him. Clean-cut doesn't usually go with cutting class.

"Maybe we should go in," I say.

Piper looks at my paintings. "When did you do these?"

"Last night."

Nick squats next to them and studies them before saying, "Wow. Just, wow."

Piper leans forward. Her tiny features arrange themselves into pure admiration. "This is your best work, Allie, for sure."

Nick stands and then reaches his hand down for me. "Let's go in so you can dazzle Mr. Kispert."

Nick hoists me to my feet. The sureness of his movements make me want to want him even more. He's solid. First-baseman solid. Nick is attentive, patient. He works the stats, he romances the score. I wish I could be more like him.

"Man, we rock," Piper says, making me feel incredible that she's including Nick and me. That she didn't leave him out. It's a surprise to me that I'm worrying about his feelings, like I used to with Max.

I hope one day I'll want to be more than friends with Nick. That my heart will heal, and I'll choose him. Because if I were able to paint Happy right now, I'm thinking it would look a lot like a small-stat-chasing first baseman with artist hands.

CHAPTER 27

When I get home, Sophie's at the door, her tail wagging like crazy and her paws climbing me. I pick her up and kiss her face.

"Come to Mommy," Leah said on the way back from the breeder. I remember like it was yesterday. Her laughter fills my ears, and it feels good to have her so near to me. Just one memory and Leah is with me again. Without the drugs or the inventions, Leah can be here.

Walking up the stairs, I hope the mess I made is not as bad as I remember, that I didn't do as much damage as I thought. But it's awful. I decimated her shrine. I retreat to the kitchen and get Ziploc bags, a box from the recycling bin, and a dustpan and brush. Sophie follows me, but I say, "Not this time, girl."

In Leah's room I fall to my knees and start cleaning. I pick up all the big pieces of glass. They flash and sparkle in the light. My eyes try to focus with all the reflections of color. And suddenly, I have to paint. Right now. I shut the door tightly behind me and race down the stairs.

But downstairs, I notice something's changed. The house feels cold, as if a breeze is running through it. The door to the backyard is flung open. I run to my studio.

I can't believe what I see. My paintings are all back. Mom's paintings are there too.

"I hope you don't mind; it's just for now." She steps from behind a group of canvases propped on easels.

"No, it's fine. I mean, it's good." I look at my paintings and compare them to hers. She painted landscapes and still lifes. But she made them feel so vibrant, like they weren't just scenes. She breathed life into the trees and the flowers. I look at her paintings, and I feel as if I could step into them and become part of each one. She removed the barrier between the viewer and the scene. You have to really understand art to do that.

"Really? I won't come down here when you're with your friends…and…"

"It's fine, Mom. I don't mind sharing. I like it."

"I might even get a job at the community college. They're looking for a drawing and painting teacher, and one of my old friends is working there, so…"

"That would be great."

"Yeah. It would." Mom looks around the studio, a satisfied smile on her face. It's nice to see her so pleased. "You really captured her," Mom says, her fingers brush the edge of the canvas that depicts Leah in her dance uniform.

"She was easy to paint."

"She was larger than life."

We both smile, and it's the first time since Leah died that we've been able to talk about her without fighting or crying.

And at this moment, I want to tell Mom how I really feel about Leah. How I always sort of felt.

"Sometimes I think I didn't really know her…" I look at my paintings of Leah and wonder how I made her feel. I made her pose for me. Was I part of the problem? Did I feed her addiction? Did I make her feel like she wasn't good enough unless she was perfect? I don't want to have been part of her disease.

"I don't think Leah let many people in." Mom moves to the picture of her in Sean's jersey. "I think she gave everyone a small piece of who she was. So if any one of them left, no one would have taken all of her, she wouldn't be completely broken."

"Maybe." It feels a little wrong to talk about Leah without her here to defend herself, but she's never going to be here and it feels good to talk about her with someone who also loved her.

"I'll let you work," Mom says as she walks out the door, leaving me with Leah—my paintings of her at least.

Dr. Applegate said my work got deeper when I stopped caring about what others thought and just tapped into my feelings. Can I do that now? I put an empty canvas on the easel and sit, looking at it. I take the Cape pictures out of my purse and try to remember what it felt like that day.

I was happy.

It was before Max. Before Max and Emery got together. It was before Mom and Dad were fighting. It was when my palette was pure. When I cared as much about what I thought as other people's expectations. The Cape Cod picture is about finding *my* colors again. The ones I've lost along the way.

I pull out the picture of Leah and me on our ski trip. For some reason, this one really speaks to me. So I give up the Cape and start on the ski slope.

I paint snow white against cobalt blue. Fir green dots the landscape. I paint eggplant purple. Royal blue snowsuit with a hot-pink stripe for Leah. I remember feeling so powerful. Sad, because of Mom and Dad, but so glad to be with Leah. We were pretending we were in college. We were unstoppable. I paint silver glimmer on the snow to make it shine, but it's missing something. I go back and grab arctic white. I layer in light pink and sweetheart-rose pink and crimson. I reach inside for the colors that are really me. The colors of sea glass, the ocean, of freedom and beauty. It's better but not perfect. Something's still missing. I get frustrated. I stand up. Why can't I do this? What's blocking me?

I close my eyes and think about Leah. She used to say she'd come to me when I called for her. Would that work now? Even without the drugs? I open my eyes and stare at the paintings. I take them all in. Every painting. Every feeling. Every color.

"Please, Leah. Please come to me."

I hold my breath and wait. Nothing. My head starts pounding, a steady drumbeat that takes up all the empty space inside me till I can't take it anymore. My hand falls to the chair next to me. I think about the broken glass and its different colors. And I get an idea.

I head to the garage. Where is it? I search the high shelves. Low ones. Middle ones. I can't find it anywhere. I push bike tools and brooms out of the way. Finally. I see it. A sledgehammer.

I pass Mom on the way through the house and back to my studio.

"You okay, Allie?" she asks.

"I will be." I don't stop to explain.

"Be careful with that thing," she calls.

I race upstairs and grab the Ziploc with the smashed frames and take them back to my studio. The glass doesn't stand a chance. Each hit is delivered carefully so as not to tear the bag but forcefully enough to grind down the glass. I take a palette knife and a spoon, and I carefully sift out the fine powder, which is all glittery and sparkly. I mix it with my whites and pinks and then apply it to the painting. When I'm done with each detail, I take a step back and look at the canvas to make sure the effect is exactly as I want it to be. Satisfied, I sit down on the cold floor.

It's only when I'm done with my painting that I realize Leah's not coming to see it. But maybe that's the way it should be. Like Dr. Applegate said, I paint better when I'm not worried about what Leah or Mr. Kispert or Nick or anyone else will think of my work.

But even with all the colors I love and the shimmer from the broken glass powder, it's not enough. I need more light because all of a sudden, I feel like that's the thing I want to show about myself; how after all this has happened, I'm still here. I take some of the pieces of the broken glass and affix them on the painting. I layer in pieces of sea glass flanked by pieces of the mirrored frames on top of the circles of color.

I build it out so the colors change in the light and the

perspective you take. It's me when I'm happy. It's Leah when she dances. It's John Strickland when he talks about Leah. It's Nick when he's found himself in his painting. When I'm done, I look at what I've created, and I feel good because I've made my world clean and pure and with no lies to mess it up. Dr. Ziggler and Dr. Applegate were right. Lies are ugly. They have no place in art. Or life.

And then I realize the word that describes me. Alive. I am *alive*.

Sophie wakes up from her perch by the window as I start to clean my brushes. She jumps on my leg, and I lift her up so she can kiss my face.

"Let's go in, Soph," I say as I turn off the lights, then lock the door to my studio and head to the house.

The clock above the stove says it's three in the morning. As I climb the stairs to my room, I whisper, "I love you, Leah," not expecting an answer, knowing that Leah has moved on and I need to also.

The post-painting headache starts to kick in, and I know it's going to be a bad one. I think about using the pain as a gateway to Leah, but I can't do that anymore. It's time to grow up.

I lift the top of Leah's last cherry ChapStick and trace my finger lightly over the waxy surface, trying not to disturb the last trace of Leah, knowing that that's impossible. I bring it to my nose and breathe in, hoping some remnant of my sister remains. Not the made-up version from my cracked mind filled with too many drugs and too much need. Real Leah. But I've got nothing. She's gone.

I let the pain hit me, invite it in. It floods my body and makes me too heavy to move. I cry until I fall asleep.

———————◦———————

When I wake up, it's light out, Saturday morning, and I feel a little better, even though I'm not sure why. I go to my desk, open the top drawer, and her ring is there. I have no idea how. Was it left behind by my sister's ghost? Or by Mom, who always wanted me to have it?

It's a sign, I think, simple and beautiful: Leah's always going to be with me. Even if she's gone. She loved me even when I didn't measure up. And I loved her back. Even when she didn't love herself. Even when I had to fill in the details and brush over her faults. I loved Leah. She was my sister. She still is.

I pull out my phone and text John Strickland.

Can you come over? My studio?

BRT

Sophie walks into the room and jumps on the bed. I pull her to me. She kisses my face and then runs to the door, barking and twirling.

"Okay, okay."

I take her with me to my studio and wait for him there, texting Dad as I do. Sunday breakfast. No Danielle. No yelling. Deal?

Dad texts back almost immediately. Deal.

A shadow falls over the studio. John Strickland is there, leaning against the door. "Hi."

"Come in." I stand. "I want to show you something."

He joins me and surveys the room. "You do all these?"

"No." I wave my hands toward the Leah pictures. "These." And then to my four new canvases. "And these."

"Who did…"

"Mom. Mom did."

"I didn't know she…"

"I know, right? I just found out myself."

"I love these." He points to my ski lift painting and the one called *Reign*.

"I thought you'd like the Leah ones."

He laughs. "I do. They look just like how she wanted people to see her. But this one"—he holds up *Downfall*—"this feels like her."

"I want to give this to you after I use it for my application to RISD. I can't thank you enough for everything you've done for me. And for Leah."

"Really? Yeah. I'd like that."

"Wait. I have something for you now." I get up and bring him Leah's box. "I'm done with this. Thanks."

Our hands touch, and he notices the ring.

"Oh, I guess I should give this back to you."

His voice gets choked up. "No. Not at all. It looks good on you." He pulls me toward him and kisses me on the forehead. "Here."

"What's this?"

He hands me a card with his number written on it. "I'm

moving. Going to Chicago. Going to try to learn to weld. Stay with my uncle. Don't know why I didn't go sooner really."

"Good luck."

"Call. Anytime you need me. I promised Leah I'd keep you safe. She said it was because she was upset about the Em and Max thing. But now I know…"

"Yeah."

"Anyway. Keep in touch. You're very special."

I watch him walk away. Sophie sits expectantly, wanting to play. I could use a little fresh air. And a first baseman with a better arm than mine. I text Nick, grab the battle plan notebook, and leash Sophie. We walk to Back Lake Park, where Nick is already waiting, hands in his pocket.

"Hey, what's up?" Nick says. "You said you needed a favor?"

"I do." I walk to the edge of the lake, Nick right behind me. I kiss the notebook, then hand it to him.

"You want me to…" He points to the center of the lake, eyebrows raised.

"As far as you can throw it."

I watch as he launches it into the water.

Sophie barks at him. "Okay, Soph, your turn. Let's play." Nick takes her off her leash, then has to pick up the pace to keep up with her little legs that run like mad.

The water in the lake sparkles with the sunlight. I watch the notebook sort of bob on top, then soak and disappear under the water. I almost think I see Leah in the water too, but when I squint and bring my hand to my eyes, it's just the sun. Leah's gone. Except in my heart and my head. How it should be.

ACKNOWLEDGMENTS

There is no way to explain how many people helped me write this book and I'm sure I'm leaving someone super important out. To that person, please accept my apology. This writing stuff is hard.

To start I'd like to thank my agent, Nicole Resciniti, for plucking me out of the slush pile and believing in this book to begin with. For saying it's too beautiful of a book to stay on my computer, and for all of the hand-holding and endless explaining she's had to do to date and will likely have to do in the future. You rock.

Next, I'd like to thank Annette Pollert-Morgan for loving this book. And the incredibly talented and hardworking team at Sourcebooks for working tirelessly to polish this book, make a beautiful cover, market it, and help me at every stage of the way.

As for my writing tribe, there are so many of you and I'm grateful for you all. Specifically, I'd like to thank Amanda Coppedge Bosky for being my first SCBWI friend and critique group leader. And Alex Flinn for being my first conference critique.

My writing journey definitely started in Florida SCBWI, but

I met Jacqueline Garlick Pyneart, Bridget Casey, and Tracy Clark in the Nevada Mentoring Program. They were my Inner Circle there, and I'm so lucky to have them in my writing life! While we are talking about Nevada, I have to thank Ellen Hopkins and Suzy Morgan Williams for their mentorship during and after that incredible program, and to my wonderful Nevada mentor who has now become a friend, Terri Farley. All of you were among the first people who saw potential in my writing. There are not enough thanks in the world for that!

While we are discussing writing mentors, Joyce Sweeney has to top the list of best evers. She's been a general when she's had to, a nursemaid, a psychologist, a teacher, a be-all-end-all. Just so you know, I write these books just to make you cry in public.

As for critique groups, I have to thank Linda Salem Marlow and Donna Gephart and the PGAs who may be the best critique group that's ever let me in. You all are the real deal and teach me by example how to live my life as a writer. Thank you also to Sylvia Andrews and the Palm Springs Group. Sylvia is such a thoughtful leader who understands how to make writing personal. A special thank you to Jill Nadler who I met in both of those groups. She's brought me chicken soup when I was sick and encouraged me when I was down. She's the true definition of friend.

Onto the Tuesdays. Jonathan Rosen has been more than the leader of that group. He's been a great friend to me and terrific coach to us all, specifically Joanne Butcher, Melody Maysonet,

Faran Fagen, and Cathy Castelli. You all have been so key in my writing life and I'm glad I have you.

To David Case and Laen Ghiloni, who saw very early drafts of this book, I thank you for your honest critique, always. Thank you to Jamie Morris who *prompted* me to write this book.

Thanks to the Wellington critique group and my coleader, Gail Shepherd, who is one of the best writers I know.

Two writing mentors don't feel like enough, so I'd like to add Lorin Oberweger to the group. She's been essential in helping me keep my sanity in a truly insane business.

And to Steven Dos Santos who has been my pace car through-out this entire journey. Watching you and having you in my corner is what gave me the courage to follow your mantra *just keep writing*. Thank you for everything. Muah!

To my HellYA girls, Marjetta Geerling, Jill MacKenzie, and Ty Shiver. Thank you for deciding that we were going to do this. HellYa we are!

Now onto my family. To Wendy Hartmann Moore who isn't technically part of my biological family, but has been in my life forever, has never given up on me, and who has been like a sister to me in all things and in all ways. I heart you, girl. The Kreiders and the Macphauls have also been like family to me. This whole writing gig started with you, Consuelo. Big smooch.

To my wonderful mother-in-law, Kathleen Ramey, thank you for always being so supportive and for that 'believe in yourself' card. It seemed to do the trick. As for the rest of the Ramey clan, specifically, the west coast Rameys, including Emerson, Miles, and Meagan, thanks for your being your beautiful selves. You are the reason my family is always California dreaming!

To my brother and sister, Bonnie and Mark. I know I kid around a lot about how you tormented me as a kid (that's all still true which is why it's in my official bio!), but to be completely honest and serious, (for once), you two have always been the best and most supportive siblings a girl could be lucky enough to have. You keep me tethered to the world. As do your beautiful children, my niece, Rachel, and baby niecey, Becca. Love them both so much. Also, big thanks to Heidi who helps make our family complete.

To my children, Andrew, Gabe, and Lexi, you are amazing and creative and so positive in a world of crazy negative people. You are my world. To my doggies, Roxy and Fetch: Woof!

To JKR, who, aside from being the most supportive spouse in history, is my universe, and without him, there is nothing.

ABOUT THE AUTHOR

Stacie Ramey learned to read at a very early age to escape the endless tormenting from her older siblings. She attended the University of Florida, where she majored in communication sciences, and Penn State, where she received a master of science in speech pathology. When she's not writing, she engages in Netflix wars with her children or beats her husband in Scrabble. She lives in Wellington, Florida, with her husband, three children, and two rescue dogs.